JOHN BARTH was born in 1930 in Cambridge, on the Maryland Eastern shore. He was educated in the public schools of Dorchester County and at Johns Hopkins University. Since 1953 he has combined writing with an academic career at Pennsylvania State University and, currently, at the State University of New York at Buffalo. THE FLOATING OPERA was his first full-length work. Barth's other books include the novels THE END OF THE ROAD, THE SOT-WEED FACTOR, and GILES GOAT-BOY, and a collection of short works, LOST IN THE FUNHOUSE.

THE FLOATING OPERA
JOHN BARTH

An Avon Library Book

AVON BOOKS
A division of
The Hearst Corporation
959 Eighth Avenue
New York, New York 10019

First Printing (Avon Library), February, 1965
Fifth Printing, May, 1969

Cover illustration by Carl Swanson

Printed in the U.S.A.

I. Tuning my piano

To someone like myself, whose literary activities have been confined since 1920 mainly to such pedestrian *genres* as legal briefs (in connection with my position as partner in the firm of Andrews, Bishop, & Andrews) and *Inquiry*-writing (which I'll explain presently), the hardest thing about the task at hand—*viz.*, the explanation of a day in 1937 when I changed my mind—is getting into it. I've never tried my hand at this sort of thing before, but I know enough about myself to realize that once the ice is broken and the ink is flowing, the pages will follow all too easily, for I'm not naturally a reticent fellow, and the problem then will be to stick to the story, and finally to shut myself up. I've no doubts on that score: I can predict myself correctly almost every time, because opinion here in Cambridge to the contrary, my behavior is actually quite consistent, and of course what is consistent is predictable. If other people (my friend Harrison Mack, for instance, or his wife Jane, or practically anyone in Cambridge) think I'm eccentric and unpredictable, it is because my actions and opinions are inconsistent with *their* principles, if they have any; I assure you that they're quite consistent with *mine*. And although my principles might change now and then— this book, remember, concerns one such change, in 1937 —nevertheless I always have them a-plenty, more than I can handily use, and they usually hang all in a piece, so that my life is never less logical simply for its being unorthodox. Also, I get things done, as a rule.

7

For example, I've got this book started now, and though we're probably a good way from the story yet, at least we're headed toward it, and I for one have learned to content myself with that. Perhaps when I've finished describing that particular day I mentioned before—I believe it was about June 23, 1937—perhaps when I reach the bedtime of that day, if ever, I'll come back and destroy these first pages of piano-tuning. Or perhaps not: I intend directly to introduce myself, caution you against certain possible interpretations of my name, explain the significance of this book's title, and doubtless do several other gracious things for you, like a hostess fussing over a guest, to make you as comfortable as possible and to dunk you gently into the meandering stream of my story—certainly useful activities, and better preserved than scrapped.

To carry the "meandering stream" conceit a bit further, if I may: it has always seemed to me, in the few novels that I've read now and then, that those authors were asking a great deal of their readers who start their stories furiously, in the middle of things, rather than backing or sidling slowly into them. Such a plunge into someone else's life and world, like a plunge into the Choptank River in mid-March, has, it seems to me, little of pleasure in it. No, come along with me, reader, and don't fear for your weak heart; I've one myself, and know the value of inserting first a toe, then a foot, next a leg, very slowly your hips and stomach, and finally your whole self into my story, and taking a good long time to do it. This is, after all, a pleasure-dip I'm inviting you to, not a baptism.

Well, where were we? I was going to comment on the significance of the *viz.* I used earlier, was I? Or explain my "piano-tuning" metaphor? Or my weak heart? Good heavens! How does one write a novel? I mean, how can anybody possibly stick to the story, if he's at all sensitive to the significances of things? As for me, I see already that storytelling isn't my cup of tea: every new sentence I set down is full of figures and implications that I'd love nothing better than to chase to their dens with you, but such chasing would involve new figures and new chases, so that I'm sure we'd never get the story started, much less ended, if I let my inclinations run unleashed. Not that I'd mind, ordinarily—one book is as good as another to me—but I really do want to explain that day (either the 23rd or the 24th) in June of 1937 when I changed my mind for the last time. We'll have to stick to the channel, then, you and I, though it's a shoal-draught boat we're sailing, and let the creeks and coves go by, pretty as they might be. (This metaphor, by the way, isn't gratuitous—but let it go.)

So. Yes, my name. Todd Andrews is my name. You can spell it with one or two *d*'s; I get letters addressed either way. I almost warned you against the single-*d* spelling, for fear you'd say, "*Tod* is German for death: perhaps the name is symbolic." I myself use two *d*'s, partly in order to avoid that symbolism. But you see, I ended by not warning you at all, and that's because it just occurred to me that the double-*d Todd* is symbolic, too, and accurately so. *Tod* is death, and this book hasn't much to do with death; *Todd* is almost *Tod*—that is, almost death—and this book, if it gets written, has very much to do with almost-death.

One last remark, may I? and then I promise I'll get on with the business. Were you ever chagrined by stories that seemed to promise some revelation, and then cheated their way out of it? Maybe I've read the wrong books, but I've run more times than I'd have chosen to into stories concerning some marvelous invention—a gravity-defier, or a telescope powerful enough to see men on Saturn if there are any, or a secret weapon capable of dislocating the solar system, or whatnot—but the mechanics of the gravity device are never explained; the question of Saturn's inhabitation is never answered; we're never told how to build our own solar-system-dislocators. Well, not so this book. If I tell you that I've figured some things out, I'll tell you what those things are, and explain them as clearly as I can. I won't pull any punches.

Todd Andrews, then. Now, watch how I can move

when I really care to: I'm fifty-four years old (does this surprise you?); I'm six feet tall, but weigh only 145. I look like what I think Gregory Peck, the movie actor, will look like when he's fifty-four, except that I keep my hair cut short enough not to have to comb it, and I don't shave every day. (The comparison to Mr. Peck isn't intended as self-praise, only as description. Were I God, creating the face of either Todd Andrews or Gregory Peck, I'd change it just a trifle here and there.) I'm well off, by most standards: I'm a partner in the law firm of Andrews, Bishop, & Andrews—the second Andrews is me—and the practice nets me as much as I want it to, up to perhaps ten thousand dollars a year, maybe nine, although I've never pushed it far enough to find out. I live and work in Cambridge, the seat of Dorchester County, on the Eastern Shore of Maryland. It's my home town and my father's—Andrews is an old Dorchester family name—and I've never lived anywhere else except for the years I spent in the Army during the First World War and the years I spent in Johns Hopkins University and the University of Maryland Law School afterwards. I'm a bachelor. I live in a single room in the Dorset Hotel, just across High Street from the courthouse, and my office is in "Lawyer's Row" on Court Lane, one block away. Although my law practice pays my hotel bill, I consider it no more my career than a hundred other things: sailing, drinking, walking the streets, writing my *Inquiry*, staring at walls, hunting ducks and 'coons, reading, playing politics, and whatnot. I'm interested in any number of things, and enthusiastic about nothing. I wear rather expensive clothing. I smoke Robert Burns cigars. My drink is Sherbrook rye and ginger ale. I read often and unsystematically —that is, I have my own system, but it's unorthodox. I am in no hurry. In short, I live my life—or have lived it, at least, since 1937—in much the same manner as I'm writing this first chapter of *The Floating Opera*.

I almost forgot to mention my illnesses.

The fact is, I'm not a well man. What reminded me of it just now was that while I was daydreaming about the name *Floating Opera*, sitting here at my table in the Dorset Hotel, surrounded by the great files of my *Inquiry*, I commenced drumming my fingers on the table, in rhythm with a galloping neon sign outside. You should see my fingers. They're the only deformity in a body otherwise quite serviceable and, it has in my life been whispered to me, not unlovely. But these fingers. Great clubbed things: huge, sallow, heavy nails. Very unattractive. I used to have (probably still have) a kind of subacute bacteriological endocarditis—heart trouble, in English—with a special complication. Had it since I was a youngster. It clubbed my fingers, and now and then I get weak, not too often. But the complication is a tendency toward myocardial infarction. What that means is that someday, any day, I may fall quickly dead, without any warning—perhaps before I complete this sentence, perhaps twenty years from now. I've known this since 1919: thirty-five years. My other trouble is a chronic infection of the prostate gland. It gave me rather severe trouble when I was younger—several kinds of trouble, as I'll doubtless explain somewhere later— but for many years now I've simply taken a hormone capsule (one milligram of diethylstilbestrol, an estrogen) every day, and except for a sleepless night now and then, the infection doesn't bother me any more. My teeth are sound, except for one filling in my lower left rear molar and a crown on my upper right canine (I broke it on a ferryboat railing in 1917, wrestling with a friend while crossing the Chesapeake). I'm never constipated, and my vision and digestion are perfect. Finally, I was bayoneted just a little bit by a German sergeant in the Argonne during the First World War. There's a small place on my left calf from it, where a muscle atrophied, but I don't limp, and the little scar doesn't hurt. I killed the German sergeant.

Am I boring you? I don't really care, I suppose, but I'd be more comfortable if I knew all this interested you. No doubt when I get the hang of storytelling, after a chapter or two, I'll go faster and digress less often.

Now then, the title, and then we'll see whether we

can't start the story. When I decided, sixteen years ago, to write this story about how I changed my mind one night in June of 1937, I had no title in mind. Indeed, it wasn't until an hour or so ago, when I began writing, that I realized the story would be at least novel-length and resolved therefore to give it a novel title. Originally, you see, in 1938, when I determined to set the story down, it was intended only as an aspect of the preliminary study for one chapter of my *Inquiry,* the notes and data for which fill most of my room. I'm thorough, if unhurried. The first job, once I'd sworn to set that June day down on paper, was to recollect as totally as possible all my thoughts and actions on that day, to make sure nothing was left out. That little job took me nine years—I didn't push myself—and the notes filled seven peach baskets over there by the window. Then I had to do a bit of reading now and then: a few novels, to get the feel of the business of narrating things, and some books on medicine, boatbuilding, philosophy, minstrelsy, marine biology, jurisprudence, pharmacology, Maryland history, the chemistry of gases, and one or two other things, to get "background" and to make sure I understood approximately what had happened. This took three years—rather unpleasant ones, because I had to abandon my usual system of choosing books in order to do that comparatively specialized reading described above. The last two years I spent editing my recollections of that day from seven peach baskets down to one, writing commentary and interpretative material on them until I had seven peachbasketsful again, and finally editing the commentary back down from seven peach baskets to two, from which I intended to draw comments rather at random every half-hour or so during the writing.

Ah, me. Everything, I'm afraid, is significant, and nothing is finally important. I'm pretty sure now that my sixteen years of preparation won't be as useful, or at least not in the same way, as I'd thought: I understand the events of that day fairly well, but as for commentary—I think that what I shall do is try not to comment at all, but simply stick to the facts. That way

I know I'll still digress a great deal—but the temptation is always great, and becomes irresistible when I know the end to be irrelevant—but at least I have some hope of reaching the end, and when I lapse from grace, I shall at any rate be able to congratulate myself on my excellent intentions.

The Floating Opera. Why *The Floating Opera?* I could explain until Judgment Day, and still not explain completely. I think that to understand any one thing entirely, no matter how minute it is, requires the understanding of every other thing in the world. That's why I throw up my hands sometimes at the simplest things; it's also why I don't mind spending a lifetime getting ready to begin my *Inquiry*. Well, *The Floating Opera*. That's part of the name of a showboat that used to travel around the Virginia and Maryland tidewater areas: *Adam's Original & Unparalleled Floating Opera;* Jacob R. Adam, owner and captain; admissions 25, 35, and 50 cents. The *Floating Opera* was tied up at Long Wharf on the day I changed my mind, in 1937, and some of this book happens aboard it. That's reason enough to use it as a title. But there's a better reason. It always seemed a fine idea to me to build a showboat with just one big flat open deck on it, and to keep a play going continuously. The boat wouldn't be moored, but would drift up and down the river on the tide, and the audience would sit along both banks. They could catch whatever part of the plot happened to unfold as the boat floated past, and then they'd have to wait until the tide ran back again to catch another snatch of it, if they still happened to be sitting there. To fill in the gaps they'd have to use their imaginations, or ask more attentive neighbors, or hear the word passed along from up-river or downriver. Most times they wouldn't understand what was going on at all, or they'd think they knew, when actually they didn't. Lots of times they'd be able to see the actors, but not hear them. Need I explain? That's how much of life works: our friends float past; we become involved with them; they float on, and we must rely on hearsay or lose track of them

completely; they float back again, and we must either
renew our friendship—catch up to date—or find that
they and we don't comprehend each other any more.
And that's how this book will work, I'm sure. It's a
floating opera, friend, chock-full of curiosities, melodrama, spectacle, instruction, and entertainment, but it
floats willy-nilly on the tide of my vagrant prose: you'll
catch sight of it, then lose it, then spy it again; and it
will doubtless require the best efforts of your attention
and imagination—together with no little patience, if
you're an average fellow—to keep track of the plot as it
sails in and out of view.

II. The Dorchester Explorers' Club

I suppose I must have waked at six o'clock, that morning in 1937 (I'm going to call it June 23). I had spent a poor night—this was the last year of my prostate trouble. I'd got up more than once to smoke a bit, or walk about my room, or jot some notes for my *Inquiry*, or stare out the window at the Post Office, across High Street from the hotel. Then I'd managed to fall asleep just before sunrise, but the light, or whatever, popped me awake on the tick of six, as it does every morning: a curious phenomenon, and a significant one, I think.

I was just thirty-seven then, remember—I was born in 1900—and as was my practice, I greeted the new day with a slug of Sherbrook from the quart on my window sill. I've a quart sitting there now, but it's not the same one; not by a long shot. The habit of saluting the dawn with a bend of the elbow was a hang-over from my college-fraternity days: I had got really to enjoy it, but I gave it up some years ago. Broke the habit deliberately, as a matter of fact, just for the exercise of habit-breaking. How I got in and out of a college social fraternity is a story in itself; perhaps I'll squeeze it in sometime, but not now.

I opened my eyes, then, and opened my bottle and took a good pull, shook all over from head to toe and looked at my room. It was a sunny morning, and even though my window faces west, enough light reflected in to make the room bright. Which was too bad: the

15

Dorset Hotel was built in the early eighteen hundreds, and my room, like many an elder lady, looks its best in a subdued light. Then, as now, the one window was dappled with little rings of dust from dried raindrops; the light-green plaster walls were filigreed with ancient cracks like a relief map of the Dorchester marshes; an empty beef-stew can, my ashtray, was overflowing butts (I often smoked cigarettes then) onto my writing desk— a bizarre item provided by the management; the notes for my *Inquiry*, then in its seventh year of preparation, filled a mere three peach baskets and one corrugated box with MORTON'S MARVELOUS TOMATOES printed on the end. One wall was partially covered, as it is yet, by a great Coast & Geodetic Survey map of Dorchester County—not so fully annotated as it is now. On another hung an amateur oil painting, atrocious by any standards, of what appeared to be a blind man's conception of fourteen whistling swan landing simultaneously in the Atlantic Ocean during a half-gale. I don't recall now how I came by it, but I know I let it hang through pure inertia. In fact, it's still over there on the wall, but once while drunk and exhibitionistic my friend Harrison Mack, the pickle magnate, painted a kind of nude on top of it in crayon. All over the floor (then, not now) were spread the blueprints of a boat that I was building at the time in a garage down by the range lights on the creek; I'd brought the prints up from the garage to do some work on them the day before.

Disorderly? Think before you say so—it's too easy a judgment. It seems to me that any arrangement of things at all is an order. If you agree, and I don't see why you shouldn't, then it follows that my room was as orderly as any room can be, even though the order was perhaps an unusual one. If you're interested in accuracy, you mustn't jump at easy judgments while reading this book.

For example, don't get the impression that my life, then or now, is "Bohemian" or "left bank." If I understand those terms correctly, it isn't. In the first place, by 1937 I wasn't enthusiastic about any kind of art, although I was and still am mildly curious about it. Neither was my room dirty or uncomfortable—just crowded. It was probably the day before the maids came to clean: they always ruin my orderliness by putting things "straight"—that is, out of sight. Finally, I live too well to be called a Bohemian. Sherbrook rye costs $4.49 a quart, and I use a lot of quarts.

So. It's really a quite adequate room, and I'm still here. I woke up that morning, then, slugged my rye, looked around my room, got quietly out of bed, and dressed for the office. I even remember my clothes, though that damned date—the 23rd or 24th—escapes me, after sixteen years of remembering: I wore a gray-and-white seersucker suit, a tan linen sports shirt, some necktie or other, tan stockings, and my straw boater. I'm sure I splashed cold water on my face, rinsed my mouth out, wiped my reading glasses with toilet paper, rubbed my chin to persuade myself that I didn't need shaving, and patted my hair down in lieu of combing it—sure, because I've done these things, in that order, nearly every morning since perhaps 1930, when I moved into the hotel. It was, if I'm not altogether mistaken, at some moment during the performance of this ritual— the instant when the cold water hit my face seems a probable one—that all things in heaven and earth quite suddenly came clear to me, and I realized that this day I would make my last; that I would destroy myself on this day.

"Of course!"

I stood erect and grinned at my dripping face in the mirror—dumb, stunned surprise.

"Of course!"

Exhilaration! I could scarcely suppress my joy. A choked snicker escaped me.

"For crying out loud!"

Momentous day! Inspiration, to have closed my eyes on the old problem; to have opened them on the new and last and only solution!

Suicide!

I tiptoed from the room to join my colleagues in

the hall, the charter members of the Dorchester Explorers' Club, for coffee.

Like the hotels of many small towns, the Dorset Hotel is bigger than it need be. Most of its fifty-four rooms are empty in the wintertime, and even with the addition of the several all-summer visitors who move in when the weather warms, there are enough rooms left empty on an average night to accommodate the personnel of any traveling circus or muskrat-trappers' convention that might come through town unexpectedly. The owners are able to stay in business, one might guess, only because the building was paid for several generations ago, and willed to the present operators unencumbered; because overhead and maintenance costs are very low; and because a number of elderly ladies and gentlemen unfortunate enough to have outlived their welcome in this world are forced by circumstances to make the hotel their last stopover on the road to the next. These supernumeraries, especially the men among them, comprise the Dorchester Explorers' Club—meetings every morning from 6:15 until 6:45. The D.E.C., founded and named by myself, is still extant, though of the charter members only I remain alive.

That morning, as I remember, just two other members were present: Capt. Osborn Jones, an eighty-three-year-old retired oyster dredger crippled by arthritis, and Mister Haecker, seventy-nine, former principal of the high school, then pensioned and, though in good health, absolutely devoid of family—the end of his line. Because Capt. Osborn had difficulty with stairs, we met in his room, on the same floor as mine.

"Morning, Cap'n Osborn," I said, and the old man merely grunted by way of reply, as was his habit. He was dressed in a shiny gray cap, a nondescript black wool sweater, and blue overalls washed nearly to whiteness.

"Morning, Mister Haecker," I said. Mister Haecker wore his usual spotless and creaseless black serge, a silk necktie, and a clean if somewhat threadbare striped shirt.

"Good morning, Todd," he answered. I remember he

was lighting his first cigar of the morning with one hand and stirring coffee with the other. I had purchased a one-burner hot plate for the Club some months before, and by mutual consent it remained in Capt. Osborn's room. "Good and hot," he said, handing me a cup of coffee.

I thanked him, and just then Capt. Osborn commenced swearing steadily, in a monotone, and striking his right leg with his cane. Mister Haecker and I watched him while we sipped our coffee.

"Can't wake her up, huh?" I offered. Every morning, as soon as Capt. Osborn dressed and sat down, his leg went to sleep, and he pounded it viciously until the blood circulated. Some mornings it took longer than others to get the job done.

"Drink your coffee, Captain," Mister Haecker said in his very mild voice. "It will do more good than all your temper."

Capt. Osborn grew dizzy from the exertion; I saw him sway for an instant and grip his chair arms to steady himself. He sighed, between clenched teeth, and took the coffee that Mister Haecker held out to him, grunting his thanks. Then, without a word, he deliberately poured the steaming stuff all over the delinquent leg.

"Hey there!" Mister Haecker exclaimed with a frown, for such displays annoyed him. I, too, was startled, afraid the coffee would scald the old fellow, but he merely grinned and struck once more at the leg with his cane.

"Smack her good," I urged admiringly.

Capt. Osborn gave up the struggle and settled back in his chair, coffee still steaming and dripping from his trouser leg onto the floor.

"Awright," he said, breathing heavily, "awright. I'm goin' to die. But I want to do it all at oncet, not a piece at a time." He regarded the offending leg with disgust. "Goddam leg," he hissed, kicking his right foot with his left. "Pins and needles, feels like. One time I could buck and wing with that leg. Even steered my boat with 'er, standin' on the other and holdin' a donkey rope in each hand! No more, sir."

"Wouldn't be so bad if he'd die in installments," I
said to Mister Haecker, who was fixing the Captain another cup of coffee. "Maybe the undertaker'll bury him a
piece at a time, and we can pay him a little each month."

This about Capt. Osborn's senility was a running joke
in the Explorers' Club, and as a rule Mister Haecker,
for all his primness, joined in the bantering, but this
morning he seemed preoccupied.

"You *are* going to die, Captain," he said solemnly,
giving Capt. Osborn the fresh coffee, "just as Todd says.
But not for a spell, we trust. In the meantime you're an
old man, same as I. Just old age, is all. Why buck it?
There's not a thing in this world you can do about it."

"Ain't nothing I can do about it," Capt. Osborn admitted, "but I ain't got to like it."

"Why not?" Mister Haecker pressed. "That's just
what I want to know, Captain."

"Why'n hell should I?" Capt. Osborn snorted. "Can't
work and can't play. Jest spit tobacco and die. You take
it; I don't want it." He drew a handkerchief from his
sweater pocket and blew his nose violently. The cushions
of his chair, the drawers of his table, the pockets of his
sweater and trousers—all were stuffed with damp or dry-
ing handkerchiefs: the Captain, like many watermen,
suffered from acute sinusitis, aggravated by the damp air
of Dorchester County, and of course would have nothing
to do with doctors. His only therapy was the half-tum-
blerful of Sherbrook that I gave him every morning
before I left the hotel. It kept him mildly drunk until
near noon, by which time the day was warmer and his
sinuses were less congested.

"Well," Mister Haecker said, still solemn, "wise men
have never run down old age. Let me read you a quote
I copied down from a book yesterday, just to read to
you."

"Oh, my. Oh, my."

"He's going to convert you, Cap'n Osborn," I warned.

"Hee, hee!" the old man chuckled. He always thought
it tremendously funny when I suggested that he was a
backslider.

"No," Mister Haecker said, spreading open a folded strip of paper and holding it to the light. "This is something I copied down from Cicero, and I want you to hear what Cicero says about being old. Here's what Cicero says, now: '. . . *if some god should grant me to renew my childhood from my present age, and once more to be crying in my cradle, I should firmly refuse. . . .*' There now, what do you think of that? I guess Cicero ought to know. Don't you think so? Eh?"

"I expect so," Capt. Osborn said grudgingly, not daring to contradict flatly the written word.

"Well, now," Mister Haecker smiled, obviously much relieved. "Then I say let's make the most of it. How does it go? *The last of life, for which the first was made.* Don't you think so?" He looked to me, nervously, for support. "Don't *you* think so?"

"Don't ask me, Mister Haecker," I said; "I'm still in the first."

"Listen," Capt. Osborn said, in that tone often employed by old men to suggest that, having indulged long enough the nonsense of others' opinions, they are about to get down to the truth. "Ye see this here arm?" He held out his bony right arm. "Well, sir, they could tie me to a cottonwood tree this minute, and hitch a team o' frisky mules to this here arm, and they could pull 'er out slow by the roots, God damn 'em, and I'd let 'em, if they'd make me forty again, with a season's pay in my pocket and all summer to live. Now, then!"

He sat back exhausted in his chair, but his face was triumphant.

"Do you think that's right?" Mister Haecker pleaded to me. "Is that the way you'd feel?"

"Nope," I said. Mister Haecker brightened considerably, but Capt. Osborn favored me with a look of disappointment.

"Ye mean ye'd spend yer time readin' nonsense to yerself?" he asked incredulously.

"Nope," I said. Now Mister Haecker seemed disappointed too.

"Well, what's your opinion about it?" he asked glumly. "Or don't you have one?"

"Him!" Capt. Osborn wheezed, snuffling with laughter and phlegm. "That one's got opinions on ever'thing! Be a cold day ye catch him without nothin' to say!"

"Oh, I've got one," I admitted. "Matter of fact, I woke up with it this morning."

"Woke up with it, did ye!" Capt. Osborn cackled, thinking my remark terribly witty. "I bet it's a hot one, now!"

Mister Haecker waited patiently, though apparently without much relish, to hear my opinion, but he was spared it, because just about then Capt. Osborn's laughter turned into coughing and choking, as it sometimes did, and the two of us had to clap him on the back until, still sputtering, he caught his breath. As soon as he could breathe normally again, I left the club meeting to fetch him his daily glass of rye from my room, for it seemed to me he needed his medicine badly.

Light step! I wanted to dance across the hall! My opinion? My opinion? S U I C I D E ! Oh, light step, reader! Let me tell you: my whole life, or at least a great part of it, has been directed toward the solution of a problem, or rather a mastery of a fact. It is a matter of attitudes, of stances—of masks, if you wish, though the term has a pejorativeness that I won't accept. During my life I've assumed four or five such stances, based on certain conclusions, for I tend, I'm afraid, to attribute to abstract ideas a life-or-death significance. Each stance, it seemed to me at the time, represented the answer to my dilemma, the mastery of my fact; but always something would happen to demonstrate the inadequacy of my conclusion, or else the stance would simply lose its persuasiveness imperceptibly until suddenly it didn't work—quantitative change, as Marx has it, suddenly becoming qualitative change—and then I had the job to face again of changing masks: a slow and, for me, painful process, if often an involuntary one. Be content, if you please, with understanding that during several years prior to 1937 I had employed a stance that, I thought, represented a real and permanent solution to my problem; that during the first half of 1937 that stance had been losing its effectiveness; that during the night of June 22, the night before the day of my story, I became totally and forcibly aware of its inadequacy—I was, in fact, back where I'd started in 1919; and that, finally and miraculously, after no more than an hour's predawn sleep, I awoke, splashed cold water on my face, and realized that I had the real, the final, the unassailable answer; the last possible word; the stance to end all stances. If it hadn't been necessary to tiptoe and whisper, I'd have danced a *trepak* and sung a *come-all-ye!* Didn't I tell you I'd pull no punches? That my answers were yours? *Suicide!* Poor Mr. Haecker, he must wait to learn my opinion (wait, wretched soul, for Judgment Day, I fear), but not you, reader. *Suicide* was my answer; my answer was *suicide*. You'll not appreciate it before I've laid open the problem; and lay it open I shall, a piece at a time, after my fashion—which, remember, is not unsystematic, but simply coherent in terms of my own, perhaps unorthodox, system.

Then, for heaven's sake, what is my system? Patience, friend; it's not my aim to mystify or exasperate you. Remember that I'm a novice at storytelling—even if I weren't, I'd do things my own way. I suggest you substitute this question for yours: Why didn't I carry Capt. Osborn's rye with me when I first left my room, so that I shouldn't need to return for it? There's a more specific question, and a more reasonable, and a less prying, and its answer involves the answer to the other. I didn't take the rye with me in the first place because it wasn't my habit to do so on previous mornings, and one of the results of my amazing new solution, my eye-opening answer, was that this day—this June 23 (I'm almost certain)—should, because of its very momentousness, be lived as exactly like every other day of my recent life as I could possibly live it. Therefore, although I knew very well that Capt. Osborn would need his medicine, I left it in my room and returned for it after coffee, as was my practice.

Is this an answer? More to the first question than to the second; you still don't know how the practice originated, any more than I do, but you know that my system for living this extraordinary day was to live it as ordinarily as possible, though every action would necessarily be charged with a new significance. And similarly, my method in telling this story will be to set down the events of that day, as barely as possible, for I know too well that in the telling I'll lose the path often enough for you to learn or guess the whole history of the question, as the audience to my untethered showboat pieces together the plot of their melodrama—and I swear by all the ripe tomatoes in Dorchester that when the excitement commences, the boat will be floating just in front of you and you shan't miss a thing.

So, then. I crossed the hall to my room, opened the door softly, and tiptoed inside to fetch the glass of rye. My intention was to rinse the drinking glass out, fill it half full, and leave as quickly as possible, but as soon as I turned the faucet at the washbasin, and it sounded its usual A♭ above high C, Jane Mack opened her marvelous green eyes and sat up in my bed: her hair, brown and sleek as a sable's, fell around her shoulders, and the bed sheet slid down to her hips; she raised her right arm to push the hair back; the movement flattened her stomach and lifted one of her breasts in a way that flexed my thighs to watch. I was still holding the quart of Sherbrook in my right hand and the glass in my left. Jane asked me, in a very sleepy voice, whether it was eight o'clock yet; I told her it was not. She scratched her head, yawned, flopped back on the pillow, sighed, and, I think, went to sleep again instantly. The sheet was still down around her hips, and she lay with her back to me. I believe that a small warm breeze was moving through the room, and I remember clearly that a little ray of sunlight reflected from something outside and streaked brilliantly across the sun-browned skin of her, where her waist grew smallest above the round angle of her hip, thrust up by the hard mattress of my bed. I drank Capt. Osborn's medicine myself, as was *not* my practice, poured him another dose, and tiptoed out.

III. Coitus

If you're still with me, then I shan't even bother explaining why I couldn't tell you that Jane Mack was my mistress until after I'd announced that this day was a momentous one: either you're familiar with the business of climaxes and anticlimaxes, in which case no explanation is necessary, or else you know even less about storytelling than I do, in which case an explanation would be useless. She was, indeed, very much my mistress, and a magnificent one in every way imaginable. To make the triangle quite equilateral, Harrison Mack was my excellent friend, and I his. Each of the three of us loved the other two as thoroughly as each was capable of loving, and in the case of Jane and Harrison, that was very thoroughly indeed. As for me—well, I'll explain it in a later chapter. And the really surprising thing is that Harrison was quite aware of the fact that between 1932 and 1937 his wife spent many, many hours in my room and in my bed (if he didn't know that I had made love to her exactly six hundred seventy-three times, it's because Jane neglected to keep score as accurately as I did).

Hell, I'll explain it now: it's a good yarn, and Capt. Osborn can wait a chapter for his rye.

I first met Harrison Mack in 1925, at a party given by a classmate of mine from the University of Maryland Law School. It was a drunken affair held somewhere in Guilford, a wealthy section of Baltimore—I've no idea whose house the party was in, or where in Guilford the house is. At the time, I should explain, I was in the early throes of a spell of misanthropic hermitism, so to speak, which lasted from 1925 until 1930. I had, for various reasons, renounced the world of human endeavors and delights, and although I continued my legal studies (principally through inertia), I was having no more to do with my fellow man and his values than I had to. Rather a saint, I was, during those five or six years—a Buddhist saint, to be sure, of the Esoteric variety. It was one of my stances, my provisional answers to the peculiar question of my life, and long after I'd outgrown it I still remembered that stance with pleasure.

For one thing, it made me appear mysterious, standing aloof in a bay window, smoking a cigarette with an air of quiet wisdom while all around me the party screamed and giggled. Some quite pleasant people, Harrison Mack among them, reasoned that I must have answers that they lacked, and sought me out; women thought me charmingly shy, and sometimes stopped at nothing to "penetrate the disdainful shell of my fear" (as one charming, if overeducated piece put it). As often as not, though, it was they who got penetrated.

On the night of this particular party I found myself being made friends with by a great handsome fellow who came over to my bay window, introduced himself as Harrison Mack, and stared out beside me for nearly an hour without speaking: some time afterwards I observed that Harrison involuntarily adopts, to a great extent, the mood and manner of whomever he happens to be with—a tendency I greatly admire in him, for it implies that he has no characteristic mood or manner of his own. We talked after a while, gruffly and brusquely, of several things: the working class, prohibition, law, the Sacco-Vanzetti affair, and Maryland. Harrison, it turned out, was well off; his father, Harrison Mack Senior, was president of a pickle company, of all things—Mack's Pickles—and was rich. Since the cucumbers that were ultimately transmogrified into

Mack's Pickles were grown on the Eastern Shore, whence
they were carried as whole pickles to the Baltimore
plant for fancy processing, the Macks had several summer homes sprinkled about the peninsula, and Harrison
was no stranger to the haunts of my youth. We talked
aloofly of pickles and wealth.

Harrison—a fine, muscular, sun-bronzed, gentle-eyed,
patrician-nosed, steak-fed, Gilman-Schooled, soft-spoken,
well-tailored aristocrat—Harrison, to his family's understandable alarm, was a communist at the time. Not
a parlor communist, either, mind: an out-and-out leaflet-
writing revolutionary who had sold his speedboat, his
Stutz automobile, and God knows what else, to live on
when his father disinherited him; who spent ten hours
a day writing and distributing party-line penny-dreadfuls
among factory workers, including the employees of the
Mack Pickle factories; who took his lumps with the
rest when strikebreakers or other kinds of bullies—including certain salaried employees of the Mack Pickle
factories—objected to his activities; who was at the
moment engaged to marry the woolliest-looking specimen of intellectual Bolshevism I've ever laid unbelieving
eyes upon, because she was ideologically pure; and whose
only remaining streak of good sense, as far as I could
see that night, was his refusal to become actually a dues-
paying member of the Party, for fear it might prove a
liability to the execution of his Muscovite schemes.

Well, as it happened, Harrison did precisely, if ac-
cidentally, the one and only thing that could possibly
have induced me to like him that night: he made it
fairly obvious, right from the beginning, that he liked
me a great deal. He was an engaging fellow, and still is,
and I saw nothing amiss in a saint's having just one
friend. The sheer oppositeness of his enthusiasm from
anything I myself could conceivably have been enthusiastic about at that time—though I had been interested
enough in social reform not too long before—drew me
to him, and, as I learned later, he was attracted by
my "transcendent rejection" (his term) of the thing
that meant life to him. In short, we were soon close

friends, and walked blindly to my rooms at dawn for
more drink, singing the *Internationale* in French all
through the mansioned and junipered roads of Guilford.

I knew him intimately for the next year, or until my
graduation from law school. I was a saint throughout
the whole year—indeed, that mask endured for four
more years—and although we argued sometimes for days
without interruption, neither of us was rational enough
to be convinced of the other's position. I say this because I know for certain that all the major mind-changes
in my life have been the result not of deliberate, creative
thinking on my part, but rather of pure accidents—
events outside myself impinging forcibly upon my attention—which I afterwards rationalized into new masks.
And I suspect that Harrison, like the chameleon whom
nature has equipped with no greater gift, simply assumes,
in time, the intellectual as well as the manneristic color
of his surroundings.

For example, when we said goodbye in 1926—I to
set up practice in Cambridge, he to assist a Party press
in Detroit—I thought I detected an ideologically impure
attitude in him toward his leaflet-writing colleagues. He
had, in fact, come to loathe them, boorish inadequates
that they were, and, it seemed to me, had begun to
prefer refuting the *Mensheviki* with me in my room to
supporting *Bolsheviki* with them in some dirty factory,
pickle or otherwise. He was not at all enthusiastic about
his new assignment, and I think he would have washed
his hands of the whole distasteful business, but that such
a defection would, to say the least, have given his arguments for universal brotherhood a hollow ring. Our sep-
aration upset Harrison a great deal more than me, whose
nirvana could hardly be ruffled by such a mundane
tragedy as losing a friend.

I saw him next in 1932, under quite different circumstances (don't be alarmed if I sketch them in briefly;
I'll return to them later): I had been admitted as a partner in the firm of Andrews & Bishop, and throughout
1927 and 1928 I enriched myself and the firm at the
rate of perhaps forty dollars a month—the folks of Cam-

bridge very wisely trust no new doctors or lawyers, even fifth-generation natives of the county. I was living with my father, a widower, in his house in East Cambridge. In 1929 Dad lost all his savings and property on the stock market, and the next year he hanged himself with his belt from a floor joist in the basement. The most I could hope for him was that he'd had other reasons besides the loss of his money for killing himself, but if he did I never discovered them. After that I made more money from the firm, despite the depression, since Dad's clients more or less inherited me as their lawyer, and when the family house and lot, a summer cottage at Fenwick Island, Delaware, and one or two timber properties down the county had been sold towards meeting Dad's debts, I moved into Room 307 of the Dorset Hotel, where I've lived ever since.

And I became a cynic, a cosmic cynic, although I didn't bother to mention the fact to Harrison when I saw him again, any more than I'd told him before, in so many words, that I was a saint.

He walked into my office in "Robbers' Row," next to the courthouse, one afternoon, very solemnly, and put a bottle of gin on my desk. He had grown stouter and a bit tired-looking, but was still bronzed and handsome.

"I'm back," he said, indicating the gin, and for the rest of the afternoon we drank straight gin—horrible thought!—and walked the several streets of Cambridge, renewing our friendship.

"What happened to your revolution in Detroit?" I asked him once. "I notice they're still making cars out there."

"Ah," he shrugged, "I got fed up with the fuzzy bastards."

"And the brotherhood of man?" I asked him later.

"To hell with the brotherhood of man!" he replied. "I wouldn't want those guys for field hands, much less brothers. A more worthless lot of politicians I never saw."

"What about Miss Moscow?" I asked later yet, referring to his woolly fiancée of 1926.

"Free lover," he snorted. "I believed all men were

brothers, but she thought all men were husbands. I didn't want ideological syphilis. I gave the whole mess up."

And so he had, for it became apparent, as he talked, that he was in fact a saint these days, of the sort I'd been earlier. He was having little or nothing to do with the world's problems any more.

"But what about social justice?" I asked him.

"Impossible to achieve, and irrelevant if achieved," he answered, and went on to explain that men aren't worth saving from their capitalist exploiters.

"They'd be just as bad as the capitalists if they were on top," he declared. "Worse, in fact, because we present capitalists are at least gentlemanly beasts, and my comrades were beastly beasts."

It was the "inner harmony" of the "whole man," he told me, that really mattered. The real revolution must be revolution in the soul and spirit of the individual, and collective materialistic enthusiasms only distracted one from the disorder of his own soul.

"Marxism," he said, "is the opiate of the people!"

Oh, he was fed up. He insisted I come to his house for dinner.

"To Baltimore? Tonight?" I exclaimed.

He blushed. "I'm living here now, Toddy boy," he said. He explained that upon his recanting the Marxist heresy, his father had reinstated him in the Mack family's good graces and excellent credit ratings, and that he was now in charge of all the cucumber patches and raw processing plants on the Shore.

"We bought a house in East Cambridge," he said, "on the water. Fine place. Just moved in. Come on and help us warm it."

"*Us?*" I inquired.

"I'm married," he said, blushing again. "The loveliest thing you ever saw. Janie. Ruxton and Gibson Island type, you know, but damned sensible. You'll love each other, Toddy."

Well, I went to Harrison's house that evening, when we were good and drunk, and I recall saying "For Christ's sake!" when I found that he'd bought Dad's old house—

the one in which I was born and raised, and which I'd
abandoned in disgust.

"Didn't know it was your family's place till I'd bought
it and searched the title," Harrison claimed, beaming.
He was extremely happy about the whole thing: he'd
heard since about Dad's debts and the fact that I'd lost
the house along with the other property, and it gave
him great pleasure to have rescued it, so to speak, from
unclean hands, and to be able to invite me to make it
my home as often as I wished. I thanked him unenthu-
siastically, and without much appetite I followed him
inside to meet his wife and eat dinner.

Jane, perhaps twenty-six at the time, met us at the
door with an indulgent smile, a mother tolerant of her
boisterous boys, and we were introduced. She was indeed "Ruxton and Gibson Island," if by that Harrison
had meant a combination of beauty and athleticism. She
wore a starched sundress and looked as fresh and sweet
as if she'd just stepped from a shower after a swim. Her
dark brown hair, almost black, was dried by the sun, as
was her skin. That night she kept reminding me of sail-
boats, for some reason or other, and she has ever
since. Whenever I think of her, I think of her as
perched on the windward washboard of a fast racing sailboat, a Hampton or a Star, perhaps tending the jib
sheet, but certainly squinting against a blinding sun in
a brilliant blue world—a sun that heats the excellent
timber beneath her thighs and buttocks, and dries the
salt spray on her face and arms, and warms the Chesapeake wind that fans her cheeks and fluffs her hair and
swells the gleaming sails to bursting. And as a matter of
fact her skin, particularly across the fine soft plateau of
her stomach, did indeed, I later learned, smell of sunshine in my nostrils, and her hair of dried salt spray;
and the smell of her in my head never failed for five
years to give me that same giddy exhilaration which, as
a boy, I always felt when I approached Ocean City on a
family excursion, and the first heady spume of Atlantic
in the air made my senses reel. To be sure, she always
insisted that it was simply the result of not washing her

hair as often as she should: she was in fact an ardent sailor.

For dinner, I believe, we were served chicken breasts and some vegetables or other. Harrison was too drunk to bother with small talk; he just ate and gave polite orders to the maid. And I was too full of gin and Jane to do much besides stare at the chickens' breasts and hers. Luckily, Harrison had told her that I was psychopathically shy—his impression of my former sainthood— and so she interpreted as a timid inability to look her directly in the face what was actually a hushed and admiring, if somewhat drunken ogling directly beneath. I've no idea what, if anything, was said that evening, but I remember clearly that, as frequently used to happen when my sexual passions were aroused and unsatisfied, my ailing prostate gland gave me much pain that night, and I was unable to sleep at all.

Of course I wanted very much to make love to her —I can't think of any attractive girl I ever saw in my youth whom I didn't want to take to bed, frankly, and young Mrs. Mack was, if somewhat solemn like her husband, a good deal more lovely and sensible than most of the women I'd encountered in my thirty-two years. Nor had I any scruples about adultery—I was a cynic, remember. Still, I know very well that left to myself I'd never have carried my attentions beyond ogling her and telling her, half seriously, in Harrison's presence, that I was in love with her body: I simply didn't choose to prejudice my friendship with Harrison, whom I really enjoyed, or to do anything which, if successful, might disturb what appeared to be an unusually pleasant marriage. There could, I decided during the first weeks of what turned out to be a close friendship between the three of us, be no doubt that in their rather grave fashion Jane and Harrison were entirely in love with each other.

But the matter was quite dramatically taken out of my hands one August weekend. Harrison had acquired one of his father's summer cottages, on Todd Point, downriver from Cambridge, and the three of us often spent weekends there, sailing, swimming, fishing, drinking, and talking. On the morning of the second Saturday in August he and Jane roused me out of bed in the hotel, loaded me into their roadster with themselves and two cases of beer, and set out for the cottage. It struck me during the ride out that they were unusually, even deliberately, exuberant: Harrison roared risqué songs at the top of his voice; Jane, sitting in the middle, had her arms around both of us; husband and wife both called me "Toddy boy" with every third breath. I sighed "Oh, hell" to myself, resolved not to wonder about their strange behavior, and emptied three bottles of beer before we finished the fifteen-mile trip to the cottage.

All morning we swam and drank beer, and the exaggerated liveliness and good-fellowship continued without letup. It was decided that after lunch we would load the rest of the beer into the Macks' sailboat—a beamy, clinker-built knock-about—and sail to Sharp's Island, in the Bay at the mouth of the Choptank, in order to sail back again. Harrison gave Jane a long goodbye kiss and set off to find ice, which he declared we needed in quantity; Jane set her browned, bathing-suited self to washing the lunch dishes, and I went to sleep on the Macks' bed in the cottage's one bedroom.

Needless to say, I dreamed of Jane. The absence of Harrison—the first time he'd left Jane and me alone together, as it happened, because of my supposed shyness—was embarrassingly obvious, and on my way to sleep I was acutely conscious of her presence on the opposite side of the plywood partition between us. I fell asleep imagining her cool brown thighs—they must be cool!—brushing each other, perhaps, as she walked about the kitchen; the scarcely visible gold down on her upper arms; the salt-and-sunshine smell of her. The sun was glaring in through a small window at the foot of the bed; the cottage smelled of heat and resinous pine. I was quite tired from swimming, and sleepy from beer. My dream was lecherous and violent—and unfinished. Embarrassingly so. For suddenly I felt a cool, shiveringly cool, hand caress my stomach. It might have been ice, so violently did all my insides contract; I fairly exploded awake, and wrenched up into a sitting position. I believe it was "Good Lord!" that I croaked. I croaked something, anyhow, and with both arms instantly grabbed Jane, who sat nude—unbelievable!—on the edge of the bed; buried my face in her, so excruciatingly startled was I; pulled her down with me, that electrifying skin against mine; and *mirabile dictu!* at the sheer enormous lust of it I did indeed explode, so wholly that I was certain liver, spleen, guts, lungs, heart, head, and all had blown from me, and I lay a hollow shell without sense or strength.

Damned dream, to leave me helpless! I was choked with desire, and with fury at my impotency. Jane was terribly nervous; after the first approach, to make which must have required all her courage, she collapsed on her back beside me and scarcely dared open her eyes.

The room was dazzlingly bright! I was so shocked by the unexpectedness of it that I very nearly wept. Incredible smooth, tight, perfect skin! I pressed my face into her; I couldn't leave her untouched for the barest sliver of an instant. I quiver even now, twenty-two years later, to write of it, and why my poor heart failed to burst I'm unable even to wonder.

Well, it was no use, and if I'd had a knife handy then, I'd have unmanned myself. I fell beside her, maddened at my impotency and mortified at the mess I'd made. That, it turned out, was the right thing to do: my self-castigation renewed Jane's courage, gave her the upper hand again.

"Don't curse yourself, Toddy," she soothed, and kissed me—sweetness!—and stroked my face.

"No use," I muttered into her breast.

"We'll see," she said lightly, entirely self-possessed now that I seemed shy again: I resolved to behave timidly for the rest of my life. "Don't worry about it, honey; I cán fix it."

"No you can't," I moaned, as strickenly as I could.

"Yes I can," she whispered, kissing my ear and sitting up beside me.

Merciful heavens, reader! If you must marry, marry from Ruxton and Gibson Island, I charge you! Such a magnificent, subtle, versatile, imaginative, athletic, informed, delightful, exuberant mistress no man ever had, I swear: she burst frequently into spontaneous, nervous laughter. . . .

Enough. I'm no gentleman—I don't really believe in chivalry any more than I believe in anything else— but I shan't go further. I shan't share it. For your purposes it's enough to know that Jane was soon able to muster enough manliness in me for us to commit jubilant adultery. Afterwards we smoked, shuddered, and talked brokenly.

"How about Harrison?" I asked.

"All right," she answered.

"All right?" I repeated.

"Yes," she said.

"How?"

"He doesn't mind."

"*Doesn't* or *won't?*"

"Doesn't."

"He knows?" I asked, incredulously.

"Approves," she said glibly.

"Don't you love each other?"

"Of course," she said. "Don't be silly."

"What the hell!"

"We talked it over," she explained, rather embarrassed again. "Harrison thinks the world of you, and I do, too. We don't see why a woman can't make love to somebody she likes a lot, just for the pleasure of it, without a lot of complications. Do you?"

"Of course not," I said quickly.

"That's how we felt," she said, relieved. I was becoming terribly curious and—may I confess it?—just a tiny bit amused. "Harrison and I love each other completely," Jane went on, speaking very solemnly and scratching a fly bite on one lovely leg. "So much that neither of us could possibly ever be jealous, or doubt the other's love. If you thought for a minute that I didn't love him because of what I've done, I'd die."

"Nonsense," I assured her, just as solemnly. "I understand everything."

"Thank heaven," she sighed, resting her head on me. "We talked it over for a long time. I was scared to death. I still don't know if I should've done it, but Harrison is so wonderful. He's so *objective*."

"I've loved you ever since the first time I saw you," I said, and though I intended it to sound convincing, the solemnity of it made me blush.

"I wish you wouldn't say that," Jane said. "I don't think there's got to be any love in it. I like you a lot, as a friend, but that's all, Toddy."

"Not for me."

"I mean it," she said. "I enjoyed making love to you, and I hope you liked it, too. That's plenty enough, I think, without falsifying it with any romance."

"I completely agree, if that's how you want it," I said sedately. "You were the finest thing in the world."

She cheered up a lot, then. She went to the icebox for beer—I noticed there was at least fifty pounds of ice inside—and when I came up behind her, held her against me, and nuzzled the back of her neck, she laughed and pressed my hands more tightly against her with her own.

"I don't know how I'll be able to face Harrison," I said, in order to please her.

"Oh," she said, pleased, "you mustn't be embarrassed, Toddy. He's so wonderful about this. He was as eager as I was. He really thinks you're fine."

"He's amazing," I said. She seemed afraid that I wouldn't appreciate his marvelousness. "He's a regular saint."

"He admires you a lot," she said. Her back was toward me while she opened the beer.

"But he's better in every way than I am," I declared to the calendar on the wall. "He's the antithesis of all my faults. How can I ever pay him back?"

Now I must confess that this last was a loaded question; nasty barrister that I am, I was curious to learn the extent to which Harrison had suggested to his wife that she go to bed with his friend.

"He doesn't expect any payment," she assured me. "I mean, I don't either. You mustn't feel obliged at *all*, Toddy. The thing is to not make much of it; it was just for the pleasure of it; that's all."

"I can't believe that any man could go on liking another man, though, after that," I said doubtfully.

"I swear he will, Toddy!" Jane cried, very urgently for one determined to make light of the whole matter. "How can I convince you, damn it? Honest, it was as much his idea as mine!"

I shook my head to indicate either the difficulty anyone might have in comprehending such an unorthodox situation, or the awe that an ordinary, unthinking, weak-willed mortal such as myself necessarily felt before such saintly objectivity and generosity as Harrison Mack's.

"Cheer up," Jane smiled, and kissed me on the nose as she handed me my beer. I was certain my attitude had been the best possible one. She was in control, sheltering and encouraging me. Somewhat self-consciously, but apparently for my benefit, she slipped off the robe she'd covered herself with and began donning lithely the bathing suit she'd stripped off to come to me earlier. The show, I supposed, was part of the gift from Saint Harrison. It was a dazzlingly good show, and I drank it in with my beer.

After the beer I calmed a little from the terrific shock of being seduced and sat in an old glider on the little screened porch of the cottage to watch the Choptank through the pines. Jane came through, smiled reassuringly at me as though to say again, "Please don't worry, now; I swear Harrison approves," and walked down the lawn and out on the pier to the sailboat. I watched her, then, with pleasure, as she pumped the bilge, sponged the hull and deck, and bent the mainsail and jib to the spars. Everything she did was graceful, efficient, and lust-provoking. Good Lord! I shook my head in astonishment at the whole business.

I heard the car drive up, and a moment later Harrison entered through the rear of the cottage. He made a great noisy show of putting the unnecessary ice away, and after a while came out on the porch with me, handed me yet another beer, and sat down on the glider. He was, of course, terribly embarrassed, and despite himself made a exaggerated show of everything: lighting his cigarette and mine, taking deep draughts of the beer, stretching out his legs, sighing, yawning. There could be no question but that he knew very well I had made love to his wife. We both rather avoided looking either at each other or at Jane, whose rangy body was conspicuously before us. The thought occurred to me that we were in the classical situation, and I smiled at the notion of Harrison's pulling a revolver from his shirt and laying me out with three slugs of lead. I began recalling all the violent consequences of adultery I'd ever heard of as a lawyer and a reader of tabloid newspapers. Was this sort of hospitable prostitution something entirely novel, or did one simply never hear of it?

"Well," Harrison croaked, in a voice that I believe was meant to be hearty, "we can either keep quiet about it, like gentlemen, or talk frankly about it, like I'd like to, to make sure we understand each other."

"Sure," I said, a little embarrassed despite my amusement, and began peeling the label off my beer bottle.

"She sure makes love well, doesn't she?" Harrison grinned.

"Oh, yes indeed!" I said.

There was a silence that Harrison didn't dare let last more than an instant.

"I want you to know it's all right with me, Toddy," Harrison said, his voice still unnatural. "I approved of it as much as Janie did. She just likes you a lot, you know, and I do too. I think it was a swell idea she had."

What could I say? I was certain now that it had been Harrison's idea.

"Janie and I love each other completely," he went on, wishing I'd help him. "We're not stupid enough to be affected by things like jealousy or conventions. [*Pause*] You can have sexual attractions apart from love. We both enjoy love-making. [*Pause*] If I was attracted to any girl, Janie wouldn't be silly enough to object to me going to bed with her, because she knows there wouldn't be any love in it."

"Of course not," I said.

"It's just like playing tennis," Harrison laughed. "Just for the fun and exercise. Some guys would get jealous if their wife played tennis with another man, or danced with him. Actually, I guess kissing is a more serious offense than love-making, because it's no fun in itself, but just a symbol of something else."

I shook my head in apparent awe.

"Don't feel obligated," Harrison laughed. "For Christ's sake don't thank me for anything. Just enjoy it. The thing is, don't make too much of it. It gets all out of proportion."

Well, I wasn't making anything out of it.

"Are any of us any different than we were?" he went on.

"I am," I said solemnly. It was clear to me that whether he realized it or not, Harrison very much wanted thanking and being obliged to, and I decided to make him feel very good.

"Oh, sure," he grinned. "But you know what I mean."

"But you don't know what *I* mean," I said, reverent as a church. "It was my first time."

"What?" he cried.

"That's right," I affirmed. I stared at my peeled beer bottle. "I was a virgin."

"No!" he breathed, realizing that this enormous fact was not to be laughed at. "How old? Thirty?"

"Thirty-two," I said. "I had prostate trouble for a long time," I added vaguely.

Harrison glanced out to where Jane was walking back up the pier toward the cottage.

"Well say," he said, "I hope we didn't do anything you didn't like." He was extremely impressed and flattered.

"No," I said. "It was fine, Harrison. Of course I've nothing to compare it with."

"Well listen," he said quickly, for Jane was coming near. "For Christ's sake don't feel obligated to me. I thought it was a swell idea. I did it—we did it—because we like you. And don't get the idea—I've heard of guys like this—don't get the idea I'm the kind of guy that has to push his wife off on his friends."

"Of course not," I replied, as though the idea was absurd.

"Well, here comes Janie," he said, relieved. "Cheer up, now. And for Christ's sake *don't feel obligated*."

"All right," I said.

The breeze that afternoon was pretty stiff, and a quietude settled on the three of us. For my part, I simply did a lot of staring at nothing, as though preoccupied with my thoughts. Harrison and Jane assumed that I was meditating on the cataclysmic thing that had happened to me, and they were flattered and uneasy, and spoke in ridiculously cheerful voices about nothing. Harrison, I could see, was bursting to tell Jane I'd been a virgin. Both behaved protectively and with exaggerated consideration for my feelings: it was, let me assure you, a real and thoroughgoing generosity in the Macks that I smiled at inwardly—nothing false about it except the manifestations, and that falsification was due to the strained situation, which I was aggravating by my silence. I could pretty much see where the whole thing was leading.

May I explain?

Really, you see, Harrison and Jane were quite normal and ordinary people, only a little more intelligent and a lot better-looking and richer than most. They had few friends—by their own choice,—preferring to be on extremely intimate terms with just one or two people. There was nothing affected in Jane's warmth—she was naturally disposed to affection—and Harrison's intelligence, while rather disoriented and not really keen, was capable of convincing the both of them that most social conventions are arbitrary. Yet I knew Harrison well enough to know that his emotions were often at variance with his intelligence—he realized the irrational nature of race prejudice, for example, but couldn't bring himself to like Negroes—and I supposed Jane had similar conflicts. Doubtless they'd thought about this great move for a long time, each titillated with the daring of the thing, the adventure; perhaps they'd discussed it in bed together, in the dark, where their embarrassment—or eagerness—wouldn't show. Neither would want to appear overenthusiastic, I imagine, for fear of making the other suspicious—that Jane was dissatisfied or Harrison perverted, neither of which suspicions was true. I'm sure they'd worked out every detail, savoring the deed before it was committed, imagining my surprise and pleasure, and my gratitude. I really liked Harrison, and for that reason I was sorry he'd initiated the affair, because I anticipated certain unpleasant consequences from it. But it was done: Jane was officially my mistress for a while —I was sure she'd be back for more—and I resolved to enjoy the thing while it lasted, for she was all that a man, shy or otherwise, could want in a bed partner.

These were the things I thought as we rounded Todd Point and sailed on a close reach directly for Sharp's Island. Jane was at the tiller—she was an excellent helmsman, of course—I tended the jib sheet, and Harrison lay supine in the bilge beside the centerboard trunk, his feet forward, the mainsheet in one hand and a cigar in the other, talking to Jane, on whose lovely bare feet his head rested. We took a swim when we reached the island, got stung by sea nettles, talked a bit about politics, and smoked cigarettes. After a while I pled fatigue and lay down to sleep on a blanket on the sand. Jane and Harrison declared they were going to walk around the island.

The time came when I felt her hand, but I had heard her returning up the beach, and so lost no manliness through surprise. I pulled her down beside me at once and kissed her.

"Where's Harrison?" I asked her.

"Oh the other side of the island," she said, and I had the bathing suit half off her before she could add, "He's getting firewood."

"Let's go in the trees," she said, a little nervously.

"They could see us from Cook's Point if they had field glasses."

"Never mind," I said, tossing the bathing suits aside. "Let's oblige me good and proper."

"Don't say that," she said.

Harrison came back as it was getting dark, dragging after him a roped bundle of firewood, and found us sitting dressed and talking on the blanket. He was not so cheerful as before, and set about silently and busily to build the fire, his stooped back half-accusing me of letting him do all the work. I let him do all the work, so that he could enjoy his persecution. He remained morose throughout the rest of the evening and during the run back to the cottage. Jane made some attempt at cheerfulness, but lapsed into silence when she got no response. I watched them benignly, wondering what had happened to everyone's objectivity.

By next day the mood was gone, replaced by Harrison's usual cheerfulness; but its very existence, though short-lived, was, I thought, indicative of chinks in the saintly armor. Of course, I tend to see significances in everything.

"It's just for the pleasure of it; that's all," Jane had told me.

"You can have sexual attractions without love," Harrison had told me.

Yet: "The truth is, I do love you in a way, Toddy," Jane said a week later in my hotel room. "Not the same way as I love Harrison, but it's more than just friendship; and it makes love-making more fun, doesn't it?"

"Of course," I said.

And: "A woman can love two or several men in the same way at the same time," Harrison declared after that, one night at dinner at his house, "or in different ways at the same time, or in the same way at different times, or in different ways at different times. The 'one-and-only-and-always' idea is just a conventional notion."

"Of course," I said.

Nor was I being especially hypocritical, reader, although I'd just as readily agreed earlier to the proposition that love is separable from copulation, and copulation from love. The truth is that while I knew very well what copulation is and feels like, I'd never understood personally what love is and feels like. Are the differences between, say, one's love for his wife, his mistress, his parents, his cats, his nation, his hobby, his species, his books, and his natural environment differences in kind, or merely in degree? If in kind, are the kinds definable to the point of intelligibility? If in degree, is the necessarily general definition which can cover them all so general as to be meaningless? Is this thing a fact of nature, like thirst, or purely a human and civilized invention? If he is in love who simply decides to say, "I am in love," then love I'd never known, for often as I'd said, "I am in love," I'd said it always to women who expected to hear it, never to myself. As for copulation, whether between humans or other sorts of animals, it makes me smile.

Despite which fact, I could assent without qualm to either of the Macks' sets of propositions, for they speak only of "a person," not of everybody; who was I to say that "a person" can or cannot divorce love from copulation, when I didn't comprehend love? That "a person" can or cannot love several others at once, when I didn't comprehend love? Assenting even simultaneously to contradictory propositions has never especially troubled me, and these of the Macks weren't simultaneous. I was not and am not interested in the truth or falsehood of the statements.

What I *was* interested in, when I thought of it now and then in the weeks that followed, was the fact that the Macks had so changed their minds, because it corresponded to my speculations about the course of the affair. I scarcely regarded myself as involved in it at all: my curiosity lay entirely in the character of Harrison and, to a lesser degree, of Jane. When I'd got home that August weekend after losing my chastity, I did a bit of conjecturing, supplementing my conjectures with notes. Here is one of the outlines I wrote of Harrison's psychic process:

ANTE COITUM FELIX

   I Desire for adventure.
  II Titillation at idea of extra-marital sex.
 III Reluctance to suggest idea to wife.
 IV Love for friend—suggests idea of ex.-mar. sex
     for wife with friend.
  V Titillation at idea.
 VI Objective discussion with wife of jealousy,
     adultery, *etc*.
VII Planning of actual affair betw. friend and
     wife.

THE ACT

 VIII Desperate objectivity: *"Don't feel obligated!"*
   IX Real wrestling with jealousy, despite intel-
     lectual tolerance. Unusual demands on
     wife's affections.
    X Moodiness at wife's enjoyment of affair, and
     refusal to hear of her canceling it.
  XI Insistence that wife continue affair with
     friend, and mounting jealousy when she
     does.
 XII Desultoriness except when wife asks what's
     up; then cheerfulness and objectivity,
     necessarily, or wife will end affair and
     chance for martyrdom.

Stages I through X, if not XII, were, to be sure, matters of history, easily enough inferred by the time I wrote
the list. But I went on as follows:

POST COITUM TRISTE

XIII Wife, to reassure herself, decides she loves
     friend "in a way."
XIV Husband doubts friend appreciates enormity
     of his good fortune in having been se-
     duced.

XV Both h. & w. become more demanding of friend; he is their property. Jealous of him, if not of each other.

XVI Want declarations of love from friend.

XVII *Friend refuses*—friendship cools.

XVIII Active dislike of friend for his ingratitude.

XIX Suspension of affair.

XX Period of mutual silence: h. & w. love each other more than before, in self-defense.

This was as far as I could see with any certainty, but from there I outlined a number of possible directions that the business might take:

I Permanent disaffection (probable)

II Resumption of affair on original basis (quite possible)

III Resumption of affair on part of wife, against husband's will (very doubtful)

IV Resumption of qualified affection, but no more sex (quite possible)

I made other outlines, as well, in the days that followed, but this one, at least as far as Stage XX, proved to be the most accurate. First of all, as I have already suggested, when the horns on Harrison's brow were but a few days old, Jane and I contrived to lengthen them a bit, whether at his instigation or not I can only guess. I had returned to my room for a nap after lunch, as was my practice even then. She was waiting for me, and not long afterwards she said, "The truth is, I do love you in a way, Toddy. Not the way I love Harrison, but it's more than just friendship; and it makes loves-making more fun, doesn't it?"

"Of course," I said.

I was sitting on the edge of my bed. She was standing directly in front of me. I believed she wanted me to tell her that I loved her.

"I love you," I said. I was right: she did want to hear it.

During the next year or so the affair went on strongly. Janie actually began spending every Tuesday and Friday night in my room—fantastic, so to schedule it!—and Harrison dropped into the office at least twice a day. They insisted that I take dinner with them every night, and Harrison even suggested that I move in with them, in their house.

"You can have your old bedroom back," he said. "I've always felt it was the Andrews' house, and that we were the guests."

The mention of my old bedroom, where I'd slept from age zero to age seventeen, reminded me of a certain adventure, and I laughed out loud.

"I can't help it," Harrison smiled, a little abashed.

"No, no, it's not that," I grinned. But I turned his proposal down, to be sure. Incredible! Yet he was, I'm sure, more manly in every way than I—it was a matter of sheer generosity and affection for me, I swear!

Well, the thing soon commenced getting out of hand, as I'd feared it would. Jane was as lovely and skillful as ever, but she was too loving, too solicitous. Harrison was planning a summer trip to the Bahamas for the three of us. Jane spoke vaguely for a while of my marrying some *intelligent* girl, but soon spoke of it not at all. Harrison mentioned it once, too, with the implication that the four of us would live precisely like one big happy family. All this out of the excess of their love for me! It was time to take measures.

Once he stopped in my office when I happened to be preparing a suit *a vinculo matrimonii* for Dorothy Miner, a plump Negro girl of eighteen, who picked crabs at one of the seafood houses. She was an entirely ignorant and uneducated girl, a good friend of mine, and she was arranging a divorce from her no-good husband of a month, one Junior Miner, who had abandoned her. Dorothy's skin, teeth, and eyes were excellent, and she snapped her gum. Our relationship was entirely Platonic.

"Hi, Harrison." I greeted him. "This is Dorothy."

Dorothy grinned hello and snapped a one-gum salute.

"How d'you do," Harrison said, scarcely noticing her. "Coming for lunch, Toddy?"

Recently he'd been taking me to lunch every day uptown.

"In a few minutes," I said. "Dorothy here is divorcing her husband, and I'm handling her suit."

"Oh?" he said, without interest. He sat in one of the chairs, lit a cigar, and prepared to read a magazine.

I peered into the waiting room. The secretary had already gone to lunch.

"She's poor," I went on, "so I take it out in trade."

Harrison flinched as though I'd slapped him and, blushing deeply, looked at me with a twisted smile.

"Are you kidding?" He looked surreptitiously at Dorothy, who at my statement had clapped her hand over her mouth to hold down the laughter and chewing gum that threatened to explode out of her.

"No indeed," I grinned. "I'm getting to be real good at this business. Isn't that so, Dorothy?"

"Whatever you say, Mister Andrews," Dorothy giggled; it was a tremendously funny joke.

"What the hell, Toddy!" Harrison laughed sharply.

"As a matter of fact," I said, moving toward her, "I believe her bill is overdue right now."

Dorothy giggled excitedly and fussed with her hair, not absolutely sure what was being said. But she rose uncertainly from her chair, brushed her skirt flutteringly, and stood facing me.

"Aw, say, Toddy!" Harrison croaked, getting up from his chair.

"Excuse me, boy," I said, turning to him. "I forgot my manners. You go on to lunch, and I'll be along in a minute."

"What the hell, Toddy!" Harrison exclaimed, aghast and angry. "I'll see you later!" He left the office as fast as he could, actually perspiring from his humiliation and embarrassment. I went to the window and watched him walk hurriedly up the sidewalk.

Dorothy, meanwhile, watched my face for some clue to my intentions. "What you up to, Mr. Andrews?" she

demanded with feigned severity, bursting into giggles
after the question.

I don't recall my answer, but I'm sure Dorothy laughed
at whatever it was, since she thought I was insane. I
went to join Harrison.

"What the hell, Toddy!" he said, sometime during
lunch, for perhaps the third time. "I'd have felt cheap
as hell!"

He was apologizing for what he feared I'd call his
prudery, to be sure, and perhaps even chastising himself
for having missed his chance; but more than that he was,
I saw clearly, deeply insulted.

"I'm not prejudiced; I just couldn't have anything to
do with a Negro girl," is what he said, but, "*You've
been unfaithful to Jane and to me; you've defiled yourself and us in that black hussy*," is what he meant.

"Do you make a practice of that?" he asked me.

"Some of 'em pay in eggs," I confessed blithely. "But
a man can use just so many eggs."

"Aw, hell, Toddy." He was really hurt.

"What's the matter, man?" I laughed. "Don't you
want me to put what I've learned into practice?"

"You may do anything you want to, of course," Harrison said. He was really wounded. "I've said that all
along."

"Hell, Harrison, you knew I wasn't a virgin, and Jane
did, too," I said. "What did you think I'd been doing
for thirty-two years?"

But of course they didn't know; they'd believe anything I told them, they loved me so much. Harrison
could only shake his head. His appetite was gone.

"You mustn't take things seriously," I said cheerfully.
"No matter how you approach it, everything we do on
earth is absolutely ridiculous." I laughed again, as I do
every time I remember what happened in my bedroom
when I was seventeen.

"Friendship's not a ridiculous thing," Harrison said,
solemn as an owl and full of emotion. "I don't see why
you've decided to hurt Jane and me."

"Friendship may or may not be ridiculous," I said, "but it sure is impossible."

"No, it's not," Harrison said. He was very near crying, I think, and it looked ridiculous in a robust fellow like him. "I just wish you hadn't hurt us. There wasn't any reason to. I'm not angry. I just wish you hadn't done it."

"Nonsense," I said, getting up from lunch. "I didn't say anything."

"Do you think love is ridiculous?" Harrison asked.

"Everything is ridiculous," I said.

"Why'd you lie about being a virgin? There wasn't any reason to."

"You deserved that for expecting to hear it, and being pleased when you heard it," I said.

Harrison practically slumped on the table. I really believe I had destroyed his strength.

"You don't love us," he declared hopelessly.

"Hell, buck up, man, this is degrading!" I said. "What difference does anything make? Of course I was acting, but you all wanted an act. How do you think Jane would've felt if I'd told her the truth? I'm on your side."

"The hell you are," Harrison grumbled; he was angry enough at me now to get up and walk out of the restaurant. He even left me with the check.

It was Tuesday, and there was a good chance that Jane was in my room, waiting for me to come up for my nap. I took my time, strolling down to Long Wharf before heading toward the hotel, so that Harrison could rescue her from my clutches. When finally I went in, no one was there, but I thought I detected the smell of her skin in the air. Perhaps it was my imagination. I sighed and, for the first time since that August weekend, really relaxed. It was a pity: the Macks were in every way superior to me, I thought. The antithesis of all my faults. They would have a bad day.

IV. The Captain's confession

Now, what was I doing? I believe I didn't even explain how Jane got to be back in my bed again by 1937, did I? Well, I'll finish the story later, as we go along: I've stayed close to the plot for a good long time now. Wait: looking back I see it was that I was incapable of great love for people, or at least solemn love. And I see I didn't explain it yet, at that. Good Lord! The last half of this book, I'm afraid, will be nothing but all these explanations I've promised and postponed. Let's forget all this for the moment and get Capt. Osborn his glass of rye, which I've been holding all this time, before he dies of thirst and old age.

Very well: I tiptoed from my room, so as not to disturb Jane again from her slumbers, and took the old rascal his drink, which he threw down neat with much sputtering and fuming.

"Ah, that's a good boy, son," he grinned upon finishing. Already his face was regaining its color. "If yer headed out, why I'll jest take yer arm, sir."

Mister Haecker had watched us listlessly all this time. That morning he seemed more nervous and preoccupied than usual, and—I swear this isn't all hindsight—I believe I suspected just then that for some reason or other this June 23 or 24 was going to be as momentous a day for him as for me.

"I'm headed out right now, Cap'n," I said. Capt. Osborn wheezed to his feet and limped over to take my arm, so that I could help him down the steps.

"Going out today, Mister Haecker?" I asked.

"No, son," Mister Haecker sighed. He looked as if he would say more; as if, in fact, the "more" were filling his head to bursting. One terrible look he flashed me, of pure panic; I've not forgotten it. I waited a moment for it to come. "No," Mister Haecker said again, flatly this time, and rose to return to his room.

Capt. Osborn and I left then, and started the slow descent of the stairs. I tried carefully to feel every step, so full was I of the wonder of this day; the wonder of my new and final answer; the wonder of my stupidity at not having thought of it sooner—years ago!

But I am not a thinker, nor have I ever been. My thinking is always after the fact: my thinking is the effect of my circumstances, never the other way round.

"This is step number nine," I said to myself. "Isn't it a nice step? This is step number ten, as you go down, or eighteen as you come up. Isn't it grand? This is step number eleven, or seventeen . . ." and so on. There was plenty of time to enjoy each step for its particular virtues, because of Capt. Osborn's lameness. I was having a fine time.

On step number seventeen going down, or eleven coming up, Capt. Osborn pinched my arm, the one supporting him, and chuckled softly, "How was it last night, Toddy boy?"

I looked at him in amused surprise. "What?"

The Captain chortled. "Ye don't s'pose a nosy old dog like me don't know what's up, do ye?" He poked me with his elbow, and actually winked.

"You lecherous old bastard!" I grinned. "I bet you've been listening at my door!"

"Naw, boy, I got ears for that kind o' carryin's-on. Shucks! Don't think I give a durn about it, boy. I'd have 'em up to my room by the clutch if I weren't most dead."

I said nothing, wondering only why he'd bothered to tell me about it.

"I been listenin' to you and her for a right smart

while now," he said seriously, but with his eyes twinkling. "She's a fine gal, and a frisky-lookin' one. You know how it is when yer old."

"How is it?" I asked.

Capt. Osborn snorted and smacked me on the shoulder. "Well, sir, I jest couldn't go on a-listenin' to ye any more, Toddy boy, without ye knew about it. 'Tweren't noways fair. I even left my door open some nights, now that's how wicked I am. Ye can think what ye like; I done told ye now and it's off my chest."

He seemed really relieved—of course he was a little drunk, too.

"How long have you been listening?" I asked him cheerfully. "Since 1932?"

"Durn near," Capt. Osborn admitted glumly. "I swear I never did no more'n leave my door open, though. I don't care, Toddy; ye can hate me if ye want."

Now he didn't dare to look me in the eye. He was overwhelmed with shame, unable to speak for shame. We were near the bottom of the steps.

"So you think she's frisky-looking, do you?" I grinned. The change in my voice gave him courage, but he still felt bad.

"I've had a bunch o' women, Toddy," he whispered to me solemnly. "My wife, God rest her poor soul, was a fine woman, despite she weren't no beauty; and a waterman—well, ye run into lots o' cheap floozies round the boats, want to help a drudgeman spend his wad. Some of 'em was mighty lively gals, too, for a small town, sir! And I been to the city, and the fancy houses, I won't lie." He smiled at the memory, then grew solemn again. "But I swear to God as I'm standin' here before ye this minute, may He smite me dead if I'm a-lyin', I never in my wicked life seen a woman yet could hold a candle to that gal o' yourn, Toddy. She's a beauty, I declare!"

"You old goat," I said after a minute.

"I shan't do it no more, Toddy," he said wretchedly.

"Indeed you shan't," I laughed, and his spirits were soon restored. I had had a wonderful idea, a magnificent idea, an idea such as one should have every day. Oh, it was going to be a lovely momentous day. "Good morning to you, Cap'n," I said when we reached the lobby. "I may go by your corner later on today. I'm going to pay my bill now."

But Capt. Osborn wasn't ready to let me go yet. He held on to my arm and chewed his coffee-stained moustache for a minute, composing what he had to say. I waited respectfully, for I was in no hurry at all.

"Do you believe that malarky o' Haecker's?" he asked finally, a little suspiciously. " 'Bout how nice it is to git old?"

"No," I said.

"I sleep light," he said after a moment, looking past me to the street door. "Some days I don't sleep a wink from one day to the next, sir, but I don't git tired, or I guess I'm the same tired all the time, sleep or no. Ye git that way when yer old; ye don't need sleep 'cause ye ain't able to do nothin' when yer awake to tire ye out no more'n ye already are. An old man hears what he ain't s'posed to hear, and don't hear half what he ought to. I've heard you and that young lady till I wanted to holler, if my head wasn't clogged up with the catarrh and my lights a-burnin' with the bronchitis and my joints stiff with the rheumatism, and I'd cuss myself for listenin', and couldn't stop to save me. I'd cuss myself for not gittin' up to close the door, but when yer old as me, gittin' up is a chore, and ye got to sort o' collect yerself, and then ye jest wait all day to git back in bed, but can't sleep 'cause ye know sooner or later that that there bed ye was so all-fired hot to crawl into is goin' to be the last time ye'll crawl into it. That ain't no fit lullaby to git sung to sleep with, Toddy! And when I'd git up and go to the door, why I could jest hear ye all the plainer, and I'd tell myself that right there was somethin' I'll never do again on this earth!"

He paused for breath; I was astonished at his volubility.

"Well, sir, Haecker might be right; he's a sight smarter'n me, but I swear I can't see one durn thing to this *old* business. The sinus keeps a-fillin' yer nose till

yer fit to drown, and yer eyes water, and yer legs go to
sleep if ye set still, and yer bones pain ye if ye move.
I'd rather be forty and feel good and be dumb as a post,
and be fit to do work, than to feel all day like I weren't
rightly alive, and hurt all the time and have to blow my
nose till it's sore, and crack a cane on my legs to keep
the blood a-goin', even if I knew all there was to know."

"Mister Haecker's just a kid," I smiled, delighted to
hear Capt. Osborn talk.

"He ain't but seventy and fit as a fiddle," the old man
snorted. "I'd of said the same thing at seventy if I'd of
commenced to think about it, which I didn't commence
to think about it till I was eighty. And I can tell you
today it's an awful thing to think about, this *dyin'*, and I
would rather be chokin' from the sinus, and not fit to
git out o' bed no more, and use a bedpan and eat dry
toast, than to be dead, sir! Any man tells ye yer goin'
to git to like the idea jest 'cause yer old, he's lyin' to ye,
and I want to tell ye right now, when the time comes
I am goin' to cuss and holler at the first angel steps into
my room, and if the rheumatism lets me, I am goin' to
kick the daylights out of 'im. I figure I'll prob'ly die halfway down these stairsteps, Toddy, a-tryin' like hell to
git outside, and if them angels think o' me what I
think o' them, I'm goin' to Hell for sure."

Well, he went on in that vein, and I remember it all,
but that's enough of Capt. Osborn for now—perhaps you
don't enjoy old men as I do. When the old fellow had said
his piece—and completely forgotten, I'm certain, what
he'd been apologizing for—he went out into the street to
take his place on the loafers' bench uptown with his
cronies in the sunshine. I love him, if I loved anyone,
I think; death for him would be the hyphenated break in
an endless, rambling, illiterate monologue, and that is a
good way for it to be if you're most people. He was fooling himself, and not fooling himself about it, so that
ultimately he wasn't fooling himself at all, and hence it
wasn't necessary to feel any pity for him. I felt much
sorrier, in my uninvolved way, for Mister Haecker, with
his paeans to old age and gracious death: he was really

fooling himself, and one could anticipate that he would someday have a difficult time of it. In the meanwhile, he must spend all his energies shoring up his delusion, and do it, moreover, alone, for his intensity and prudishness found him no friends; Osborn, on the contrary, sniffed and wheezed and creaked and spat, and cursed and complained, and never knew a gloomy day in his life.

I remembered my little plan and went to the registration desk. Jerry Hogey, the manager, was on duty. He was a friend of mine, and it was due to his understanding of the world that Jane had been able to come to my room despite hotel policy at any time for the last five years. I bid him good morning as usual, and borrowing a sheet of hotel stationery from him, scribbled a note to Jane.

"This is for the young lady, Jerry," I said, folding it and giving it to him.

"Sure."

Then, as I had done every morning since 1930 (and still do), I wrote out a check for one dollar and fifty cents payable to the Dorset Hotel, for the day's lodging.

V. A *raison de coeur*

That's right, I pay my hotel bill every day, and reregister every day, too, despite the fact that the hotel offers weekly and monthly and even seasonal rates for long-term guests. It's no eccentricity, friend, nor any sign of stinginess on my part: I have an excellent reason for doing so, but it is a *raison de coeur*, if I may say so—a reason of the heart and not of the head.

Doubly so; literally so. Listen: eleven times the muscle of my heart contracted while I was writing the four words of the preceding sentence. Perhaps six hundred times since I began to write this little chapter. Seven hundred thirty-two million, one hundred thirty-six thousand, three hundred twenty times, since I moved into the hotel. And no less than one billion, sixty-seven million, six hundred thirty-six thousand, one hundred sixty times has my heart beat since a day in 1919, at Fort George G. Meade, when an army doctor, Captain John Frisbee, informed me, during the course of my predischarge physical examination, that each soft beat my sick heart beat might be my sick heart's last. This fact—the fact that having begun this sentence, I may not live to write its end; that having poured my drink, I may not live to taste it, or that it may pass a live man's tongue to burn a dead man's belly; that having slumbered, I may never wake, or having waked, may never living sleep—this for thirty-five years has been the overwhelming condition of my existence, the great fact of my life: had been so for eighteen years already, or five hundred forty-nine

57

million, sixty thousand, four hundred eighty heartbeats, by June 23 or 24 of 1937. This is the enormous question, in its thousand trifling forms (Having heard tick, will I hear tock? Having served, will I volley? Having sugared will I cream? Having eithered, will I or? Itching, will I scratch? Hemming, will I haw?), toward answering which all my thoughts and deeds, all my dreams and energies have been oriented. This is the problem which, having answered it thrice before without solving it, I had waked this one momentous morning with the key to, gratuitously, gratis, like that! This question, the fact of my life, is, reader, the fact of my book as well: the question which, now answered but yet to be explained, answers, reader, everything, explains all.

Well, perhaps not all, or at least perhaps not clearly. It doesn't directly explain, for example, why I chose and choose to pay my bill daily, every morning, instead of weekly or seasonally. Don't think, I beg you, that I fear not living to get my money's worth if I pay too far ahead: lose money I might, but fear losing it, never. There's nothing in me of Miss Holiday Hopkinson, my ninety-year-old neighbor and senior member of the D.E.C., who buys her one-a-day vitamin pills in the smallest bottles—for her, the real economy size—and sleeps fully dressed, her arms folded funereally upon her chest, so as to cause, by her dying, the least possible trouble for anybody. No, I pay my buck-fifty every morning to remind myself—should I ever forget!—that I'm renting another day from eternity, remitting the interest on borrowed time, leasing my bed on the narrow chance I may live to sleep on it once more, for at least the beginning of another night. It helps me maintain a correct perspective, reminds me that long-range plans, even short-range plans, have, for me at least, no value.

To be sure, one doesn't want to live as though each day may be his last, when there is at least some chance that it may be only his next. One needs, even in my position, something to counterbalance the immediacy of a one-day-at-a-time existence, a life on the installment plan. Hence my *Inquiry,* properly to prepare even for the beginning of which, as I see it, would require more lifetimes than it takes a lazy Buddhist to attain Nirvana. My *Inquiry* is timeless, in effect; that is, I proceed at it as though I had eternity to inquire in. And, because processes persisted in long enough tend to become ends in themselves, it is enough for me to do an hour's work, or two hours' work, on my *Inquiry* every night after supper, to make me feel just a little bit outside of time and heartbeats.

So, I begin each day with a gesture of cynicism, and close it with a gesture of faith; or, if you prefer, begin it by reminding myself that, for me at least, goals and objectives are without value, and close it by demonstrating that the fact is irrelevant. A gesture of temporality, a gesture of eternity. It is in the tension between these two gestures that I have lived my adult life.

VI. Maryland beaten biscuits

Now you know my secret, or an important part of it,
at least. No one else—except Dr. Frisbee, I suppose—
ever knew it, not even my excellent friend Harrison.
Why should I have told him? I never told him I was a
saint, and yet he became one himself soon enough afterwards. I never told him in so many words that I was
a cynic, and yet he's one today, as far as I know. If I
had told him of my heart condition he'd only have tried
to acquire one too, and I've no particular wish to
make anyone unhappy. No, I long ago learned that one's
illnesses are both pleasanter and more useful if one keeps
their exact nature to himself: one's friends, uncertain as
to the cause of one's queer behavior and strange suffer-
ings, impute to one a mysteriousness often subtly convenient. Even Jane never suspected my ailing heart,
and though she well knew—from how many painful
nights!—that something was wrong with me, I never
told her about my infected prostate, either. As a result,
she often attributed to herself failures in our intercourse
that were incontestably mine, and Jane—proud Jane—
is never lovelier or more desirable than when contrite.

Enough: I paid my hotel bill, then, and stepped onto
High Street just as the clock on the People's Trust
building struck seven. Already the air was warm; it
promised to be a blistering hot day, like the day before,
when temperature and humidity both were in the
nineties. Very few people were about yet, and only an

occasional automobile wandered down the quiet expanse of the street. I crossed diagonally against the traffic—to the corner of Christ Episcopal Church, whose lovely stones were softly greened, and strolled from there down the left side of High Street toward Long Wharf, eating my breakfast as I walked.

May I recommend three Maryland beaten biscuits, with water, for your breakfast? They are hard as a haul-seiner's conscience and dry as a dredger's tongue, and they sit for hours in your morning stomach like ballast on a tender ship's keel. They cost little, are easily and crumblessly carried in your pockets, and if forgotten and gone stale, are neither harder nor less palatable than when fresh. What's more, eaten first thing in the morning and followed by a cigar, they put a crabberman's thirst on you, such that all the water in a deep neap tide can't quench—and none, I think, denies the charms of water on the bowels of morning? Beaten biscuits, friend: beaten with the back of an axe on a sawn stump behind the cookhouse; you really need a slave system, I suppose, to produce the best beaten biscuits, but there is a colored lady down by the creek, next door to the dredge builder's. . . . If, like a condemned man, I had been offered my choice from man's cuisine for this my final earthly breakfast, I'd have chosen no more than what I had.

Few things are stable in this world. Your morning stomach, reader, ballasted with three Maryland beaten biscuits, will be stable.

High Street, where I walked, is like no other street in Cambridge, or on the peninsula. A wide, flat boulevard of a street, gently arched with edge-laid yellow brick, it runs its gracious best from Christ Church and the courthouse down to Long Wharf, the municipal park, two long, stately blocks away. One is tempted to describe it as lined with elegant mansions, until one examines it in winter, when the leaves are down and the trees are gaunt as gibbets. Mansions there are—two, three of them—but the majority of the homes are large and inelegant. What makes High Street lovely are the trees and the street itself. The trees are enormous, for the most part: oaks and cottonwood poplars that rustle loftily above you like wind pennants atop mighty masts; that when leaved transform the shabbiest houses into mansions; that corrugate the concrete of the wide sidewalks with the idle flexing of their roots. An avenue of edge-laid yellow bricks is the only pavement worthy of such trees, and like them, it dignifies the things around it. Automobiles whisper over this brick like quiet yachts; men walking on the outsized sidewalk under the out-sized poplars are dwarfed into dignity. The whole boule-vard terminates excellently in a circular roadway on Long Wharf—terminates, actually, in the grander boule-vard of the Choptank. Daniel Jones, upon whose plan-tation the whole city of Cambridge now rests, put his plantation house near where this street runs. Colonel John Kirk, Lord Baltimore's Dorchester land agent, built in 1706 the town's first house, "The Point," near where this street runs. There are slave quarters; there are porch columns made of ships' masts; there are ancient names bred to idle pursuits; there are barns of houses housing servantless, kinless, friendless dodderers; there are brazen parades and bold seagulls, brass bands, eminence, and imbecility; there are Sunday pigeons and excursion steamers and mock oranges—all dignified by the great trees and soft glazed brick of the street. The rest of Cam-bridge is rather unattractive.

As was my custom, I strolled down to the circle and over beside the yacht basin. The river was glassy and empty of boats, too calm to move the clappers of the bell buoy out in the channel, a mile away. A single early motor truck inched across the long, low bridge. The flag above the yacht club predicted fair weather. With a great sense of well-being I tossed the last hard half of my breakfast biscuits at a doubler crab mating la-zily just beneath the surface. As was *their* custom, the gentleman did the swimming while the soft lady be-neath, locked to him with all her legs, allowed him his pleasure, which might last for fourteen hours. Crabbers refer to the male and female thus coupled in their sport as one crab, a "doubler," just as Plato imagined the human prototype to be male and female joined into one being. My biscuit landed to starboard of the lovers, and the gentleman slid, unruffled, six inches to port, then submerged, girl friend and all, in search of the tasty missile that had near scuttled his affair. I laughed and made a mental note to make a physical note, for my *Inquiry*, of the similarity between the crabbers and Plato, and to remind Jane that there were creatures who took longer than I.

I lit my first cigar and completed the circle, coming around to the side nearest the creek. Work was commencing in the lumber mill and shipyard across the creek mouth from where I stood: a weathered bugeye, worn by forty or fifty years of oyster-dredging, was hauled up on the railway, and a crew of men scraped barnacles and marine growth from her bottom. I surveyed the whole scene critically and with pleasure, but no more intently than usual, despite the fact that I might never see it again, for I was determined to preserve the typicality of this great day. I had knocked the first ash from my cigar and was preparing to walk part way up High Street to the garage where my boat lay a-building, when my satisfied eye caught something new in the picture: a brightly lettered poster tacked to a piling at the farthest corner of the wharf, where the creek joined the river, and at the foot of the piling a small package or bale tied with a string. I walked over, of course, to investigate.

ADAM'S ORIGINAL & UNPARALLELED FLOATING OPERA, announced the poster; *Jacob R. Adam, Owner & Captain.* 6 BIG ACTS! it went on to declare: DRAMA, MINSTRELS, VAUDEVILLE! *Moral & Refined!* TONIGHT TONIGHT TONIGHT TONIGHT! *Admission 20¢, 35¢, 50¢!* TONIGHT TONIGHT! FREE *Concert Starts 7:30 P.M.! Show Starts 8:00 P.M.!*

The bundle at the foot of the piling contained printed handbills advertising the show in more detail; it was obviously dumped there temporarily by the showboat's advance man. I took a handbill from the bundle, stuck it

into my coat pocket to read at my leisure, and continued
my morning walk.

I smoked my way back onto High Street, the handbill
folded in my pocket and my mind preoccupied with
scampering ideas as flitting as idle mice. In thirty seconds I'd forgotten all about the poster, the handbill, and
ADAM'S ORIGINAL & UNPARALLELED FLOAT-
ING OPERA.

VII. My two unfinished boats

When I think of Cambridge and of Dorchester County, the things I think of, quite understandably, are crabbing, oystering, fishing, muskrat-trapping, duckhunting, sailing, and swimming. It is virtually impossible, no matter what his station, for a boy to grow to puberty in the County without experiencing most of these activities and becoming proficient in one or two of them.

Virtually, but not entirely impossible. I, for example, though I was not a sheltered child at all, managed to attain the age of twenty-seven years without ever having gone crabbing, oystering, fishing, muskrat-trapping, duckhunting, sailing, or even swimming, despite the fact that all my boyhood companions enjoyed these pursuits. I just never got interested in them. Moreover, I've never tasted an oyster; I can't enjoy crabmeat; I'd never choose fish for dinner; I detest wild game of any sort, rodent or fowl; and although Col. Henry Morton, who owns the biggest tomato cannery on God's earth, is a peculiar friend of mine, the tomatoes that line his coffers upset my digestion. But lest you conclude too easily that this represents some philosophical position of mine, let me add that I *have* done some sailing since I set up my law practice here in 1927—though I still can't handle a sailboat myself—and I'd become, as a matter of fact, something of an expert swimmer by the time of this story. And this *does*, in a small way, reflect a philosophical position of mine, or at least a general practice, to wit: being just a little bit less than consistent in practically everything, so that any quick characterization of me, or general statement about me, will probably be untrue, or at least inadequate. To be sure, many people make such characterizations anyway—I get the impression at times that doing so constitutes a chief activity of the town's idle intelligences—but I have the not-inconsiderable satisfaction of knowing that they're wrong and of hearing them contradict one another (and thereby, I conclude, cancel one another out).

All this, deviously, by way of introduction to my boat-building, for my next step, after completing my morning stroll around Long Wharf, was to turn off High Street into an alley running down to the creek. There, in a two-car garage loaned me by a friend and client of mine, every morning I did an hour's work on the boat I'd been building for some years.

My boats—what shall I say of them? In my life I've built two. The first I started when I was perhaps twelve years old. I had devoured every yachting magazine I could lay my hands on, had "sent away" for countless blueprints and specifications, had tossed and dreamed of hulls and spars and sails until I was dizzy with yearning. To build a boat—that seemed to me a deed almost holy in its utter desirability. Then to provision it, and some early morning to slip quietly from my mooring, to run down the river, sparkling in the sun, out into the broad reaches of the Bay, and down to the endless oceans. Never have I regarded my boyhood as anything but pleasant, and the intensity of this longing to escape must be accounted for by the attractiveness of the thing itself, not by any unattractiveness of my surroundings. In short, I was running *to*, not running *from*, or so I believe.

But I could never be content with anything even remotely within my power to achieve. My father, delighted at the idea of my building a boat, suggested various types of skiffs, scows, prams, dinghies, and tenders, and even a simple catboat: he would help me, of course, with the steaming of the frames and strakes. But what! Go to Singapore in a dinghy? Cap the black growlers of the

northern ocean in a row-skiff? Dare the broiling Bay of
Bengal in a common catboat? For me it was more a
problem of choosing between a fifty-foot auxiliary sloop
and a fifty-foot auxiliary schooner. The sloop rig, I
remember arguing to myself, lent itself more readily to
one-man cruising, and I'd not need to rely for help on
the indistinct but delicious young girls I somehow saw
always lying about the deck; on the other hand, if in a
typhoon, say, I should be dismasted, that would be all,
brother, were I to put my eggs in one basket as the sloop
rig does. A divided rig—schooner, yawl, or ketch, in the
order of my preference—would leave me some hope of
limping bravely to port under the remaining mast. To
be sure, these delicate arguments had to be kept to myself. I allowed my father to buy me enough lumber for a
skiff, and I remember quite clearly regretting then that
he and Mrs. Aaron, the current housekeeper, weren't
dead, so that I could commence work on my schooner
without their scoffing to embarrass me.

Finally I more or less began work on the skiff, declaring it to be a lifeboat for my schooner. Alas! I was
horribly clumsy with tools, if deft and ingenious with
daydreams. My measurements were all wrong, my lines
out of plumb and out of symmetry, my saw cuts rough
and crooked, my nails askew. All summer I worked on
the thing, correcting one error with another, changing
the length and shape of a miscut strake to fit a mis-
measured frame, laying a split batten over a gaping
seam, ignoring fatal errors into nonexistence, covering incompetence with incompetence, and pretending that the
mere labor and bulk of the thing would somehow rectify
all the fundamental mistakes implied in the very first
step (rather, misstep) of construction. I made it known
that I desired neither help nor advice, and my father,
chalking the cost of the lumber up to my education, left
me alone.

When autumn came I lost interest in boatbuilding.
Why labor so on a dinghy, when what I wanted was a
schooner? And a schooner, of course, I could never build
where there were people to watch and scoff. Left to my-

self, absolutely to myself, I was certain I could build one
and surprise everybody with the finished product. But
it must be only the finished product that they judge me
by, not the steps of construction: there would be a
grandeur in the forest, so to speak, transcending and re-
deeming any puny deficiencies in the individual trees.
All through the winter the half-framed hull weathered
untouched in the back yard, like a decomposing carcass
whose ribs are partly exposed; by spring I was interested
in nothing but horses. The skiff remained in the yard, a
silent reproach to my fickleness, for perhaps six years.
Then one year, while I was in the Army, a hurricane
blew the boat off its sawhorses, and the rotting planks
sprang from the frames. My father used it for firewood, I believe.

I tell you this story because it's rather representative
of a great many features of my boyhood. My daydreams, my conceptions of how things should be, were
invariably grandiose, and I labored at them prodigiously
and always secretly. But my talent for doing correctly
the small things that constitute the glorious whole was
unfailingly defective—I never mastered first principles
—and so the finished product, while perhaps impressive
to the untutored, was always mediocre to the knowl-
edged. To how many of my young achievements does
this not apply! I dazzled old ladies at piano recitals, but
never really mastered the scales; won the tennis cham-
pionships of my high school—a school famously indifferent to tennis—but never really mastered the strokes;
graduated first in my class, but never really learned to
think. And so on: it's a painful list.

Now a deficiency like this, which doubtless stems from
overeagerness to shine in the eyes of one's neighbors, can
be damnedly hard to throw off, and I'm confident I
should have it yet, but that the Army cured me of it.

Not the Army as such—heavens no. The Army as
such was a terrible experience in every way. I shan't
even speak of it. I enlisted impulsively in 1917—God
alone knows why—and realized before the bus left
Cambridge what a really distasteful experience I was

going to have. And I had it too: every unpleasant thing that could happen to a soldier in that insane army happened to me, except being gassed and being killed. Certainly I wasn't patriotic. I had no feelings at all about the issues involved, if there were any (I've never been curious enough really to find out).

Well, this isn't a book about my war experiences, though I certainly could write a good long book about them, and it wouldn't resemble any war book you've ever read, either. Except for a single incident—and I mean to tell you about it at once—my army career was largely without influence on the rest of my life. This one incident, during the battle in the Argonne Forest, I find significant in two ways, at least: it in some way cured the tendency described above, and it provided me with the second of two unforgettable demonstrations of my own animality.

The Argonne fighting was well under way before my outfit was sent in to replace a rifle company that had been virtually destroyed. It was my first and only battle. I was, of course, inadequate fighting material—what intelligent boy isn't?—but I was no more afraid as the lorries drove us to the front than were any of my fellows, and I've never been cowardly, to my knowledge, in matters of physical violence. It was late afternoon when we arrived, and the Germans were laying down an incredible barrage on our positions. We were hustled out of the lorries onto the ground, and it was much as I imagine jumping from an airplane would be: relative calm, and then bang! horrible confusion. We were all paralyzed. None of us remembered anything, not anything that we'd been told. Frightful! Horrifying! The air, I swear, was simply split with artillery. The ground— you couldn't stand on it, no matter how loudly your officers shouted. Really, we all simply fell down: fortunately for us, I guess. I suppose most of you, if you are men of this century, have experienced the like, or worse.

I've no idea what we did. Indeed, I've often wondered, if there were many soldiers like me, how in heaven the Allies won the war. God knows how much the government had spent on my training, hurried as it was, and then I—all of us—simply collapsed. No cowardice, no fear (not yet); we were simply robbed of muscle by the noise.

Just before dark, I remember, I found myself belly-down on a sort of ridge. All around were splintered tree stumps, perhaps three feet high. I had no idea what I was doing there. The sun was almost down, and there was a great deal of smoke in the air. A number of uniformed figures seemed to be attending to some business of theirs in a hollow below me. The barrage, I think, had ceased, or else I was totally deaf.

"Why," I said to myself, rather drunkenly, "those men are German soldiers. That is the enemy."

I could scarcely believe it. For heaven's sake! German soldiers! It occurred to me that I was supposed to kill them, and that I was equipped with a Springfield rifle designed for that purpose. I didn't even look around to see if the rest of the United States Army was with me; I simply fired my rifle any number of times at the men working in the hollow. None of them dropped dead, or even seemed to notice their danger—don't ask me why. It seems to me they should have counter-attacked, or taken cover, or something. No, sir. I remember very carefully reloading and firing, reloading and firing, reloading and firing. It was a hell of an easy war, but how in the world did you go about killing the enemy soldiers? And where was everyone else?

The next thing that happened (for scenes changed in this battle exactly as they do in dreams) happened in the dark, because suddenly it had been nighttime for a while. This time it was I who was in a hollow, on all fours in a shell hole half full of muddy water. I still had my rifle, but it was empty, and if I owned any more ammunition I didn't remember how to put it in the rifle. I was just there, on hands and knees, my head hanging down, staring at the water. Everything was quiet again; only a few flares made a hissing noise as they drifted down through the air. And now there came the real fear, quickly but not suddenly, a purely physiological sensation. It swept over me in great shuddering waves from my thighs and buttocks to my shoulders and jaws and back again, one shock after another, exactly as though rolls of flesh were undulating. There was no cowardice involved; in fact, my mind wasn't engaged at all—either I was thinking of something else or, more probably, I was just stupefied. Cowardice necessarily involves choice, but fear is independent of choice. When the waves reached my hips and thighs I opened my sphincters; when they crossed my stomach and chest I retched and gasped; when they struck my face my jaw hung slack, my saliva ran, my eyes watered. Then back they'd go again, and then return. I've no way of knowing how long this lasted: perhaps only a minute. But it was the purest and strongest emotion I've ever experienced. I could actually, for a part of the time it lasted, regard myself objectively: a shocked, drooling animal in a mudhole. It is one thing to agree intellectually to the proposition that man is a species of animal; quite another to realize, thoroughly and for good, your personal animality, to the extent that you are actually never able to oppose the terms *man* and *animal*, even in casual speech; never able to regard your fellow creatures except as more or less intelligent, more or less healthy, more or less dangerous, more or less adequate *fauna;* never able to regard their accomplishments except as the tricks of more or less well-trained beasts. In my case this has been true since that night, and no one—not my father, nor Jane, nor myself—have I been able even for a moment to regard differently.

The other part of the incident followed immediately. Both armies returned from wherever they'd been hiding, and I was aware for the first time that a battle was really in progress. A great deal of machine-gun fire rattled across the hollow from both sides; men in ones and twos and threes stalked or crawled or ran all around, occasionally peering into my shell hole; the flares blazed more frequently, and there was much shooting, shouting, screaming, and cursing. This must have

lasted for hours. With a part of my mind I was perfectly
willing to join in the fighting, though I was utterly
confused; if someone had shouted orders at me, I'm
quite certain I'd have obeyed them. But I was left entirely alone, and alone my body couldn't move. The
waves of fear were gone, but they'd left me exhausted,
still in the same position.

Finally the artillery opened up again, apparently laying their fire exactly in the hollow, where the hand-to-
hand fighting was in progress. Perhaps both sides had
resolved to clean up that untidy squabble with high-ex-
plosive shells and begin again. Most of the explosions
seemed to be within a few hundred feet of my shell
hole, and the fear returned in force. There was no question in my mind but that I'd be killed; what I feared
was the knowledge that my dying could very well be
extremely protracted and painful, and that it must be
suffered alone. The only thing I was able to wish for
was someone to keep me company while I went through
with it.

Sentimental? It certainly is, and I've thought so ever
since. But that's what the feeling was, and it was tremendously strong, and I'd not be honest if I didn't speak
of it. It was such a strong feeling that when from no-
where a man jumped into the mudhole beside me, I fell
on him instantly and embraced him as hard as I could.
Very sensibly he assumed I was attacking him, and with
some cry of alarm he wrenched away. I fell on him
again, before he could raise his rifle, but he managed,
in our tussling, to run the point of his bayonet into
the calf of my left leg, not very deeply. I shouted in
his ear that I didn't want to fight with him; that I
loved him; and at the same time—since I was larger
and apparently stronger than he—I got behind him and
pinioned his arms and legs. He struggled for a long time,
and in German, so that I knew him to be an enemy
soldier. How could I make everything clear to him? Even
if I were able to talk to him and explain my intentions,
he would certainly think me either a coward or a lunatic,

and kill me anyway. He had to understand everything, all of me, at once.

Of course, I could have killed him, and I'm sure he understood that fact; he was helpless. What I did, finally, was work my rifle over to me with one hand, after rolling my companion onto his stomach in the muddy water, and then put the point of *my* bayonet on the back of his neck, until it just barely broke the skin and drew a drop of blood. My friend went weak—collapsed, in fact—and what he cried in German I took to be either a surrender, a plea for mercy, or both. Not wanting to leave any doubts about the matter, I held him there for several minutes more, perhaps even pressing a trifle harder on the bayonet, until he broke down completely, lost control of all his bodily functions, as I had done earlier, and wept. He had, I believe, the same fear; certainly he was a shocked animal.

Where was the rest of the U.S. Army? Reader, I've *never* learned where the armies spent their time in this battle!

Now you must read this paragraph with an open mind; I can't warn you too often not to make the quickest, easiest judgments of me, if you're interested in being accurate. The next thing I did was lay aside my rifle, bayonet and all, lie in the mud beside this animal whom I'd reduced to paralysis, and embrace him as fiercely as any man ever embraced his mistress. I covered his dirty stubbled face with kisses: his staring eyes, his lolling tongue, his shuddering neck. Incredibly, now that I look back on it, he responded in kind! The fear left him, as it had left me, and for an hour, I'm sure, we clung to each other frenziedly. We were one man.

If the notion of homosexuality enters your head, you're normal, I think. If you judge either the German sergeant or myself to have been homosexual, you're stupid.

After our embrace, the trembling of both of us subsided, and we released each other. There was a complete and, to my knowledge, unique understanding between us. I, in fact, was something like normal for the first time since stepping out of the lorry. I was aware, now, with all my senses. A great many shells were whistling overhead, but none were bursting very near us, and the hand-to-hand fighting had apparently moved elsewhere.

The German and I sat on opposite sides of the shell hole, perhaps five feet apart, smiling at each other in complete understanding. Occasionally we attempted to communicate by gestures, but for the most part communication was unnecessary. I had dry cigarettes; he had none. He had rations; I had none. Neither had ammunition. Both had bandages and iodine. Both had bayonets. We shared the cigarettes and rations; I bandaged the wound in his neck, and he the wound in my leg. He indicated the seat of his trousers and held his nose. I indicated the seat of my trousers and did likewise. We both laughed until we cried, and fell into each other's arms again—though only for an instant this time: our fear had gone, and normal embarrassment had taken its place. We regarded each other warmly. Perhaps we slept.

Never in my life have I enjoyed such intense intimacy, such clear communication with a fellow human being, male or female, as I enjoyed with that German sergeant. He was a little, grizzled, unlovely fellow, considerably older than I; doubtless a professional soldier. I saw him more clearly as the day dawned. While he slept I felt as jealous and protective—I think *exactly* as jealous and protective—as a lion over her cub. If any American, even my father, had jumped into the shell hole at that moment, I'd have killed him unhesitatingly before he could kill my friend. What validity could the puny artifices of family and nation claim beside a bond like ours? I asked myself. What difference did it make that we would go our separate ways, never having learned even the other's name, he to kill other Americans, I perhaps to kill other Germans? He and I had made a private armistice. What difference (I asked myself) did it make even if we were to meet each other again, face to face, in the numberless chances of war, and without a smile of recognition, go at each other with bayonets? For the space of some hours we had been one man, had understood each other beyond friendship, beyond love, as a wise man understands himself.

Let me end the story. My rhetorical questions, as you may have anticipated from the way I just phrased them, raised after a while the germ of a doubt in my mind. To be sure, I understood perfectly how *I* felt about our relationship. But then, I had instigated it. My companion had indeed responded, but from beneath the pointed end of my bayonet, his face down in the mud. Again, he'd not turned on me, though he'd had many opportunities to do so since our tacit truce; but, as I remarked, he looked like an old professional soldier, and I, remember, was only eighteen. How could I be certain that our incredible sympathy did not actually exist only in my imagination, and that he was not all the while smiling to himself, taking me for a lunatic or a homosexual crank, biding his time, resting, smoking, sleeping—until he was good and ready to kill me? Only a hardened professional could sleep so soundly and contentedly in a mudhole during a battle. There was even a trace of a smile on his lips. Was it not something of a sneer?

In the growing light everything seemed less nightmarish. Doubtless the fighting had moved considerably away from our position. Was I in German territory, or was he in Allied territory? He was indeed an unlovely fellow. Common-looking, and tough. No intelligence in his face. Heaven knows he looked incapable of conceiving or appreciating any such *rapport* as I'd envisioned. Hadn't he speared my leg? Of course, I'd jumped him first. . . .

I grew increasingly nervous, and peered out of my hole. Not a living soul was visible, though a number of bodies lay in various positions and degrees of completeness on the ground, in the barbed wire, on the shattered stumps, in other holes. The air was full of smoke and dust and atmospheric haze, and it was a bit chilly. My leg hurt. I sat back in the hole and stared nervously at the German sergeant, waiting for some sign of his awakening. I even took up my rifle (and moved his

away), just to be safe. I was getting jumpier all the
time, and began to worry that the fear might return.

Finally I decided to sneak quietly out of the hole and
make my way to the Americans, if I could find
them, leaving the German asleep. A perfect solution! I
rose to my feet, holding my rifle and not taking my eyes
from the German soldier's face. At once he opened his
eyes, and although his head didn't move, a look of terrible
alarm flashed across his face. In an instant I lunged at
him and struck him in the chest with my bayonet. The
blow stunned him, and my weight on the rifle held
him pinned, but the blade lodged in his breastbone and
refused to enter.

My God! I thought frantically. *Can't I kill him?* He
grasped the muzzle of my rifle in both hands, trying to
force it away from him, but I had better leverage from
my standing position. We strained silently for a second.
My eyes were on the bayonet; his, I fear, on my face.
At last the point slipped up off the bone, from our combined straining—our last correspondence!—and with a
tiny horrible puncturing sound, slid into and through his
neck, and he began to die. I dropped the rifle—
no force on earth could have made me withdraw it—and
fled, trembling, across the shattered hollow. By merest
luck, the first soldiers I encountered were American,
and the battle was over for me.

That's my war story. I told it—apropos of what?
Oh yes, it cured me. In fact, it cured me of several
things. I seldom daydream any more, even for an instant.
I never expect very much from myself or my fellow animals. I almost never characterize people in a word or
phrase, and rarely pass judgment on them at all. I no
longer look for the esteem or approbation of my acquaintances. I do things more slowly, more systematically, and
more thoroughly. To be sure, I don't call that one incident, traumatic as it proved to be, the single cause of
all these alterations in me; in fact, I don't see where
some of them follow at all. But when I think of the alterations, I immediately think of the incident (specifically, I confess, of that infinitesimal puncturing noise),

and that fact seems signficant to me, though I'll allow the possibility of the whole thing's being a case of *post hoc ergo propter hoc,* as the logicians say. I don't really care.

So, when I was mustered out of service in 1919 and entered Johns Hopkins University, I began to relearn, correctly, a number of things that I'd half-learned before—among them the technique of thinking clearly. I found, for example, that when I handled a tennis racket correctly, I had little aptitude for tennis. On the other hand, my golf game improved considerably. I gave up playing the piano. And, when in 1935 I again took a mild interest in boats, I did everything correctly right from the beginning. Not that I believe, as many people do, that there is some intrinsic ethical value in doing things properly rather than improperly. I don't subscribe, as an ethical premise, to the proposition that anything worth doing is worth doing well. It's simply that I've been incapable, temperamentally, of doing things otherwise than correctly since 1918, just as prior to then I was very nearly incapable of doing anything just right.

My boat is a thirty-five-foot work boat, "torpedo-backed" and narrow-beamed in the manner of the tong boats used hereabouts. Her frames, keel, and floor timbers are of stout white oak, and her side, deck, and bottom planking of good white cedar. A very seaworthy little craft, carefully, slowly, and correctly built. By this morning in 1937 I'd been working on her for two years, doing perhaps an hour's work each day. Many mornings I remember, I simply sat in the garage and stared at her, thinking out the wisest next move, or at the wall, thinking of nothing.

On this particular morning I laid some floor planking: I'd finished planking the sides and bottom and had turned the hull right side up. As usual, I didn't bother to change my clothes or even roll my sleeves; in hat, coat, and tie I set to work laying 3/4" × 3" tongue-and-groove cedar planks to the floor beams, fastening them with bronze screws and galvanized wire nails, countersunk and puttied over. I'd cut the planks the day before, so that

at the end of my hour most of the deck was laid and I
wasn't even sweating. I brushed the knees of my trousers (they weren't dirty, for I kept my wood clean), lit
my second cigar of the day, surveyed my work for several
minutes, and then left for the office, closing the garage
door behind me. If anyone ever took the trouble to
finish my boat, I reflected without sorrow, he'd have
himself an excellent vessel.

VIII. A note, a warning

A note, a warning, if I may?

I got from my father the habit of doing manual work in my good clothes. Dad always made a fetish of it, like the nineteenth-century surgeons who affected evening clothes in the operating rooms and prided themselves on executing difficult surgery without bloodying their starched and studded shirt fronts.

"It teaches a man to be careful," Dad declared, "and to work easily. Hard work isn't always good work."

In the same attire he'd worn that afternoon in court, boutonniere and all, Dad would spade the vegetable garden before supper, spray the catalpa trees for caterpillars (mixing the unslaked-lime spray himself), and perhaps whitewash the foundation piers of the house or hose off the car. He never got dirty or wet, or even ruffled. When one day in 1930 I came home from the office and found Dad dead in the cellar, one end of his belt spiked to the floor joist and the other fastened around his neck, there was not a smudge of dirt anywhere on him, though the cellar was quite dusty. His clothes were perfectly creased and free of wrinkles, and although his face was black and his eyes were popped, his hair was neatly and correctly combed.

I agree with Dad that doing manual labor in one's office clothes teaches one to work carefully and neatly, and I follow his practice almost consistently. But I suspect that he attributed to the habit some terminal value; it was, I think, related to some vague philosophy of his. With me that is not the case, and I caution you against inferring anything of a philosophical flavor from my practice. There is in my daily routine a great deal that legitimately implies my ideas about things, but you mustn't work from the wrong things or you'll go astray. Perhaps I shouldn't even have mentioned working on my boat in my good clothes.

IX. The handbill

I didn't choose the practice of law as my career, except perhaps passively; it had been assumed from earliest memory that I was to study for the Maryland Bar and enter Dad's firm, and I never protested. Certainly I've never been dedicated to anything, although as with many another thing I've always maintained a reasonable curiosity about the meanings of legal rules and the workings of courts.

May I say that I am perhaps the best lawyer on the Eastern Shore? Perhaps I shouldn't, for you'll take the statement as self-praise. If I thought the practice of law absolutely important, then my statement would indeed be as much a boast as a description; but truthfully I consider advocacy, jurisprudence, even justice, to have no more intrinsic importance than, say, oyster-shucking. And you'd understand, wouldn't you, that if a man like myself asserted with a smile that he was the peninsula's best oyster shucker (I'm not), or cigarette roller, or pinball-machine tilter, he'd not be guilty of prideful boasting? It requires small subtlety to grasp that, I think.

I am the legal equivalent of a general practitioner in medicine. I handle criminal cases, torts, wills, deeds, titles, bonds, articles of incorporation—everything that a lawyer can get his fingers into. I've argued in orphans' courts, circuit courts, federal courts, admiralty courts, and appellate courts—once in the U.S. Supreme Court. I seldom lose cases; but then I seldom plead a case that

I'm not fairly happy about to begin with. I must confess that I pick and choose among my possible clients,
not to find easy cases, but to find interesting ones. I'd
rather sit idle than do work I'm not interested in.

My partners, fortunately for the firm, are not so
choosy; they keep fairly busy and earn good incomes.
Harry Bishop, of the original Andrews & Bishop, was
sixty-three at the time of this story (he died in 1948).
He and Dad founded the firm in 1904, when both were
fairly young men. Jimmy Andrews—no relation to me—
is the other partner. In 1937 he was perhaps twenty-
seven or -eight, just beginning his practice, and I'd
suggested bringing him into the firm if only for the convenience of being able to use the same letterhead we'd
used before Dad hanged himself.

Our office, whither I went at last after my hour of
boat-building, is a little frame building. We each have a
private office, but we share the same waiting room, lavatory, and secretary.

The last-mentioned, Mrs. Lake, a lady of fifty, was
typing when I entered and paid my usual respects.

"No one waiting for me, I suppose?" I asked.

"Mrs. Mack was in," Mrs. Lake said.

"Oh? What for?"

"She left a note," Mrs. Lake said. "I put it on your
desk."

I straightened my tie, using the waiting-room mirror.

"No word yet from Charley this morning?"

"Not yet."

Charley was Charley Parks, an attorney whose office
was next door to ours. He was an old friend and poker
partner of mine, and currently we were on opposite sides
in a fantastically complicated litigation that had developed out of a trifling automobile accident. The suit
was several years old already and hadn't even been tried
yet: both parties being wealthy and "litigious," as we
barristers say, Charley and I were having a field day
fencing with procedural disputes. I'll describe the case
eventually.

"How about the pickle barrel?" I asked, stubbing

out my cigar in Mrs. Lake's ashtray and picking up my mail from her desk.

"I think there's a letter there from Baltimore," she said.

This had to do with my major case at the moment, another venerable one, involving the contested will of Harrison Mack Senior, the pickle king, who had died in 1935. It too was a labyrinthine affair: suffice it for the moment to say that Harrison had retained me to rescue his jeopardized millions (nearly three millions, in fact), and that since January things had been looking up for our adversaries, much to Harrison's concern, if not mine.

I took my letters into my office then and began my last day's work at the law. Two of the letters were advertisements, and I threw them out unopened. Another was a check for one thousand seven hundred dollars from William Butler, my client in the automobile litigation mentioned before—an installment on his bill. I put it aside for Mrs. Lake to handle. Another was a personal note from Junior Miner, the ex-husband of the little colored girl in Chapter III, whose divorce I'd handled five years before. It read, in part:

> I will kill you m———g son of a bich if come
> on Pine street m———g son of bich you now
> why. J.M.

The deleted words (he, not I, deleted them, by the way) are, of course, present participles suggesting that I was addicted to that activity characteristic of King Oedipus. I've no idea why Junior deleted that word in his weekly letter to me; perhaps he was prudish. He believed I arranged Dorothy's divorce in order to make her my mistress, and sent me threatening letters of this sort every six or eight days for a number of years. I put this one aside for Mrs. Lake to file with the others, hoping, as I always did on these occasions, that Junior would not be foolish enough to carry out his threat. Our state's attorney, Jarman James, was an avid

Negro-hanger whom I detested for no particular reason,
and it would have distressed me to present him with such
an easy case. To be sure, if Junior didn't carry out his
threat within the next several hours, he would be safe.

The next letter I recognized at once from my own
handwriting on the envelope—I'd addressed it to myself.
It was postmarked *Baltimore,* and it was, or could be,
tremendously important. But I wasn't ready to read it
yet; I propped it against my desk lamp.

The other letters had to do with various works in
progress. I read them, spending some minutes after each
to stare out of my window at the county jail and make
mental notes. Then I put them aside and read Jane's
message.

> Darling, if you hoped in some way to hurt me
> again with your note this morning, you failed.
> I'm not disturbed at all. I will do exactly what
> you suggest, my dear, if you will see Marvin
> Rose for a complete physical, to find out why
> you're such a pansy. Love, Jane.

"Touché!" I said, impressed at Jane's rhetoric. Really,
she had come a long way since I first met her! I must
explain that Marvin Rose is a doctor and a golfing friend
of mine, and that in naming a visit to him as the condition for her granting my request—remember the note
I sent her earlier, by way of Jerry Hogey—Jane believed herself safe: not since 1924 had I visited a doctor
except socially, and Jane knew that my refusal to do so
was no less strong for its being unreasonable.

Jane's note, too, I put aside for Mrs. Lake to file, first
replacing it in its envelope. I think I may safely suggest,
reader, that no one—no one—in Cambridge could bring
suit against me with reasonable hopes of winning. In
cases where I can't persuade judge or jury with rhetoric
or legal gambit, I usually have something in my files to
do the trick as evidence. Certainly I could forsee no circumstances in which this note might prove useful, especially since my slight involvement in the world would be

terminated that very day. Despite which fact, I put it aside for Mrs. Lake.

Then I called the doctor.

"I'd like an appointment to see Dr. Rose just before lunch," I told his receptionist.

"I'm sorry, sir, Dr. Rose will be busy until this evening."

"Would you tell him it's Todd Andrews?" I asked. "I want a physical. Maybe he can look at me during his naptime." I knew that Marvin was in the habit of napping in his office, on the examination table, before lunch.

"Hold on." I heard her cover the mouthpiece and speak to Marvin.

"Hello? Todd?" It was Marvin who spoke now.

"Yes. How about a minute of your naptime today, Marv?"

"What the hell, Toddy, you sick?" he asked incredulously.

"Nope."

"Somebody suing me?"

"Nope. I just want an examination."

He was speechless. For years he and I had argued, at golf or over highballs, about medicine and law, or rather health and justice, and although he had no inkling of my cardiac ailments, he knew that I was unhealthy and that I didn't care to consult a physician about it.

"Sure, Toddy, come on up, boy," he laughed. "Say, are you pulling my leg?"

"Nope. I want the whole works. Eleven o'clock?"

"Make it eleven-fifteen," Marvin said. "I want to sharpen my needles and things. I don't get you often."

"All right," I said. "I'll bring witnesses."

We talked for a minute or two of other things, and then I went to my files, got out the dossier on the litigation over Harrison Mack Senior's estate, and prepared to begin work in earnest.

But again I interrupted myself. I had bitten the end off my third cigar, and finding my matchbook empty, I slapped my coat pockets to search for another. What I

found was the handbill I'd pocketed earlier on Long
Wharf and had forgotten to read.

"Let's see, here." I unfolded it and spread it out on
my desk.

COMING

BIGGER & BETTER THAN EVER!

ADAM'S

ORIGINAL   A N D   UNPARALLELED

"Ocean-Going"

FLOATING
OPERA

Jacob R. Adam, Owner & Captain

AT: Long Wharf, Cambridge, June [23 or 24]

Tickets on Sale All Day at the Ticket Office
ADMISSIONS: 20¢, 35¢, 50¢

---

* *   SEATING CAPACITY 700   * *

LARGEST FLOATING THEATRE ON
THE EASTERN SEABOARD

($60,000 Actually Invested to Date)

A
Choice Company
of
Players,
Presenting the Finest in DRAMA,

MUSIC,

MINSTRELS,

VAUDEVILLE

ONE LONG LAUGH!

Great Moral Show
The High-Water Mark of Mirth, Melody, & Minstrelsy

A   N
  L   E
    L   W

Up-to-date Comedians, Dazzling Dancers,
Cultivated Singers.

| MORAL AND REFINED | **GORGEOUS** | Cooled by the breezes of the sea |

You Are Cordially Invited to Visit America's
Finest & Safest Floating Theatre During the Day

[On the inside of the folded sheet was more information about the virtues of Adam's Floating Opera, and a program of the evening's entertainment.]

---

*FREE Concert Begins at 7:30 PM; Show Begins
8:00 PM

PROF. EISEN'S
$7,500 CHALLENGE ATLANTIC &
CHESAPEAKE MARITIME BAND

Composed of the Finest Musicians in the *U.S.A.!*

Listen for the C A L L I O P E !

Watch for the B A N D   P A R A D E!

EVERY PROMISE MADE
FAITHFULLY KEPT

Come early for the Band Concert and Stay for the
East Coast's Finest Show

✳ *SEE* ✳

THE MARY PICKFORD OF
THE CHESAPEAKE

!! MISS CLARA MULLOY !!

IN
a new, side-splitting one-act comedy

THE

Hilarious! P A R A C H U T E *Heartwarming!*

Moral!

GIRL

** ** S E E ** **
The Chaste & Inimitable

ETHIOPIAN TIDEWATER
MINSTRELS
U.S.A.'s Greatest Sable
Humorists

** ** S E E ** **
J. Strudge, the Magnificent Ethiopian Delineator,
The Black Demosthenes, in
His Original Burlesque Stump Speech

Sweet Sally Starbuck, the Singing Soubrette,
with Melodies of Heart, Hearth,
& Home.

T. Wallace Whittaker, Famous Southern Tenor, Singing
Pastoral Lays of the Corn & Cotton Fields

SPECIAL FEATURE!

Burley Joe Wells, World Renowned Imitator, With His
Impressions of Steam Calliopes, Sawmills, Model-T
Fords, Hound Dogs, and the Famous Race Between
the Sternwheelers *Natchez & Robert E. Lee,* Con-
cluding and Climaxing with the Terrible & Terrific
Explosion of the Steamboat *James B. Taylor,* Which
Tragedy Occurred at Natchez-Under-The-Hill, Mis-
sissippi, on February 19, 1892.

Concluding With A

WONDERFUL
PANITHIOPLICONICA

DON'T MISS IT!
KEEP YOUR EYE ON THE
DATE!

Bring the Kiddies

Approved By Press, Public, & Clergy Alike.

Well! Far be it from me to miss the Wonderful Panithiopliconica.

"Mrs. Lake," I called, "will you telephone Mrs. Mack sometime this morning and ask her if I may take Jeannine to see the showboat when it pulls in?"

"Okay," Mrs. Lake said. "What time?"

"Late this afternoon, I guess. About four? Am I supposed to do anything after four?"

"I'll look. . . . No."

The famous race between the stern-wheelers *Natchez* and *Robert E. Lee*. I wouldn't miss it for anything. But I didn't keep my eye on the date, as Capt. Adam's handbill suggested; indeed, I crumpled the bill and threw it away just then, and I've never been able to remember whether all this occurred on the twenty-third or twenty-fourth of June. To be sure, at some time during the nine years I spent recollecting the events of this day, I could with small effort have gone to the files of the *Daily Banner* and dug out the showboat advertisement to fix the date. But I've never bothered to. Is it the Navajo Indians who make it a point always to leave in their woven rugs and other artifacts some slight imperfection, an odd stitch or a bump of clay, in order not to compete with the gods? I think it is. Well, I have no gods, and so I can't justify my shortcomings as do the Navajos. But it has, I must say, seemed unwise to me from the beginning to verify that date. Perhaps I can't explain why.

Indeed, I shan't try.

X. The law

That will-o'-the-wisp, the law: where shall I begin to speak of it? Is the law the legal rules, or their interpretations by judges, or by juries? Is it the precedent or the present fact? The norm or the practice? I'll not define it. I think I'm not interested in what the law is.

Surely, though, I am curious about things that the law can be made to do, but this disinterestedly, without involvement. A child encounters a toy tractor, winds it up, and sets it climbing over a book. The tractor climbs well. The child puts another book here, so, and angles the first. The tractor surmounts them, with difficulty. The child opens the pages of the first book, leans the second obliquely against it, and places his shoe behind the two. The tractor tries, strains, spins, whirrs, and falls helpless like a turtle on its back, treads racing uselessly. The child moves on to his crayons and picture puzzles, no expression on his face. I don't know what you mean, sir, when you speak of justice.

It may well be that, like Capt. Osborn, you have come to believe that I have opinions about everything, and absurd ones at that. Very well. But of most things about which people hold some sort of opinion, I have none at all, except by implication. What I mean is this: the law, for example, prescribes certain things that shall not be done, or certain ways in which things shall be done, but of most specific human acts it has nothing to say one way or the other. Yet these extra-legal acts, or most of them, are certainly influenced and conditioned, implicitly, by the laws pertaining to other things. People, for example, aren't allowed to kill us while we're performing our extra-legal acts. In the same way, though I have no opinion one way or the other on whether suicide, for instance, is a sin, I have certain opinions on a few other things that made it possible for me to contemplate suicide in 1937, and actually to resolve to destroy myself.

All right. I have, then, no general opinions about the law, or about justice, and if I sometimes set little obstacles, books and slants, in the path of the courts, it is because I'm curious, merely, to see what will happen. On those occasions when the engine of the law falls impotently sprawling, I make a mental note of it, and without a change of expression, go on to my boat or my *Inquiry*. Winning or losing litigations is of no concern to me, and I think I've never made a secret of that fact to my clients. They come to me, as they come before the law, because *they* think they have a case. The law and I are uncommitted.

One more thing, before I explain the contest over Harrison Mack Senior's will: if you have followed this chapter so far, you might sensibly ask, "Doesn't your attitude —which is, after all, irresponsible—allow for the defeat, even the punishment, of the innocent, and at times the victory of the guilty? And does this not concern you?" It does indeed allow for the persecution of innocence— though perhaps not so frequently as you might imagine. And this persecution *concerns* me, in the sense that it holds my attention, but not especially in the sense that it bothers me. Under certain circumstances, to be explained later, I am not averse to pillorying the innocent, to throwing my stone, with the crowd, at some poor martyr. Irresponsibility, yes: I affirm, I insist upon my basic and ultimate irresponsibility. Yes indeed.

It did not deeply concern me, as I said before, whether Harrison received his inheritance or not, though I stood to profit by some fifty thousand dollars or more if he did. In any world but ours, the case of the Mack estate would be fantastic; even in ours, it received considerable publicity from the Maryland press.

Old man Mack, whom I've come to admire tremendously though I never met him, died in 1935, after years of declining physical and mental health. He left a large estate: stock in the Mack Pickle Co. amounting to 58 per cent of the total shares, and worth perhaps two million dollars in fairly good times; stock in various other business concerns, some more prosperous than others; a large house in Ruxton, another in West Palm Beach, and cottages in Nova Scotia and Maryland (including the one I was seduced in); extensive farmlands, especially cucumber farms, the crop from which was bought by the Mack Pickle Co.; perhaps a hundred thousand dollars in cash; assorted automobiles, cabin cruisers, horses, and dogs, and, through the majority stockholdings, the potential presidency of the pickle company, which office carried a salary of twenty-five thousand dollars a year. It was, undeniably, an estate that many people would consider worth going to court about.

Now of the several characteristics of Harrison *père,* three were important to the case: he was in the habit of using his wealth as a club to keep his kin in line; he was, apparently, addicted to the drawing up of wills; and, especially in his last years, he was obsessively jealous of the products of his mind and body, and permitted none to be destroyed.

You perhaps recall my saying that when I first met Harrison Junior, in 1925, he was undergoing an attack of communism, and had been disinherited as a result? It seems that disinheritance, or the threat of it, was the old man's favorite disciplinary measure, not only for his son, but also for his wife. When young Harrison attended Dartmouth rather than Johns Hopkins; when he studied journalism rather than business; when he became a communist rather than a Republican; he was disinherited until such time as he mended his ways. When Mother Mack went to Europe rather than to West Palm Beach; when she chose sparkling burgundy over highballs, Dulaney Valley over Ruxton, Roosevelt and Garner over Hoover and Curtis; she was disinherited until such time as she recanted her heresies.

All these falls from and reinstatements to grace, of course, required emendations of Father Mack's will, and

a number of extra-familiar circumstances also demanded
frequent revision of his bequests. His country club admits
someone he doesn't like: the club must be disinherited.
A pickle-truck driver runs down a state policeman checking on overloaded vehicles: the driver must be defended
in court and provided for explicitly in the will. After
the old man's death, when his safe was opened, a total
of seventeen complete and distinct testamentary instruments was found, chronologically arranged, each beginning with a revocation of the preceding one. He hadn't
been able to throw any of his soul-children into the fire.

Now this situation, though certainly unusual, would in
itself have presented no particular problem of administra-
tion, because the law provides that where there are
several wills, the last shall be considered representative
of the testator's real intentions, other things being equal.
And each of these wills explicitly revoked the preceding
one. But alas, with Mr. Mack all other things weren't
equal. Not only did his physical well-being deteriorate in
his last years, through arthritis to leukemia to the grave;
his sanity deteriorated also, gradually, along the con-
tinuum from relative normalcy through marked eccentricity to jibbering idiocy. In the first stages he merely
inherited and disinherited his relatives and his society; in
the second he no longer went to work, he required
entertainment as well as care from his nurses, and he allowed nothing of his creation—including hair- and nail-
clippings, urine, feces, and wills—to be thrown away; in
the last stages he could scarcely move or talk, had no control whatever over his bodily functions, and recognized
no one. To be sure, the stages were not dramatically
marked, but blended into one another imperceptibly.

Of the seventeen wills (which represented by no means
all the wills Mack had written, but only those written
since he acquired his mania for preserving things), only
the first two were composed during the time when the
old man's sanity was pretty much indisputable; that is,
prior to 1933. The first left about half the estate to
Harrison Junior and the other half to Mother Mack,
provided it could not be demonstrated to the court that

she had drunk any sparkling burgundy since 1920. This one was dated 1924. The other, dated 1932, left about half the estate to Mrs. Mack unconditionally and the rest to Harrison, provided it could not be demonstrated to the court that during a five-year probationary period, 1932-37, Harrison had done, written, or said anything that could reasonably be construed as evidence of communist sympathies. This clause, incidentally, ran through most of the subsequent testaments as well.

Of the other fifteen documents, ten were composed in 1933 and 1934, years when the testator's sanity was open to debate. The last five, all written in the first three months of 1935, could be established without much difficulty, in court, as being the whims of a lunatic: one left everything to Johns Hopkins University on condition that the University's name be changed to Hoover College (the University politely declined); others bequeathed the whole shebang to the Atlantic Ocean or the A.F.L.

Luckily for the majesty of Maryland's law, there were only two primary and four secondary contestants for the estate. Elizabeth Sweetman Mack, the testator's widow, was interested in having Will #6, a product of late 1933, adjudged the last testament: it bequeathed her virtually the entire estate, on the sparkling-burgundy condition described above. Harrison Junior preferred #8, the fruit of early 1934; it bequeathed *him* virtually the whole works, on the clean-skirts condition also described above. Misses Janice Kosko, Shirley Mae Greene, and Berenice Silverman, registered nurses all, who had attended old Mack during the first, second, and third stages, respectively, of his physical invalidity, liked Wills #3, 9, and 12, in that order: therein, apparently, their late employer provided them ample remuneration, posthumously, for services rendered beyond the line of duty. The final contestant was the pastor of the Macks' neighborhood church: in Will #13 the bulk of the estate was to pass to that church, with the express hope that the richer and more influential organized religion became, the sooner it would be cast off by the people. (Mr. Mack, whose anticlericalism was stronger than his knowledge of history, believed that the predominance of the Catholic church in Europe during the Middle Ages had led to its virtual overthrow by intelligent atheists in the French Revolution.)

Ah, it was an edifying spectacle! Mrs. Mack retained Messrs. Dugan, Froebel, & Kemp, of Baltimore, to defend her legal rights; her son retained Andrews, Bishop, & Andrews, of Cambridge; the nurses and the minister each retained separate attorneys. Everyone was a little afraid to carry the thing to court immediately, and for several months there was a welter of legal nonsense, threats, and counterthreats, among the six firms involved. Five of us joined forces to oust the clergyman from the sweepstakes—it was enough for the three nurses to agree that Mack was definitely insane by the time Will #13 was composed. A month later, by pretty much the same technique, Misses Kosko and Greene induced Miss Silverman to withdraw, on the solemnly contracted condition that should either of them win, she would get 20 per cent of the loot. Then, in a surprise maneuver, Bill Froebel, of Dugan, Froebel, & Kemp, produced sworn affidavits from two Negro maids of the Mack household, to the effect that they had seen Miss Greene indulging in "unnatural and beastly" practices with the deceased—the practices were described in toothsome detail—and suggested to that young lady that, should she not decide the contest wasn't worth the trouble, he would release the affidavits to the newspapers. I never learned for certain whether the affidavits were true or false, but in either case they were effective: the additional attraction of several thousand dollars, payable when Mrs. Mack won the case, induced Miss Greene to seek her happiness outside the courts.

The field was cleared, then, in 1936, of half the entries, before the race even began. Only Miss Kosko, Harrison Junior, and Mrs. Mack remained. Each of them, of necessity, must attempt to prove two things: that Father Mack was still legally sane when the will of their choice was written, and that by the time the subsequent wills were written, he no longer could comprehend what he was about. On this basis, Miss Kosko, I should say, had the strongest case, since her will (dated February, 1933) was the earliest of the three. But love was her undoing: she retained as her attorney her boy friend, a lad fresh out of law school, none too bright. After our initial out-of-court sparring I was fairly confident that he was no match for either Froebel or myself, and when, late in 1936, he refused on ethical grounds a really magnanimous bribe from Froebel, I was certain.

And sure enough, when the first swords clashed in Baltimore Probate Court, in May of 1936, Froebel was able, with little trouble, to insinuate that the young lawyer was a presumptuous ass; that the nurse Miss Kosko was a promiscuous hussy out to defraud poor widows of their honest legacies by seducing old men in their dotage; that Mrs. Mack, out of the kindness of her bereaved heart, had already offered the brazen slut a gratuity infinitely more munificent than she deserved (this news was ruled out as incompetent evidence, of course); and that even to listen tolerantly to such gross and ill-concealed avariciousness was a tribute to the inexhaustible patience and indulgence of long-suffering judges. In addition, Froebel must have offered some cogent arguments, for surrogate courts, even in Baltimore, are notoriously competent, and the judge ruled in his favor. When Froebel then offered Miss Kosko another settlement, considerably smaller than the first, the young barrister accepted it humbly, coming as it did on the heels of his defeat, and didn't even think of appealing the judgment until it was too late.

Then, in June of the same year, Froebel filed suit for Mrs. Mack, charging flatly that Mr. Mack had been of unsound mind when he wrote Will #8, Harrison's will, and never again regained his sanity. If the court so ruled, then Mrs. Mack's will, #6, would become the authentic testamentary instrument, since Miss Kosko was out of the running. If the court ruled against him, then our document, #8, would automatically revoke his.

There was not much difference between Mack's mental state in late 1933 and his mental state in early 1934. I introduced statements from Misses Kosko and Greene that in both years he required them to save the contents of his bedpan in dill-pickle jars, which were then stored in the wine cellar, and I got the impression that the judge—a notoriously staid and conservative fellow—believed Mack was insane from the beginning. The newspapers, too, expressed the opinion that there was no particular evidence on either side, and that, besides, it was a disgraceful thing for a mother and her son to squabble so selfishly. All the pressure was for out-of-court settlement on a fifty-fifty basis, but both Harrison and his mother—who had never especially liked each other—refused, on the advice of their attorneys. Froebel thought he could win, and wanted the money; I thought I could win, and wanted to see.

Will #6, remember, gave all the estate to Mrs. Mack, provided she hadn't tasted sparkling burgundy since 1920. Our will left the money and property to Harrison, if he had steered clear of Moscow since 1932, and, in addition, bequeathed to Mrs. Mack the several hundred pickle jars just mentioned. Both documents included the extraordinary provision that, should the separate conditions not be fulfilled, the terms were to be reversed.

Froebel's arguments, essentially, were two: 1) That a man has not necessarily lost his business sense if he provides once for a complete reversal of bequests, of the sort seen in Will #6, assuming he is really dead set against sparkling burgundy; but then to reverse himself completely in the space of a few months indicates that something has snapped in his head, since there were no dramatic external changes to account for the new will. 2) That the bequest of the pickle jars appeared in no wills before #8, and in all the wills from #8 through #16, and that such a bequest is evidence tending to show that Mack no longer understood the nature of his estate.

"Not necessarily," I suggested. "Suppose he didn't love his wife?"

"Ah," Froebel replied quickly, "but he left the pickle jars to a different person each time, not to Mrs. Mack every time."

"But remember," I said, "he saved the mess because he liked it; the bequest of it, then, is an act of love, not of hate. Would you call love insane?"

"Indeed not," Froebel answered. "But if he'd loved her, he'd have given her the property as well as the— excrement."

"No indeed," I countered. "Remember that in one will he bequeathed all his money to the church because he disliked the church. Couldn't the bequest to my client be such an act, and the bequest to yours the real gift?"

"It could indeed," Froebel grinned. "Will you say that that's the case?"

"No, I shan't," I said. "I merely suggested the possibility."

"And in doing so," Froebel declared, "you suggest the possibility that Will Number 8 is as insane as Will Number 13, the church will you mentioned. Anyone who bequeaths three millions of dollars as a punishment, I suggest, is somewhat out of perspective."

Oh, I tell you, Bill Froebel was a lawyer. When it came to impromptu legal sophistry, he and I had no equals at the Maryland Bar.

My arguments were 1) that the inclusion of the pickle jars was hardly sufficient evidence of a sudden loss of understanding, when Mack had been collecting them since Will #3 or 4; 2) that therefore the testator was either sane when he composed both instruments or insane when he composed them; 3) that if he was sane both times, Will #8 was official; 4) that if insane both times, some earlier will was official and must be brought forward, or otherwise Mack could be deemed to have died intestate (in which case Harrison would get all the money, Mrs. Mack retaining only dower).

The judge, Frank Lasker of the Baltimore bench, agreed. Froebel appealed the decision through the Court of Appeals to the Maryland Supreme Court, and both appellate courts affirmed the lower court's judgment. It seemed as if Harrison were a wealthy man: all that remained was to wait until January of 1937—the end of his probationary period—and then to demonstrate that

Harrison had kept clear of communist sympathy since 1932. He assured me that nothing could be suggested which could be called fellow-traveling, even remotely. Froebel threatened for a while to institute a new suit, in favor of Will #2, but nothing came of his threat.

The final test was in the form of a hearing. Harrison and I appeared at the Baltimore courthouse early in January; Judge Lasker read the terms of Will #8 and declared that if no one present could offer evidence of such sympathies as were therein interdicted, he was prepared to declare the matter settled and to order the will executed at once. Froebel then appeared, much to my surprise, and announced that he had such evidence, enough to warrant the reversal of bequests provided for by our will, and was ready to offer it to the court.

"You told me there wasn't anything," I reminded Harrison, who had turned white.

"I swear there isn't!" he whispered back, but nevertheless he began perspiring and trembling a little. I sat back to see what Froebel had cooked up.

"What will you attempt to prove?" the Judge asked him.

"That as recently as last year, Your Honor, while his poor father was in the grave—perhaps speeded there (who knows?) by his son's regrettable irresponsibility—that just last year, Your Honor, this son, who is now so eager to take from his mother what is rightfully hers, was aiding and abetting actively, with large gifts of money, that infamous communist doctrine against which his father's entire life was such an eloquent argument; confident, I doubt not, that he could conceal his surreptitious Bolshevism until such time as he was in a position to devote the whole of the Mack estate towards overthrowing the way of life that made its accumulation possible!"

Froebel—need I point out?—was a past master of the detached noun clause: judge and spectators were stirred.

"For heaven's sake!" Harrison whispered. "You don't think he means my Spanish donations!"

"If you were silly enough to make any, then I daresay

he does," I replied, appalled anew at Harrison's innocence.

And indeed, the "Spanish donations" were precisely what Froebel had in mind. He offered in evidence photo-stated checks, four of them, for one thousand dollars each, made out to an American subscription agency representing the Spanish Loyalist government. They were dated March 10, May 19, September 2, and October 7, and all were signed *Harrison A. Mack, Jr.*

Judge Lasker examined the photostats and frowned. "Did you write these checks?" he asked Harrison, passing the pictures to him.

"Of course!" Harrison yelled. "What the hell's that—"

"Order!" suggested the Judge. "Aren't you aware that the Loyalist movement is run by the Communist Party? Directed from the Kremlin?"

"Aw, come on!" Harrison pleaded, until I poked him and he sat down.

"May I point out," Froebel continued blandly, "that not only is a gift to the Loyalists in essence a gift to Moscow, but this particular subscription agency is a notorious Party organization, under F.B.I. surveillance. A man may donate to the Loyalists through honest, if vague, liberalism, I daresay; but one doesn't send checks to this subscription outfit unless one is sympathetic, to say the least, with the Comintern. Young Mr. Mack, like too many of our idle aristocrats, is, I fear, a blue-blood with a Red heart."

I believe it was this final metaphor that won Froebel the judgment. It was too good to let pass. I saw the newspaper people virtually doff their unpleasant hats in tribute, and scribble the immortal words for the next editions of their papers. Even the Judge smiled benignly upon the happy trope: I could see that it struck him square in the prejudices, and found a welcome there.

There was some further discussion, but no one listened closely; everyone was repeating to himself, with a self-satisfied smile, that all young aristocrats are blue-bloods with Red hearts. *Blue-bloods with Red hearts!* How could mere justice cope with poetry? Men, I think, are ever attracted to the *bon mot* rather than the *mot juste,* and judges, no less than other men, are often moved by considerations more aesthetic than judicial. Even I was not a little impressed, and regretted only that we had no jury to be overwhelmed by such a purple plum from the groves of advocacy. *A blue-blood with a Red heart!* How brandish mere reasonableness against pure music? Should I hope to tip the scales with puny logic, when Froebel had Parnassus in his pan? In vain might I warn Judge Lasker that, through the press, all America was watching, and Europe as well, for his decision.

"My client, a lover of freedom and human dignity," I declared, "made his contributions to the oppressed Loyalists as a moral obligation, proper to every good American, to fight those Rebels who would crush the independence of the human spirit, and trample liberty under hobnailed boots! How can you charge him with advocating anarchy and violent overthrow, when in a single year he gives four thousand dollars to support the Spanish government against those who would overthrow it?"

And on I went for some minutes, talking like a congressional candidate, trying to make capital out of the Spanish confusion, wherein the radicals were the *status quo* and the reactionaries the rebels. It was, I must say, an admirable bit of casuistry, but I knew well that my cause was lost. Only Froebel, I think, had ears for my rhetoric; the rest of the room was filled with *blue-bloods with Red hearts.*

And Judge Lasker, as I mentioned before in another connection, was a famous conservative. Though by no means a fascist himself—he was probably uncommitted in the Spanish revolution—he epitomized the unthinking antagonism of his class toward anything pinker than the blue end of the spectrum: a familiar antagonism that used to infuriate me when, prior to 1924, I was interested in such things as social justice. When finally he ruled, he ruled in Froebel's favor.

"It does not matter whether there is a difference between the Moscow and Madrid varieties of communism," he declared, "or whether the Court or anyone else approves or disapproves of the defendant's gifts or the cause for which they were intended. The fact is that the subscription agency involved is a communist organization under government surveillance, and a gift to that agency is a gift to communism. There can be no question of the donor's sympathy with what the agency represented, and what it represented was communism. The will before me provides that should such sympathy be demonstrated, as it has been here, the terms of the document are to be reversed. The Court here orders such a reversal."

Well, we were poor again. Harrison went weak, and when I offered him a cigar he came near to vomiting.

"It's incredible!" he croaked, actually perspiring from the shock of it.

"Do you give up?" I asked him. "Or shall I appeal?"

He clutched at the hope eagerly. "Can we appeal?"

"Sure," I said. "Don't you see how unlogical Lasker's reasoning is?"

"Unlogical! It was so logical it overwhelmed me!"

"Not at all." I assured him. "He said the subscription agency was sympathetic to communism. You give money to the agency; therefore you're sympathetic to communism. It's like saying that if you give money to a Salvation Army girl who happens to be a vegetarian, you're sympathetic to vegetarians. The communists support the Loyalists; you support the Loyalists; therefore you're a communist."

Harrison was tremendously relieved, but so weak he could scarcely stand. He laughed shortly, nervously.

"Well! That puts us back in the race, doesn't it? Ha, I'd thought there for a while—Christ, Toddy, you've saved my ass again! Damned judge! We've got it now, boy!"

I shook my head, and he went white again.

"What the hell's wrong?"

"I'll appeal," I said, "but we'll lose again, I guess."

"How's that? Lose again!" He laughed, and sucked in his breath.

"Forget about the logic," I said. "Nobody really cares

about the logic. They make up their minds by their prejudices about Spain. I think you'd have lost here even
without Froebel's metaphor. I'd have to talk Lasker
into liberalism to win the case."

I went on to explain that of the seven judges of the
Court of Appeals who would review the decision, three
were Republicans with a pronounced antiliberal bias,
two were fairly liberal Democrats, one was a reactionary
"Southern Democrat," more antiliberal than the Republicans, and the seventh, an unenthusiastic Democrat, was
relatively unbiased.

"I know them all," I said. "Abrams, Moore, and
Stevens, the Republicans, will vote against you. Forrester, the Southern Democrat, would vote for you if it
were a party issue, but it's not; he'll go along with the
Republicans. Stedman and Barnes, the liberals, will go
along with you, and I think Haddaway will too, because he likes me and because he dislikes Lasker's bad
logic."

"But hell, that's four to three!" Harrison cried. "That
means I lose!"

"As I said."

"How about the Maryland Supreme Court?"

"That's too much to predict," I said. "I don't know
that they've declared themselves on Spain, and I don't
know them personally. But they've affirmed almost every
important verdict of the Court of Appeals in three years."

Harrison was crushed. "It's unjust!" was all he could
say.

"You know how these things are," I smiled.

"Aw, but what the hell!" He shook his head, tapped
his feet impatiently, pursed his lips, sighed in spasms. I
expected him to faint, but he held on tightly, though he
could scarcely talk. The truth was, of course, that it is
one thing—an easy thing—to give what Cardinal New-
man calls "notional" assent to a proposition such as
"There is no justice"; quite another and more difficult
matter to give it "real" assent, to learn it stingingly,
to the heart, through involvement. I remember hoping

that Harrison was strong enough at least to be educated by his expensive loss.

I appealed the judgment of the Court.

"Just to leave the door open," I explained. "I might think of something."

That evening, before I left Baltimore with Harrison, we had dinner at Bill Froebel's club, as his guests. I praised his inspiration, and he my logic-twisting. Harrison was morose, and although he drank heavily, he refused to join in the conversation. He couldn't drive home. On the way, he would clutch my arm and groan, "Three million bucks, Toddy!"

I looked coldly at him.

"Hell, man," he protested, "I know what you're thinking, but you should know me better. I don't want the money like another man might, just to go crazy on. Think what we could do on three million bucks, the three of us!"

It was the first time since Jane and I had resumed our affair in 1935 that Harrison had spoken again of "the three of us," as he had used to do.

"A million apiece?" I asked. "Or a joint account?"

Harrison felt the bristles and flinched, and all the way home he felt constrained to pretend that the loss of three million dollars touched his philosophical heart not at all. I watched the effort from the corner of my eye, and marveled sadly at his disorientation.

Finally he broke down, as we were crossing the Choptank River bridge, pulling into Cambridge. The water was white-capped and cold-looking. Dead ahead, at the end of the boulevard that the bridge ran onto, Morton's Marvelous Tomatoes, Inc., spread its red neon banner across the sky, and I smiled. The town lights ran in a flat string along the water's edge, from Hambrooks Bar Lighthouse, flashing on the right, to the Macks' house in East Cambridge, its ground-floor windows still lit, where Jane was waiting.

"I give up, Toddy," he said tersely; "I'm no philosopher. I can't say I wouldn't have been happy at one time without the money—I *did* get myself disinherited a few

times, you know. But once it came so close and seemed
so sure—"

"What is it?" I snapped.

"Ah, Christ—Janie and I had plans, boy." He choked
on his plans. "How the hell can I say it? I just don't feel
like living any more."

"You *what?*" I sneered. "What'll you do—hang yourself in the cellar? There's a handy twenty-penny nail
right there, in a joist—you'll find it. It's already been
broken in. And I know an undertaker who can turn
black faces white again."

"All right, all right," Harrison said. "I don't care what
you think. I said I'm no philosopher."

"Forget about philosophy," I said. "You don't lack
philosophy, buddy; you lack guts. I suppose you're going
to ask me to marry Jane afterwards, so the two of us can
remember you? You're wallowing, Harrison. Cut it out
—it's swinish."

"I'm weak, Toddy," he said. "I can't help it. Don't
you think I'm not ashamed of it, man."

"Then cut it out," I suggested curtly. "Don't give me
any of this psychic determinism crap. Just cut it out."

"You can't just cut it out," Harrison protested, and
I sensed that he was growing stronger. "I'm past believ-
ing that people can change."

"You don't want to cut it out," I said.

"Sure I do. It doesn't matter whether I do or not; I
can't do it. I'm weak in some ways, Toddy. You don't
understand that."

I flicked my cigarette out of the ventilator in a shower
of sparks. We were off the bridge then, coasting along the
dual highway in the Macks' big Cadillac.

"I know what weakness is. But you make your own
difficulties, Harrison. It's hard because you never thought
of it as easy. Listen. An act of will is the easiest thing
there is—so easy it's laughable how people make mountains of it."

Harrison had by this time actually subjugated the idea
of his loss and was following the thought.

"You know better," he said. "You can't discount psychology."

"I'm not saying anything about psychology," I maintained. "Psychology doesn't interest me. What I'm saying is that the free-will/determinism business is irrelevant to us, because if we're predetermined, we can't know in which direction. We act as if we could choose, and so we can, in effect. All you have to do to be strong in this is stop being weak."

"Impossible."

"You never tried it."

Nor, alas, did he want to just then: I could see that plainly enough. We went into the house for a last drink. Jane had heard the news, of course, by telephone, and she cried awhile. I told her flatly that I had no sympathy for either of them while they behaved like that.

"What would *you* do, damn it!" she cried impatiently.

I laughed. "I've never lost three million bucks," I said, "but I'll tell you what I did once, after Dad hanged himself for losing a few thousand."

I told them then, for the first time, the story of my adventures with Col. Henry Morton—which story, reader, I'll pause to tell you, too, sooner or later, but not just now. I had decided that I didn't want Harrison to brood over his money: he wasn't ready to be strong of his own choosing yet, apparently, and so I opened the way towards turning him into a cynic, in emulation of me. He was ripe for it anyhow, it seemed to me, and even the one story might do the trick.

There's little need for weakness, reader: you are freer, perhaps, than you'd be comfortable knowing.

As I left, Jane asked me: "You don't have anything up your sleeve, Toddy?"

"I shan't commit myself," I said. "But Harrison might as well believe he's out three million bucks, at least for a while."

"What will he do?" she asked anxiously. "Did he say anything to you coming home?"

"He'll either grow stronger or hang himself," I predicted. "If he grows stronger it won't matter to him whether he gets the money or not, really, and then I wouldn't mind seeing him get it. If he kills himself over it, I'll be just as glad he's dead, frankly. Sissies make me uncomfortable. That goes for you, too. You're not ready for three million bucks yet. You don't deserve it."

Then I left. I suppose if *I* ever lost three million dollars I'd holler like a stuck hero. Or perhaps not: one really can't tell until the thing is upon one.

Well, the will case dropped out of the papers then; the Court of Appeals wouldn't hear the appeal for at least six months, though for reasons of my own I doubted that they'd wait much longer than that. In the meantime, Lizzie Mack, Harrison's mother, couldn't use up the old man's estate (except for running expenses for the house), though it was temporarily hers.

I conducted, during the next few months, a rather intensive investigation into the characters of the appellate court judges—my findings, as I'd anticipated, only confirmed my original estimate of the situation. As far as one with much information could guess, the decision would be four to three for Lizzie if the hearing were held when tentatively scheduled.

And if it weren't? I considered that question, sitting in my office, staring at my staring-wall opposite the desk. What advantage was there in delay, if any? And how could one delay the appeal? The advantage was negative: that is, I was certain of defeat if there were no delay; if there were any, I might very possibly still be defeated, but there would be more time for something to turn up. So, I suppose, a condemned man snatches at a day's reprieve, still hoping for a god on wires to fetch him off, and on the very gibbet, his neck roped, pleads eye-to-sky for the saving car. Who knows? Perhaps, hooded and dropped, he yet waits in a second's agony for God's hands on him, till the noose cracks neck and hope in one sick snap. To be sure, ours was but a matter of money, but the principle was the same. By September the Loyalists might be winning, or it might become dangerous over here to like the Fascists, the way Hitler was behaving. By October Franco might win, and the poor crushed Loyalists be pitied, then when they were no longer a threat to anything. Anything could happen to swing one more vote our way. November was an off-year election month: perhaps some party issue would ally John Forrester, the reactionary Democrat, with his more liberal colleagues. Perhaps—

I smiled, moved my feet off the desk, and went to the file. I looked up each of the judges, checking the length of their incumbencies and the number of years in office remaining to each.

"Ah, Freddie Barnes, you old whoremonger," I cooed; "so you're up to the post again this year, are you?"

That fact mattered little, since Roosevelt was going great guns and Barnes was a popular figure in Maryland: he'd be re-elected without difficulty. Of the other Democrats, Forrester had two years to go, Haddaway had four, and Stedman had six. I checked the Republicans: Abrams had two years yet; Stevens, six; Moore—

"Well, well, well!" I grinned. "You rascal, Rollo! Time to run again, eh?"

Mrs. Lake, at my request, spent the rest of her afternoon telephoning various Baltimorians for me, some eminent and some shady, some honest and some flexible, some friendly and some employable. By quitting time I was one of perhaps seven people, other than God, who knew as a fact, beyond puny speculation, that Judge Rollo Moore, despite the backing of Maryland Republicanism, was going to lose his coming election by a well-insured margin to Joseph Singer, who, bless his heart, was a chronic if somewhat fuzzy liberal—a man after Harrison's own heart.

We would win, by God, almost certainly, if we could hold off the appeal until November! No, until January of 1938, after the new officeholders had been sworn in. Nearly a year! I racked my brain, in my thorough but unenthusiastic way, to think of some stalling maneuver, but of the few I could imagine, none was satisfactory. What I needed was something diverting, something tenuous and intricate, that I could go on complicating indefinitely, if need be. Nothing crude would do: my maneuver, whatever it was, must be subtle even if its motives were clear to the professional eye, or else I should lose the respect, and possibly the vote, of men like Judge Haddaway, for instance, whose decisions were more often influenced by such things as the symmetry and logical elegance of a brief than by more mundane considerations like the appellant's politics.

Ah, nonsense, there was nothing. The months passed; it was spring; August and judgment would soon be upon us. Harrison sweated but kept silent. Jane wept a little, and sometimes failed to come to my room when I expected her, but kept silent. They were learning; they were strengthening, or else they were naïve enough to have some canine faith in me. At least they kept silent about it, though I often caught them looking at me intently, at supper or wherever. In fact, they often stared at me, and sometimes didn't even notice when I noticed them.

As for me, I stared at my wall. I have in my office, opposite the desk, a fine staring-wall, a wall that I keep scrupulously clear for staring purposes, and I stared at it. I stared at it through February, March, April, and May, and through the first week of June, without reading on its empty surface a single idea.

Then, on the very hot June 17th of 1937, our Mrs. Lake, who is as a rule a model of decorum, came sweating decorously into my office with a paper cup of iced coffee for me, set it decorously on my desk, accepted my thanks, dropped a handkerchief on the floor as she turned to leave, bent decorously down to retrieve it, and most undaintily—oh, most indecorously—broke wind, virtually in my coffee.

"Oh, *excuse* me!" she gasped, and blushed, and fled. But ah, the fart hung heavy in the humid air, long past the lady's flight. It hung, it lolled, it wisped; it miscegenated with the smoke of my cigar, caressed the beading oil on the skin of my nose, lay obscenely on the flat of my desk, among my briefs and papers. It was everywhere, but I had learned, even then, to live with nature and my fellow animals. I didn't flinch; I didn't move.

Through its dense invisible presence I regarded my oracular wall, and this time fruitfully.

"By God, now!" I cried.

I heard a small sound in the outer office.

"Mrs. Lake!" I rushed to my door. "Where's all the crap?"

"Oh, Mr. Andrews!" she wailed, and buried her face in her arms, weeping. Harry Bishop and Jimmy Andrews peered skeptically from their doorways.

"No!" I said, patting Mrs. Lake furiously on the head. "No, I mean old man Mack's pickle jars. Where've they been all this time? Where does Lizzie keep them?"

"I don't know," Mrs. Lake sniffed, wiping her eyes bravely.

"What was it?" I hurried back to my file, began pushing things around, and finally found the inventory of the Mack estate. "One hundred twenty-nine bottles of it, in the wine cellar!"

"Well," remarked Mr. Bishop, and returned to his work. Jimmy Andrews hung around to see what was up.

"Call 'Stacia," I said to Mrs. Lake. "No, hell no, don't. I'll run up to Baltimore." I looked at my watch. "Will you run me to the bus, Jim? I bet I can catch the four o'clock."

"Sure," Jimmy said. He drove insanely; I made the bus with two minutes to spare, and was soon off to Baltimore.

Eustacia Callader was an old Negro servant in the Mack household, whom I'd met during the course of the litigation. She had virtually raised Harrison Junior and was quietly on our side in the contest over the estate, though she grasped little of the controversy. She it was whom I sought now. Arriving in Baltimore four hours later, I stopped in a drugstore to buy envelopes and stamps, and then took a taxi out to Ruxton, getting out at the driveway of the Mack house. The sun had just set, and I actually hid myself on the grounds in the rear of the house—it was all quite theatrical—and waited, I suppose, for 'Stacia to come out of the kitchen for something. An unlikely plan, I'll confess, but then my whole scheme, my suspicion, was unlikely: when the great Negro woman did, as a matter of fact, waddle out just forty-five minutes later, en route to the garbage cans down by the big garage, I took her appearance as a good omen. Following her out of earshot of the house, I approached her.

"Lord 'a mercy, Mister Andrews!" she giggled enormously. "What y'all doin' up here? Come see Lizzie?"

" 'Stacia, listen, kid," I whispered urgently. "I've got a five-buck question." I gave her the five, and she giggled helplessly: all Negroes consider me insane.

"Where does Lizzie keep the old man's fertilizer?" I asked. "Is it still in the wine cellar?"

"De fertilize'?" 'Stacia chortled. "What fertilize'?" She laughed so hard that I knew she didn't understand.

"The crap, 'Stacia," I demanded. "How does Lizzie feel about all those bottles of crap?"

"Oh," 'Stacia wheezed. "Dat's what you mean de fertilize'!"

"A hundred and twenty-nine jars of it," I said. "Used to be in the wine cellar. Are they still there?"

When 'Stacia regained control of her risibility, she admitted that she didn't know, but she promised to find out and tell me. I gave her an impassioned buss on the cheek and took up lodgings in a huge clump of forsythia bushes near the garbage cans, while 'Stacia returned to the house to question the other servants who lived in. I was prepared, if it should prove necessary, to bribe somebody heavily to destroy those pickle jars for me secretly, but I didn't look forward to taking that step, since it opened the way for blackmail. Still, it seemed highly unlikely to me that Mrs. Mack had ordered them removed herself, although it was exactly that possibility which had occurred to me on the occasion of Mrs. Lake's *faux pas*.

I was pleasantly surprised, then, when three hours later—it was after midnight—'Stacia lumbered back with the announcement that though the bottles were indeed still in the wine cellar, Mrs. Mack had observed last week to R. J. Collier, the gimpy, dusty old fellow who tended

the gardens, that the seals on the jars were apparently
not airtight, and had mentioned the possibility of someday disposing of the collection. Indeed, 'Stacia verified
that with the coming of hot weather the jars had begun
to smell noticeably, and that the odor was creeping up
occasionally to the ground floor. Two days before, R. J.
Collier had taken it upon himself to pile the whole stack
into the far corner of the wine cellar and to cover it
with a wet tarpaulin, hoping thereby to check the
bouquet, but his experiment had yielded no apparent results. Mrs. Mack was growing annoyed. R. J. Collier had,
that very day, broached the suggestion that his late employer's singular remains be put to work around the
flower gardens—the zinnia beds, especially, could use the
nourishment, he declared. All the servants considered
the suggestion more touching than tactless, and I, too,
sensed a seed of poetry in the gardener's practicality. But
Lizzie had remained noncommittal.

"Listen, 'Stacia," I said, "you mustn't say a word
about the pickle jars, or about me being here. I'm going
to give you ten dollars, honey—"

"Hoo, Mr. Andrews!" Her eyes widened.

"—here, ten bucks. Now I want you to keep a close
watch on those jars. Make sure you know everything
that Liz or R. J. Collier or anybody else does to them.
Look. I'm giving you all these envelopes with stamps on
them. They're addressed to me, so keep them hidden, and
there's paper inside. Now, then, every time even one of
those bottles is moved from where it is now, you write to
me and tell me. Understand?"

'Stacia giggled and shook and grunted, but I was fairly
sure she understood.

"For Christ's sake don't say a word," I cautioned her
again. "If everything turns out right, Harrison will give
you a brand-new car. A yellow roadster, he'll buy you.
Okay?"

'Stacia could scarcely stand for laughing. But she stuck
the envelopes deep between her endless bosoms and rum-
bled off to the house, shaking her head indulgently at my
derangement. I walked out to the road and hiked two

miles to a telephone. Next day I was back in my office, smoking cigars and staring at my wall. I didn't bother to tell Harrison anything about my trip—perhaps nothing would come of it after all.

And except for the infrequent parries with Charley Parks, the attorney next door, over our automobile suit— you'll recall I mentioned it earlier?—I had done nothing else, no work at all on any case, since then: nearly a week. I was waiting for 'Stacia's letter, and thinking steadily about possible alternative plans of action. I'd decided to sit thus until July 1. If nothing had happened to the jars by then, I'd take the risk of bribing R. J. Collier to destroy some of them.

Then, this morning, there was 'Stacia's letter, one of the self-addressed envelopes I'd given her. It could contain anything from nonsense to the key to three million dollars, and it was merely as a disciplinary exercise that I'd postponed reading it until after I'd read the other letters and the handbill, and had called Marvin Rose. But I shan't exact such discipline from you, reader. Here is the letter:

> *Mr. Andrew. Mrs. Mack, has put pickle jars in grenhouse. R. J. Coler, has put on zinas. Eustacia M. Callader. R. J. Coler, has put 72 bottles on zinas. Eustacia M. Callader.*

I put the letter in the dossier with the other documents pertaining to the Mack will case, returned the dossier to the file, and locked the filing cabinets. For nearly two hours I stared at my wall, and then I left the office to stroll uptown for my appointment with Marvin.

A good morning's work, reader: I opened a few letters and put one in the file. An excellent morning's work for one's last morning on earth, I should say.

My friend Harrison is three million dollars richer for it.

XI. An instructive, if sophisticated, observation

The thermometer outside the offices of *The Daily Banner* read eighty-nine degrees when I walked past it on my way uptown. Few people were on the streets. At the curb in front of a large funeral parlor a sleek black hearse was parked, its loading door closed, and several mourners, along with the black-suited employees of the establishment, stood quietly about in the yard. As I approached, a fat black pussycat, scarred with experience and heavy with imminent kittens, trotted wearily out of a hydrangea bush beside the undertaker's porch into the sun, and for no discernible reason curled plumply in the middle of the sidewalk and closed her eyes. Just then the door opened, and the pallbearers came out bringing the casket. Their path was diverted, but not greatly, by the pregnant cat. Some of the pallbearers smiled, and an employee of the funeral home, nudged the cat aside with his toe. She got up, stretched, yawned, and padded off to find some less-traveled thoroughfare to sleep in; the loading door of the hearse was swung open, and the casket loaded gently inside.

I smiled and walked on. Nature, coincidence, can often be a heavy-handed symbolizer. She seems at times fairly to club one over the head with significance such as this clumsy "life-in-the-face-of-death" scenario, so obvious even in its details that it was embarrassing. One is constantly being confronted with a sun that bursts from behind the clouds just as the home team takes the ball; ominous rumblings of thunder when one is brooding desultorily at home; magnificent sunrises on days when one has resolved to mend one's ways; hurricanes that demolish a bad man's house and leave his good neighbor's untouched, or vice-versa; Race Streets marked SLOW; Cemetery Avenues marked ONE WAY. The man whose perceptions are not so rudimentary, whose palate is attuned to subtler dishes, can only smile uncomfortably and walk away, reminding himself, if he is wise, that good taste is, after all, only a human invention.

But it's not easy to keep one's patience in the face of the world's abundant ingenuousness. For instance, when I came to the corner of High and Poplar Streets and stopped to chat awhile with Capt. Osborn and two of his idle cronies, installed on their loafer's bench in front of George Melvin's store, I had to put up with a prominent MEN WORKING sign near an open manhole in the street before them; a senile clock in the store window, which, like the store and the old men, had ceased to mark the passage of time; a movie-theater poster directly behind Capt. Osborn's head, advertising a double bill—*Life Begins at Forty* and *Captains Courageous;* a pigeon perched recklessly on a NO PARKING sign—I could go on for a page. Really, to resist the temptation to use such ponderous, ready-made symbols taxes one's very integrity, and I'm certain that if I were writing stories for my bread and butter, my resistance would weaken. I recall once reading a story that ended with the hero dead on the floor—was he a suicide or a homicide?—beneath a cash register announcing: THIS REGISTERS THE AMOUNT OF YOUR PURCHASE. The machine, as one familiar with life's elephantine ironies might have anticipated, registered zero, and I for one take it as a mark of the author's lack of acumen that he couldn't ignore that cash register, or make it read $4.37 or some other meaningless figure. It's too easy otherwise, like using clichés.

So, reader, should you ever find yourself writing about the world, take care not to nibble at the many tempting symbols she sets squarely in your path, or you'll be baited into saying things you don't really mean, and offending

the people you want most to entertain. Develop, if you
can, the technique of the pallbearers and myself: smile,
to be sure, but walk on and say nothing, as though you
hadn't noticed.

XII. A chorus of oysters

Socially, as well as economically, Capt. Osborn and his colleagues of the loafer's bench were exclusively consumers. They ate food, wore clothing, and smoked cigars, but they produced nothing. They sat immobile on their antique bench like a row of crusty oysters and ingested with their eyes everything that passed, but they did not participate. They were out of it—uninvolved, for the most part. The life of Cambridge passed by and through them like sea water through an oyster's gills: they strained from it what nutrition they wanted as it passed, digesting people and events with a snort or a comment, but they never moved from their position. They were a chorus of ancient oysters, stolidly regarding the fish that swam through their ken. Their infrequent voices were slow, nasal, high-pitched, and senile.

A bright blue roadster, for example, would roar by.

"Eee, there rides young Mowb Henly!" one would observe.

" 'E's a hot one," another would add. "Ol' Mowb's boy. Can't do nothin' with that youngster."

"No, *sir*," a third would agree.

"Eee, ol' Mowb's boy!" the first would repeat, rumbling his way up to a wet cackle of mirth and expectoration.

" 'E's bad as 'is ol' man," the second would remark.

"Ye know what they say," would crow the third. "*Like father, like son.*"

The first would choke and strangle then, his red

119

rheumy eyes a-twinkle, his red cracked face all grinning, the small saliva spilling over his brown teeth and thin red lips, and begin the refrain again:

"Eee! Hmph! *Hawk!* Sploo! Ol'—*thoo!* Thff! Ol'—Hawk! Thff! *Thoo!* Ol' Mowb Henly! *Thooie!*"

I had a few minutes to spare, so I took a seat at the shady end of the bench—the old men liked the sun—and listened to their hoary music for a while. Presently the loaded hearse drove by from the funeral parlor, two cars with lighted headlights following behind. The procession paused at the intersection and then moved on through the red light, heading for Greenlawn Cemetery, out toward the country club.

"Whose funeral?" I asked.

"Why, that's Clarence Wampler's wife, ain't it, Osborn?" offered my neighbor, watching the hearse move off.

"Yep," assented Capt. Osborn. "Died Monday night."

"That the Henry Street one, come from Golden Hill?" asked the third.

"Naw, that's *Lewis* Wampler's wife yer thinkin' of," Capt. Osborn declared. "Yer thinkin' of ol' Jenny Fairwell."

"Ol' Jenny?" the first cackled. "Ol' Jenny?"

"Ol' Jenny," Capt. Osborn grinned, stretching his leg. "There was a hot one."

"Ol' Jenny!" the first snuffled happily.

"This here's *Clarence* Wampler's wife," Capt. Osborn explained. "Lived on Ross Street, down by the creek."

"Sure," the first said. "I b'lieve she was a Canlon, weren't she?"

"Now let's see," Capt. Osborn mused. "She was the oldest Canlon girl—must of been Louise Mae."

"Louise Mae Canlon. Hell, she weren't so durned old, was she?"

"Louise Mae Canlon," Capt. Osborn repeated. "She was the oldest—ol' Cap'n Will Canlon's girls, down to Golden Hill. Louise Mae Canlon must of been twenty when Clarence Wampler married 'er. I remember that was the year ol' Cap'n Canlon lost 'is schooner in the ice—I was just startin' out with my own boat that season, the *June Phillips*, I bought 'er off ol' man George Phillips, down to Fishin' Creek. That'd be 'bout 1885, I s'pect."

"Cap'n Canlon's schooner?" asked the third old fellow, who had remained silent. "Ye mean the *Samuel T. Brice?*"

"Naw, that was 'is ol' boat," Capt. Osborn declared. "I b'lieve the *Samuel T. Brice* burned up one time, tied up to Long Dock in Baltimore. This was Cap'n Will's new boat—what was 'er name? *LaVerne Canlon?* Yep, that's it, *LaVerne Canlon*, after 'is wife. Well, sir, Cap'n Will hadn't no more'n put 'er in the water, spankin' new, ever' line and whipstitch, 'fore we had that big freeze-up in the Bay, and be durned if 'e didn't git froze up in 'er, and the ice wrecked 'er. Weren't no icebreakers them days."

"No, sir," the others agreed.

"I durned near lost the *June Phillips* that winter, out off Sharp's Island. Durned water was icin' up so fast ye could watch it skim over, ever' time the wind let off. Then the breeze would puff up and we'd go a-scrunchin' a little farther. I had a extra-heavy chain for a bobstay, thank the Lord; I'd told Walter Jones to hang a big one on 'er when 'e was fittin' 'er out, and I mean I didn't know which would win, us or the ice. Thank the good Lord that breeze was up, kept us a-scrunchin' right through, don't no bobstay in the world would of cut that ice, I'm tellin' ye."

"Eee!" chuckled the first. "Don't freeze up no more like that!"

"Ol' Cap'n Jamie Snyder—you remember Cap'n Jamie? Cap'n Jamie Snyder says to me, 'e saw Walter Jones a-hangin' that big chain bobstay on the *June Phillips*, up in 'is yard, 'e says to me, 'Osborn,' 'e says, 'yer goin' to need six darkies in yer dinghy,' 'e says, 'jest to keep 'er sailin' trim!' Well, sir, I says to Cap'n Jamie, 'Cap'n Jamie, it looks like ice to me, this winter,' I says, 'and I'd a sight rather ship six darkies in my dinghy, than have to git out and walk home!' "

"Eee!"

"Yes, sir!"

"Well, sir, I didn't think no more about it," Capt. Osborn went on. "Then come that big ice, and the *June Phillips* come a scrunchin' home from Sharp's Island—took us till past dark—with that big bobstay jest a-chewin' that ice like a lean hog chews corncobs, and a good load o' oysters piled in the bow to give 'er weight. Next day I seen Cap'n Jamie down to the creek, lookin' where the ice had ground the paint off the *June Phillips's* cutwater, all round that chain, and a-shakin' 'is head. 'Osborn,' 'e says, when 'e saw me watchin' 'im, 'I didn't think nothin' at the time,' 'e says, 'but I got to admit yer one up on me.' 'How's that?' I says. 'Why,' 'e says, 'don't ye know I left the *B. John Gore* fast in the ice yesterday, right off Horn Point, stuck like a minner in a gill net? Didn't I walk ever' step o' the way from the *B. John Gore* to Sim Riley's farmhouse, to git a horse, jest like ye said? I'm eatin' humble pie, Osborn,' 'e said. Then be durned if 'e didn't laugh it off and buy me a drink. That was ol' Cap'n Jamie fer ye!"

"Ol' Cap'n Jamie!"

"Eee! *Thoo!*"

Poor Louise Mae Canlon Wampler: the oysters would, perhaps, sing of her another day.

I rose to leave—it was eleven-fifteen—and smiled all the way up Poplar St., en route to Marvin Rose's office. I felt very good about Capt. Osborn, and very happy that I was not going to live to be an old man, because the old man I'd want to be, I think, would be much like him, half archetype and half stereotype, and I am too self-conscious and inconsistent (and for better or worse, too sophisticated) to play the grand old man with comfort—though knowing my predilections, I shall doubtless end up playing that part anyway, comfortable or not.

I'll have to end this chapter by mentioning, reluctantly, that one can see one's reflection sharply in the tile front of a jewelry store on Poplar St., across from the poolroom, and that as a matter of historical fact I paused for a moment there to adjust the knot in my necktie, which

I'd loosened a bit during my morning's work. What is embarrassing about this mirror—for the tile reflects like a dark mirror—is its convenience, not only on the street but in my narrative: the next story I have to tell you is a mirror-story, the story of what happened in my bedroom on my seventeenth birthday, and it's unfortunate, considering what I said a few pages ago about life's naïve symbolisms, that I must employ such a too-perfect, Hollywoodish bridge to reach that story, but there's no help for it.

And I lose even by so explaining my discomfiture concerning these juxtaposed mirrors—the one on the street and the one in my bedroom—because the explanation itself is arch, painfully so, and my pointing out its archness archer still, until, like any image caught between facing mirrors, this conclusion loses itself, like a surrealist colonnade, in an infinite regress of archness. I apologize.

XIII. A mirror up to life

My mother having died when I was only seven years old,
I grew up under the inconsistent tutelage of my father
and a succession of maids and housekeepers. My father
always expressed great concern over my welfare and
proper guidance, but from either necessity or disinclina-
tion he seldom gave me a great deal of personal attention.
As for the maids and housekeepers, some liked me and
some didn't, but all had their own affairs to mind while
Dad was working, and so I was left to myself much of
the time.

Let me say at once, though, that I was almost never an
ill-behaved child. Not at all. I was quiet, but not un-
communicative; reserved, but not reclusive; energetic at
times, but seldom enthusiastic. There were few restrictions on my behavior, nor were many needed. I was (and
am) temperamentally disposed to observing rules—my
desires seldom fell without their pale. And because I so
rarely gave him cause for concern, my father was notably
incurious about my activities.

Therefore, when I really wanted to do something of
which I was certain he wouldn't approve, it was not
difficult for me to do it.

My sex life, reader, up to my seventeenth year, was so
unspectacular as to be unworthy of mention. I did all
the things that young anthropoids delight in while growing up; my high-school amours were limited to hot, open-
mouthed kisses and much risqué conversation—until my
alliance with Miss Betty June Gunter.

Betty June, at age seventeen, was a thin, almost scrawny little thing, most ungainly and sharp in the face, with good eyes, crooked teeth, coarse blond hair, fine skin, and no hips or breasts to speak of. She was not considered unattractive in my set, though socially she was certainly of an inferior caste. Betty June was a poor student, but she was a spirited girl, and there was a sharpness in her speech that bespoke a mind livelier than those of a number of more scholarly girls in our class. Besides—and this was her chief attraction—Betty June was sophisticated, worldly, informed, in a way that none of the thoroughly respectable girls of my acquaintance could approach. Her father was dead, and her mother—well, one wasn't sure what to think about her mother. The girl had little to do with her classmates, especially with the other girls, although there were a few notable exceptions: one or two girls of the most respectable sort claimed her as their close friend. We boys lusted after her with our eyes and our speech, of course, but before her cool, experienced manner we were clumsy and abashed. She regarded the lot of us as puppies, I'm sure.

The relationship between Betty June and me commenced when she fell in love with one Smitty Herrin, a twenty-seven-year-old bachelor who lived two houses from me. Smitty ignored her existence, she was devoted to him, and she got the habit that winter of spending much time in and around my house, hoping that Smitty would notice her. I was delighted. Betty June told me all her troubles—and they were such dramatic, such *real* troubles! Woman had never loved man, it seemed to me, as she loved Smitty, and yet he ignored her. She wouldn't have cared what he did to her—he might beat her and curse her (what a thrilling notion to a seventeen-year-old!)—if only he'd acknowledge her devotion, but he ignored her. She would even have suffered torture for him (together we dreamed up the tortures she'd be willing to suffer, considering each solemnly); would even have died for him (we discussed, in detail, various unpleasant deaths) for the slightest crumb of reciprocal passion. But Smitty remained oblivious. I was violently

sympathetic, and helping her articulate her grievances
I discovered that I could converse more easily and
naturally with her than with anyone in my experience:
there was no stultifying embarrassment, as there was
with other girls, nor was there the necessity to impress
that falsified all my communication with my male companions. Moreover, the things Betty June discussed
were of a new and thrilling order—I felt mature and
wise and confident, discussing them, and I found myself
able to think more liberally, compassionately, and judiciously than I'd ever thought before.

In fact, reader, I should say that it was here, at just
this point, that I lost my innocence. Of what concern is it
to me that eventually I made love to her? But Betty
June, thin skinny Betty, she broke the seal of my mind,
which had been before her coming an idle enough instrument; took from me my intellectual virginity, which
is childishness and naïveté, and opened my eyes to the
world of men and women—and this gently, and with
warmth. A lucky virgin, I, to fall into those meager arms
and pathetic problems; what she took from me, I lost
with pleasure!

She came to the house nearly every afternoon, after
school, and stayed until the housekeeper came to prepare
supper. On Saturdays she often spent nearly the whole
day with me. We would sit alone, either in the living
room or in Dad's study—I preferred the study—and I
would fix drinks for us, often lacing them with rum or
whiskey filched from the butler's pantry. And we talked
and talked and talked, easily, sympathetically, wed-
ding her experience with my articulation. I could feel
myself expanding, maturing in the bath of her lean life,
flexing the muscles of my rationality and my understanding. I've no real way of knowing how Betty June
felt—whether she sensed the growing power in me or regarded me merely as a harmless colt.

There came a time, alas, when, colt no more, I felt
every inch a stud, a stallion, a stone-horse! and regarding her leanness, perched on the couch, with nostrils
all but quivering. Those were embarrassing times. I sus-

pected that, should I ever be so crude as to approach her, our peculiar *rapport* would vanish. Besides—the chasm yawned, the mystery—what if she were to submit?

"Your ice is melting," Betty June would observe, and I would hide myself in my drink.

Up to this point—late winter, perhaps February—I had, be it said to my credit, remained fairly objective about the matter. I understood that Betty June was in love with Smitty; that she found in me only a sort of spiritual brother; that both she and Smitty were people whom, at bottom, I did not really respect; that, finally, one of her chief attractions was her *possibility:* the tantalizing fact that unlike most of the girls in my set, Betty June was experienced, and that it was therefore not *entirely* impossible that—

How many aching, perspiring nights I placed on the altar of that remote, teasing possibility!

One afternoon she came over to where I sat in Dad's leather study chair, to light my cigarette. She held the match expertly, and while I drew on the cigarette she ran her free hand playfully through my hair. I gasped and caught her arm instantly; she laughed and fell into my lap. I took the cigarette from my mouth and crushed her lips with a violent kiss. She grew skittish, playful, but she didn't move away, and I kissed her again and again, passionately. I could scarcely believe my good fortune; I was so emotional I couldn't speak. Betty June still laughed softly, and kissed back—no girl had done that to me!—and pinched, and nuzzled, and caught my ears, nose, and eyebrows gently in her teeth. I began pawing her flat chest clumsily, sure I'd be slapped, but she stretched and made no objection. Incredible! I had a field day. At three-thirty she left me to marvel at my good luck.

From that day on our relationship was of a different sort. She still regarded me as harmless, I'm certain, but now we played instead of talking. It was wonderful, beautiful sport; every afternoon ended with my transgressing the boundaries she'd tacitly drawn, pleading with

her to surrender to me—confident in the knowledge that
she would not. Then she would leave.

How my opinion changed! My objectivity was peeled
off with her chemise, and tossed unwanted into the corner.
I came to loathe Smitty; to rail at him inwardly—for
Betty June allowed not a word of criticism; to lay
elaborate plans for his ruin. I wept furiously whenever she
spoke of her love for him, and she pressed my wet face
to her small breast. I solemnly regarded *my* love—it had
never been voiced—as a thing inviolable, out of reach; a
hot, virginal intercourse of souls. I went about looking
wan and distracted, brooding, melancholy. My friends
kept a respectful distance; none, I think, knew of Betty
June's visits. I regarded us as lost souls, condemned by
the Fates (Clotho, Lachesis, and Atropos—I remember
looking them up, and weeping at the justice of their
names) never to consummate our love, separated by prior
commitments and by barriers of position and caste (be
sure I never mentioned *this* to her!), *etcetera, etcetera*.

Thus until March 2, 1917—my seventeenth birthday.
I wasn't expecting Betty June until that afternoon, and
I had decided to spend the morning—it must have been a
holiday—knocking down the weathered frame of my unfinished boat, which still stood rotting in the back yard.
But no sooner had Dad gone to court, and the housekeeper to her sister's place, as she always did, than
Betty June came running into the house, weeping crazily.
I grabbed her and held her tightly, and when she refused
to calm herself I shook her by the shoulders—it seemed
a manly thing to do, and it worked. She still sobbed
and whimpered, but less violently.

"What's the matter with you?" I demanded, so fright-
ened by her emotion that I actually felt nauseous, and my
knees trembled under me.

"Smitty's married!" she cried, jerkily.

"What?"

She nodded, sniffing and shuddering. "He's been married secretly to Mona Johnston for a year," she said,
"and all that time I was—"

"Shut up!" I commanded dramatically. "Don't even say it!" I had decided to be strong.

"Now he's got her in trouble, and her folks are making them announce it."

"Good for them!" I said toughly. "Serves the bastard right!"

"No!" Betty June wailed, loosing fresh tears. "Now he's enlisted in the Army, because he can't stand Mona any more! He's going overseas, Toddy! I'll never see him again!"

She threatened to break down completely.

"Tough luck!" I sneered, very proud of my new strength.

Betty June ran into the study and collapsed on the leather couch, weeping volubly. I sniffed, strode into the butler's pantry, and took a good pull of bourbon, right from the bottle. It scalded clear to my stomach, set my blood on fire. I gave Betty June a few minutes to cry (and to wonder what I was doing); then I took another swig of bourbon, choked on it, replaced the bottle, and went to the study, walking with exaggerated precision. Betty June, her eyes red, looked up at me dubiously, not knowing what to expect.

I said nothing (couldn't have if I'd wanted to). I sat carefully on the edge of the couch and with one wrench opened her blouse. Ah, I was in no mood for trifling!

"Don't rip it," Betty June whimpered, recovering her composure.

"That's your problem," I growled, and gave her a bruising kiss. "If you don't want 'em ripped, take 'em off yourself."

She sat up at once and slipped off her blouse and chemise. I stood up and watched impassively.

"You quitting there?" I demanded sarcastically, just as a matter of form.

Betty Jean regarded me for a moment with a new expression on her face: a deliberating, calculating expression. Then she stood up, and unbuttoning her placket, let her long skirt fall to the floor. Quickly she stripped off her petticoat, and without the least hesitation, her shoes, stockings, and bloomers, and stood before me nude. I very nearly swooned. Luckily I had the presence of mind to embrace her at once, so that I was out of range of her eyes.

"Take me upstairs," she moaned.

I was petrified, now that the opportunity was at hand. Take her upstairs! My mind raced frantically, seeking honorable excuses.

"Suppose somebody comes home?" I croaked.

"I'll run to the bathroom," she whispered. Obviously she was no novice at this sort of thing. "Come on, get my clothes." She broke away from me and ran, all pink skin, to the stairs. I retrieved her clothing and followed after, scared to death; soon, in my bedroom, cluttered like a museum with the relics of my boyhood, she received that boyhood happily, and kissed me, as I chose to think, for making her its custodian. I should have kissed her, for no hot bump of a boy ever had defter instruction. I have been uncommonly lucky with women, surely through no virtue of my own.

What follows is perhaps indiscreet, but it is the point of the story.

A seventeen-year-old boy is insatiable. His lust is like a tall weed, which crushed repeatedly under the mower springs up again, green and unbowed. He is easily aroused and quickly satisfied, and easily aroused again. New to the manners of the business, I cried like a baby, bleated like a goat, and roared like a lion, by turns. The time came, the lesson, when I was stallion indeed . . . need I explain?

And then I looked into the mirror on my dresser, beside us—an unusually large mirror, that gave back our images full-length and life-size—and there we were: Betty June's face buried in the pillow; me gangly as a whippet and braying like an ass. It was marvelously funny; I exploded with laughter!

"What's the matter?" Betty June asked sharply.

I tossed and rolled and roared with laughter; Betty June was blindly angry.

"Well I don't see anything funny!"

I couldn't answer. I couldn't comfort the nervous
tears that ran from her, though I swear I tried. I couldn't
help her at all, or myself. I bellowed and snorted with
laughter, long after Betty June had fumed out of my bed,
out of my room, out of my house, for the last time. I
laughed through lunch, to Dad's amusement (and subsequent irritation). I laughed that night when I undressed.

I have said that my experience in the Argonne, not
very long afterwards, was the second of two unforgettable
demonstrations of my animality, and so it was. This was
the first. Nothing is *intrinsically* funny, to be sure, but to
me nothing is so consistently, profoundly, earth-shakingly
funny as we animals in the act of mating. Reader, if
you are young and would live on love; if in the flights
of intercourse you feel that you and your beloved are fit
models for a Phidias, for a Michelangelo—then don't, I
implore you, be so foolish as to include among the trap-
pings of your love-nest a good plate mirror. For a mirror
can reflect only what it sees, and what it sees is scream-
ingly funny.

Well. I never laughed at poor Betty June again, because a few days after my birthday I enlisted in the
Army. Smitty was killed; I was not. Mona Johnston married someone else. Betty June, I learned upon my return
from service, had become a prostitute during the war,
first in Cambridge, and then—when after the Armistice it was no longer patriotic to sleep with soldiers—in
Baltimore. When I next saw her, it was under entirely
different circumstances. I've not heard anything from her
for years.

Think me heartless—I'm sure I am—but even as I
write this now, thirty-seven years later, though my heart
goes out to pitiful Betty, generous Betty, nevertheless I
can't expunge that mirror from my mind; I think of it
and must smile. To see a pair of crabs, of dogs, of people—even lovely, graceful Jane—I can't finish, reader,
can't hold my pen fast to the line: I am convulsed; I
am weeping tears of laughter on the very page!

XIV. Bottles, needles, and knives

A good habit to acquire, if you are interested in disciplin-
ing your strength, is the habit of habit-breaking. For one
thing, to change your habits deliberately on occasion
prevents you from being entirely consistent (I believe I
explained the virtues of limited inconsistency earlier?);
for another, it prevents your becoming any more a vas-
sal than you have to. Do you smoke? Stop smoking for a
few years. Do you part your hair on the left? Try not
parting it at all. Do you sleep on your left side, to the
right of your wife? Sleep on your stomach, on her left.
You have hundreds of habits: habits of dress, of manner,
of speech, of eating, of thought, of aesthetic taste, of
moral conduct. Break them now and then, deliberately,
and institute new ones in their places for a while. It
will slow you up sometimes, but you'll tend to grow
strong and feel free. To be sure, don't break *all* your
habits. Leave some untouched forever; otherwise you'll
be consistent.

Now, in deciding to see Marvin Rose for a physical examination I was accomplishing two things at once: the
appointment was extraordinary, and that fact gave an
element of inconsistency to my last day on earth, which
I'd decided to live routinely. At the same time, I was
breaking a thirteen-year-old habit of not seeing doctors.

Marvin Rose had last attended me in 1924, when he
prescribed for my infected prostate. At the time, I had
just enrolled in law school and he was interning at the
Johns Hopkins Hospital; we had been fraternity brothers

as undergraduates at the University, and were dependable, if not intimate, friends. It was a terrible morning that I went to him—drunken, bloody, half-conscious, aching—where he worked in the outpatient department of the old brown hive. He washed me up, gave me some kind of pill to swallow, perhaps even administered a needle. What he said, finally, was, "Stay here for a few days, Toddy."

I intended to refuse, but it seems I fainted; when I was conscious again I was hospitalized, and within a few hours, upon my being examined—painfully!—the infection was discovered. Although I wasn't aware of it at the time, Marvin's words had terminated a phase of my life, for upon my discharge from the hospital a month later, I was an entirely different person. I had stumbled in a drunken animal; I walked out a saint. The story is neither religious nor long.

Of the noises in my life, one of the very loudest in my memory is the tiny popping puncture of my bayonet in the German sergeant's neck—that sergeant with whom I choose to think my soul had lain for a while. Were I ever so foolish as to try, I'm quite sure I could close my eyes and hear that puncture as distinctly now as I heard it then, and the soft slide of my metal into his throat. To a noise like that, thirty-six years is a snap of the fingers, a blink of the eye.

Of the human voices I have heard, one of the very clearest in my memory is the gravelly, somnolent Missouri voice of Capt. John Frisbee, the army doctor who examined me after a heart attack just prior to my discharge. Here are his very words:

"Ah sweah, Cawpr'l, if that isn't endocahditis yew got! How in the heyell did yew git in the Ahmy, boy? Yew too young to have a haht attack, now ahn't yew?"

He shook his head, examined me again to make sure, and then wrote his report, which he explained to me as gently as his naturally blunt manner would permit.

"The endocahditis isn't so bad, son; that's what clubbed yew fingahs, and it should of kept yew a civilian. It won't git no worse. The bad thing is that yew liable to have a mocahdial infahction—and that can very likely kill yew. Might be any second; might be a yeah from now; might be nevah. But yew just as well know 'bout it. Ah don't subscrahb to this secrecy hoss-m'nure, d'yew?"

Can you understand at once—you must, for I neither can nor will explain it—that I was relieved? To say that the puncture had deranged me in any way would be too crude, but—well, I was relieved, that's all, to learn that every minute I lived might well be my last.

My first impulse, after my discharge, was to rush home as quickly as possible, in order to say farewell to Dad and my town before I fell dead. Every time the train slowed for a crossing I squirmed and fidgeted, sure I'd never reach Cambridge alive. But I did. Dad welcomed me warmly, and seemed so happy to have me safely home that I hadn't the courage to tell him the tragic news at once—though of course I mustn't wait too long, or my sudden death might surprise him, coming unprepared-for. I decided to gamble on a week, during which time I idled nervously around the big house, unable to concentrate on anything.

But at the week's end, when one night Dad called me into his study, and I resolved to tell him at once, he forestalled me by speaking first.

"Cheer up, Toddy," he laughed—I must have looked glum. "I didn't call you in to scold you, like I used to when your mother was alive! What I've got on my mind is serious, but it isn't solemn."

He was feeling very good, very affectionate. He handed me a cigar, and I sat on the leather couch and smoked it.

"Todd, the first thing I want you to do, if it's all right with you, is take a vacation—from now till fall. Don't feel obliged to stay here unless you feel like it—go anywhere you want to. For spending money you've got a pretty good wad in Liberty bonds that I banked for you while you were away."

I just listened, hoping my heart would last until he finished, so that I could explain.

"Then when September comes, son, nothing could make me happier than if you'd go to school." He grinned. "I shan't specify Johns Hopkins, but I must say that that's where the bright men are coming from, lately. Then, if you *really* want to humor me, study law. And do it right, in a law school; not in an office like I did. But again, I shan't even specify the law. I do want you to go to school, though, son—after a vacation. See if you can spend your whole bank account by September!"

I must say that at that moment I felt wonderful about my father. His concern over me, the (for him) remarkable psychology of his approach, his generosity—all these, I see now, were ordinary sentiments, not unusual in themselves; but then I was a very ordinary sort of young man, too, at the time, and the sentiments, if commonplace, were nonetheless uncommonly strong. My ailing heart felt lodged in my throat; I couldn't speak.

Seeing my hesitation, Dad busied himself attending to his cigar. His smile perhaps set a little, but it did not disappear.

"Don't answer," he said then. "Don't say anything one way or the other, yet."

"No," I protested, "no, it's—"

"Not a word," Dad insisted, sure of himself again. "What a crude fellow I am, calling you in here without a word of notice and springing a whole life's plan on you! A fine son you'd be, come to think of it, if you ever agreed to anything that drastic without a little thought first!" His spirits were high again. "Get out now," he ordered cheerfully. "Go get a little tight or something, like a veteran's supposed to. I shan't listen to a word you say about this at least until tomorrow, if not next week. Go on, now, *git!*" And he buried his attention in pretended business on his desk.

Well, I worried for a day or so—and he did too, poor fellow, thinking I didn't like his proposal—and finally decided that, since I was after all still alive, and

might be for several months, I might as well leave Dad
happy by enrolling in college: he would have the satisfaction of knowing he'd done all a father could do for
me. Besides, why tell him about my heart? Why make
both suffer, when there was no help for it?

"I'm going to Hopkins, Dad," I announced one
morning at breakfast, "and then to Maryland Law School,
if it's all right with you. And I don't know if this is
right or not to ask, but I'd like it if when I get out I
could eventually set up here in town, like you did,
maybe as a junior partner or something."

Dad didn't say a word. He was so happy his eyes
watered, and he had to fold his napkin and get up
from the breakfast table. I was certainly glad I'd said
what I said.

So I went to Johns Hopkins, enrolled in the pre-law
curriculum. At Dad's suggestion I joined a fraternity—
Beta Alpha Order, a Southern outfit—and lived in the
fraternity house. I must say that if one has to go to
college under the conditions I went under, the early
twenties was an excellent time to go. It seemed to me
that nearly all of my fraternity brothers expected, like
myself, to fall dead any moment, for they lived each
day as though it were to be their last. Their way of life
suited my feelings exactly, and I soon made myself one
of them. We stayed drunk for days at a time. We set
fire to the men's rooms in night clubs, ignited smudge
pots in the streets, installed cows in unexpected places.
We brawled and fought, made nuisances of ourselves,
spent nights in jail sobering up. We kept women in the
house overnight, in violation of University and chapter
rules—night-club strippers, prostitutes, strange ladies,
college girls—and we paid fines for it; some of us were
justifiably expelled from the University. We went on
adulterous weekend trips to Washington and New York,
beach parties at Beaver Dam and Betterton, and once a
fantastic bullfrog hunt in the Dorchester Marshes south
of Cambridge. We fell from speeding automobiles, and
were hospitalized; occasionally even fought real honest-
to-goodness duels, and were hospitalized. One of us died

in an automobile crash, drunk. Two of us were obliged
to marry girls inadvertently made pregnant. Three of
us were withdrawn from the University by irate parents.
One of us committed suicide with sleeping pills and was
discovered at the autopsy to be syphilitic. Three of us
turned into chronic alcoholics. Perhaps a dozen of us
were dismissed from school for failing courses.

Does this sound like a satire, a parody of student life
in the early twenties? It is, indeed, a thing easily
parodied, but remember that the parodies didn't appear
out of the air: they were written mostly by men who
lived through just this sort of life. It reads like a parody
to me, too—but that's how it was.

One thing more, which perhaps distinguished my
crowd from similarly exuberant groups of undergraduates
at other colleges at the time: those of us who didn't flunk
out got an education—it is difficult to remain long at
Hopkins and escape education. It was we who followed
the real tradition of the chapter and, to some extent,
of the University: *student-ensleben,* in the manner of
the old German universities. We drank hard, caroused
hard, studied hard, and slept little. We crammed for examinations, drank black coffee, chewed cigarettes, took
Benzedrine—and read books, quizzed each other for
days, and read more books, and asked more questions.
The ones who failed were not really a part of us: the
goal was to drink the most whiskey, fornicate the most
girls, get the least sleep, and make the highest grades.
I for one am thankful that studying was part of the
sport, because otherwise I certainly shouldn't have
bothered with it, knowing I'd not live to take my bachelor's degree. To be sure, most of us remembered nothing
two days after the final examinations; but some of us
did, and myself among them. It was the men, the pro-
fessors, the fine, independent minds of Johns Hopkins—
the maturity, the absence of restrictions, the very air
of Homewood, that nourished the strong seeds of reason
in our ruined bodies; the disinterested wisdom that refused even to see our ridiculous persons in the lecture
halls; that talked, as it were, to itself, and seemed

scarcely to care when some of us began to listen, to listen intently, fiercely, passionately.

I lived through 1920, through 1921, through 1922, through 1923. In the summers I lived on at the fraternity house and worked as a stonemason, a brush salesman, a factory laborer, a life guard at one of the city pools, a tutor of history, even, and once actually a ditchdigger. To my great surprise I was alive on commencement day, if not entirely sober, and lived to walk off Gilman Terrace with my diploma—pale, weak, educated. I had lost twenty pounds, countless prejudices, much provincialism, my chastity (what had remained of it), and my religion. I had gained a capacity for liquor and work; an ability to take beatings; a familiarity with card games, high society, and whorehouses; a taste for art and Marxism; and a habit of thinking that would ultimately lead me at least beyond the latter. My college years are as interesting, to me, as my time in the Army, but no more of them than what I've mentioned is relevant here.

Because at summer's end I was still alive and had to have something to do, I went ahead with my program and began reading the law at the University of Maryland Law School, in downtown Baltimore. I no longer lived in the fraternity house—in an adolescently idealistic moment I had proposed amending the Order's constitution to admit Jews and Negroes, and had brought the righteous wrath of Beta Alpha upon my head. Instead, I had a marvelous fourth-floor room in a huge, ancient row-house—it must once have been palatial—on Monument Street, very near Hopkins Hospital: a room suggested to me by Marvin Rose. My neighbors and companions were medical students; the atmosphere was intense, electric with work, exhausting—more deadly serious than before, perhaps (for we were no longer undergraduates), but not more sober. With Marvin I rode in ambulances on night duty, learned first aid, hardened my stomach to carnage that equaled Argonne's, made love to certain nurses and strange—very strange! —female patients, and drank.

I read Justices Holmes and Cardozo, and the Spanish and Italian legal philosophers; I studied criminal law, torts, wills, legal Latin. With the medical students, achievement, competence, even brilliance, were still part of the sport: I drove myself, disciplined myself, whipped myself; drank much, read much, slept little. When I was discharged from the Army I'd weighed 180 pounds; on commencement day at Hopkins I weighed 160; by the end of my first year at law school I was down to 145.

"Less work for the pallbearers," I told myself—for no one else suspected my Damocletian heart.

One night in mid-December of 1924 (I believe it was the last night before the Christmas holiday at both the law school and the medical school, though this is uncertain—it may have been before some sort of examination), Marvin and some of his colleagues proposed going out on the town, and since I happened to have thirty dollars, I agreed. I was the more eager to drink because all that day I'd had strange, sharp pains in my lower abdomen—too low for appendicitis. Walking hadn't soothed them, nor had lying down, and so I looked forward to a pleasant general anesthesia.

"Dinner," Marvin announced, and six of us took two cabs to Miller Brothers' for crab imperial. I ached all through the meal.

"Drink," he announced later, and we took a bus out to a speakeasy near the hospital, one patronized by the medical students, and got somewhat drunk. I shifted and squirmed with pain.

"Divertissement!" announced someone a few hours later—we were five, then, because Marvin had to go on duty in the outpatient department for the rest of the night—and the whole party adjourned to a house of joy that someone else had heard of on North Calvert Street, about halfway to the University.

We rode out in a cab. Someone put something in the one whiskey bottle from which most of us drank—I'm no toxicologist, and so I can't say what it was. When we disembarked we were loud, rough, and on the verge of helplessness. Twice in the next half hour I nearly fainted, and not from liquor but from the fiery pains in my abdomen. I could scarcely wait to get a woman, for apart from the blessing of lying down, I had an inebriate notion that sex might relieve the pain.

Someone must have done my selecting for me; I'm sure I neither saw nor cared which of the girls I went upstairs with.

But "Toddy!" one of my companions hollered from down a hallway, just as my girl and I were entering a bedroom. "Hol' on!"

"No," I called back politely.

"Hol' on!" my colleague hollered again, and came lurching down the hall, pulling a girl behind him. "I got a lady here knows you all from 'way back, boy."

"Oh," I said, and went into the room where my girl was waiting.

"*Oh* nothing!" the medical student cried, striding in behind me. "Why take a total stranger when right here's an ol' buddy? I'm swappin' with you."

The new girl was apologizing to my girl for being dragged in.

"You guys better get straightened out quick," my girl snapped, "or I'm callin' Cozy to bounce you."

I fell on the bed, dizzy almost to vomiting. I felt as though a hot needle, a hot bayonet, were piercing— what? My liver? My spleen?

Then I was standing in the center of the room, holding on to a bedpost for support, and Betty June Gunter, not a day older than she had been in 1917, was sitting on the bed, holding a cigarette in her hand, dangling a slipper from one foot, smiling mockingly at me.

I could see now; in fact I felt much more sober, but I was certainly suffering to the point of delirium.

"Glad to see you, Toddy," Betty June said sarcastically.

"I'm not going to talk, if you don't mind," I said carefully, holding on to my pain. "We'd never get it all said, and if it's all the same to you, I—"

What happened was that I collapsed then. After that Betty June had slipped off her one-piece whore's dress and I was holding her. If six years of prostitution had changed her at all, I couldn't see how. I remember wishing I were entirely sober and painless so that I could appreciate the grotesque coincidence of my meeting her, and also talk to her coherently. As far as I can tell, I was passing out every few minutes from my pain. At one point she asked me, "Do you hurt, Toddy boy?"

"I'm damn near dead," I admitted.

Then she was leaning over me, rubbing my chest and arms with rubbing alcohol.

"What the hell."

"Service of the house," she grinned.

There was a tremendous racket outside in the hall and downstairs. I believe my medical colleagues were destroying the whorehouse.

My original plan for relief occurred to me, but it was apparently out of the question: the pain unmanned me. I was perspiring.

Now Betty June was sitting perched at my feet, and was massaging my legs with the alcohol. Her business had not improved her bustline, I observed, but neither had it hardened her good eyes. I wished I were sober so that I could judge better how she felt about me. She certainly appeared affectionate enough. What an incredible coincidence! I wondered whether she knew Smitty was dead.

"You know Smitty's dead," I remarked.

Her expression, a puckered smile, didn't change. Her eyes followed her hands, rubbing my legs.

What I finally said—rather loudly, for the noise outside the door was incessant—was, "Damn it, honey, I owe you an apology. I wish this pain weren't so bad, I'd do things right for you, no laughing. That time in my room back home, I swear, I—"

That was when, still without any change of expression at all, Betty June emptied the whole bottle of rubbing alcohol in the worst possible place.

I hollered and leaped from the bed; I clutched myself and rolled on the floor. Stupendous pain! The two together were inconceivable! To make things worse, Betty

June fell upon me, still smiling. She struck at me with the alcohol bottle, coolly, putting all her small strength into each blow, and although I was able to parry nearly every assault, the crack of the bottle on my arm or elbow was punishment enough in itself. I pushed and kicked her away, but to stand up was beyond my power. I felt exactly as though I were on fire.

Betty June had got the bottle broken by this time, and she came at me with the jagged neck of it. I rolled away and struck desperately at her, but it was a losing fight. Every parry cost me a slash on the arm, across the knuckles, in the palm of my hand. When I finally got a grip on her right wrist, she kicked and bit violently. What I wanted to do, what I tried to do, was break her arm, if possible, to slow her up. That's what I was attempting when the room filled with people.

"Cozy!" Betty June cried.

There was an enormous din. I didn't dare let go of Betty June's arm, although I was apparently too weak to break it. Much blood was on us both. I felt like going to sleep; I had the strongest impulse to say, "Let's be friends, honey," and go to sleep right on her poor thin arm, there on the floor. *Why isn't the whole thing a sailboat?* I remember wondering through the pain that was crucifying me; then I could let go of everything, tiller and sheets, and the boat would luff up into the wind and hang in stays, and I could sleep.

Cozy must have been a quite competent bouncer. I daresay he rabbit-punched me, considering the circumstances and the additional pain in the back of my neck when I woke up next, but I didn't even feel the blow when it fell. Cozy had stuffed me into the back seat of somebody's parked automobile, on the floor. I had my shirt and trousers and shoes on, loosely, but no underwear, necktie, stockings, coat, or overcoat. Three-inch adhesive tape had been rolled roughly around my slashed arm—Cozy's employer hadn't wanted me to die near the premises—and since no major blood vessels had been severed, the bleeding had virtually stopped, but not before daubing my clothes. My neck exploded with

throbbing pains; I still burned, though not quite so
severely—horrible few minutes!—and the mysterious
original pain continued undiminished.

I crawled out of the car after a while. I still had my
wrist watch: it was four in the morning. What part of
town was I in? I kept close to the wall of row-houses
along the street, both to steady myself and to shelter
myself from the cold, and walked as best I could to the
corner gas lamp. As is usual in the poorer neighborhoods,
the street signs around the lamp were broken off. I turned
the corner and walked numbly for an infinity of unin-
habited city blocks, all fronted with infinities of faceless,
featureless, identical row-houses and nightmare lines of
marble steps like snaggled teeth. Then came the second
coincidence of the evening: I had been walking in an
absolutely lightless alleyway, as quiet and black as
the remotest cranny of the universe; I half-fell around
a corner, and I was on Monument Street—civilized,
brightly lighted, filled with automobiles and street-
cars even at four o'clock. The brown Victorian pile of
Hopkins Hospital stood waiting, just across the street,
disgorging frequent screaming ambulances into the city,
and swallowing others as frequently. A flurry of lights
and a succession of strong smells, and presently I was
sitting in a hard chair in a corridor of the hospital. There
was much glare; soft hustlings of carts, stretchers,
nurses, orderlies; muffled clinkings of instruments and
glass; laughter in the distance; activity, busyness, all
around my hard chair where I sat holding my head
tightly. Everybody was awake in the hospital; I felt so
safe I wanted to vomit.

Marvin Rose was saying, "Stay here for a few days,
Toddy."

Then I was in the ward—had slept for a long time and
was in little pain—and when I opened my eyes a
lean nurse was holding my left arm. Before I could
explain to her whatever it was that I felt explosively
needed explaining, her needle had made quite the wrong
small popping puncture (more felt than heard, to be

sure) in the white underskin of my forearm, and I
fainted another time.

Few things, I venture, are more sickeningly uncomfortable to a man than a needle biopsy. The horrible
instrument opened the secret of my pain to the doctor
who attended me. A severely infected prostate—most unusual in a twenty-four-year-old man. And my health was
generally broken down. I remained in the ward for a
month, with little to do but think.

Here are the things I thought about, lying long hours
immobile with closed eyes: my imminent, instant death;
the futility, for me, of plans and goals; the tight smile
on Betty June's lips (she hadn't laughed); the sound
of punctured skin. I thought at times coherently, at
times dizzily, moving from one subject to the next and
starting over again. I would not attempt to sort the
causes from the effects in my month's thinking, but
when I was finally discharged I had decided with my
whole being that I was "out of it"; that the pursuits,
the goals, the enthusiasms of the world of men were
not mine. My stance had been wrong, I concluded:
the great fact with which I had to live was not to be
escaped in whiskey and violence, not even in work.
What I must do, I reasoned, is keep it squarely before
me all the time; live with it soberly, looking it straight
in the eye. There was more to my new attitude, but it
was a matter of the rearrangement of abstractions, not
really important here. The visible effects on my behavior were primarily these: I still drank, but no longer
got drunk. I smoked, but not nervously. I took women
to bed only in the rare cases when it was they who had
assumed the initiative, and then I was thorough but
dispassionate. I studied and worked hard and steadily,
but no longer intensely, no longer in frenzied spasms.
I talked less. I began in earnest what was to be a long
process of assuming hard control over myself: the sub-
stitution of small, specific strengths for small, specific
weaknesses, regarding the latter with the same unresent-
ful disfavor with which one regards a speck of dust

on one's coat sleeve, before plucking it quietly off. I unconsciously began to regard my fellow men variously as more or less pacific animals among whom it was generally safe to walk (so long as one observed certain tacitly assumed rules), or as a colony of more or less quiet lunatics among whom it was generally safe to live (so long as one humored, at least outwardly, certain aspects of their madness).

There have been other changes in my attitude during my life, but none altered my outward behavior and manner so markedly as this one. I was uninvolved; I was unmoved; I was a saint. I was, or so I believed then, in precisely the position of those South American butterflies (e.g., the female *Papilio cenea*—I did learn my zoology between drinks) who, themselves defenseless, mimic outwardly the more numerous species among which they live: appropriately, the so-called "nauseous" Danais, whose bad taste and smell render them relatively safe. At least when walking their streets, I had to pretend to be like all the other butterflies—but at heart I knew I was of another species entirely, perhaps a less nauseous one.

I continued, therefore, my study of law, as part of the mimicry; at Marvin's prescription I began taking a capsule of diethylstilbestrol every day; and I awaited more quietly the moment of death. In my good time I meditated, disinterestedly, that tight, puckered smile on the face of the female human being who had intended to kill me. And, for the next thirteen years, though the prostate continued to give me frequent pain, I ceased to share that pain with physicians. Who ever heard of a saint's crying for a doctor?

"Well, well, well!" Marvin shouted (in 1937) when I stepped into his office. He rubbed his hands gleefully. "Coming home to die, are you? What'll it be, Todd my lad, euthanasia or homicide? What the hell, you pregnant?"

"A plain old physical examination, Marv," I said.

"Going to buy some insurance, man? I'll lie for you. Hell, boy, I'll euthanaze you."

"None of your business. Come on, examine."

But we smoked a cigar first, and Marvin reminisced about Baltimore. When he got around to examining me, I said:

"Will you go along with me on something, Marvin?"

"Where's the body? Who we got it in for? What'd you do, Todd?"

"You can examine me to your heart's content," I said, "but I don't want you to say a word about anything you see or find; don't even change expression."

"I won't even examine you if you say so, you big sissy. I'll call Shirley in here and let her look at you. What you say, boy?"

"Just write it all down," I smiled, "and either mail it to me or drop it off at the hotel. The point is that I don't want to know anything at all, at least until to-morrow. Okay?"

"Okay," Marvin grinned; "you're the doctor."

He then went through the examining routine, talking all the while he checked my height, weight, eyes, ears, nose, throat, and teeth. Then I stripped to the waist, and with stethoscope, watch and sphygmomanometer he checked my heart, my pulse, and my blood pressure, keeping the expressionless face I'd asked for. Then he tapped my chest and back, listening for congestion, and felt my vertebrae. Finally I removed trousers and under-wear, and he tapped my knee, testing for *locomotor ataxia*, felt for hernias, and looked for hemorrhoids and flat feet, all without any alteration of expression.

"How about a blood test and a urinalysis?" he asked.

I produced a urine specimen, but declined the blood test.

"How's the old prostate? Been keeping her empty?"

"No trouble," I said.

"Sure raised hell that one time, didn't it? I swear I wanted to cut her out for you, Toddy; you wouldn't have had another twinge. But that screwball Hodges—remember him? the resident?—he was having a feud with O'Donnell, the surgeon, that year, over politics, and wasn't letting anybody get cut. Goddam Hodges! I swear he'd have tried to amputate a leg with his damn internal medicine! What a bunch!" He made some notes on an examination form and slipped it into an envelope. "Here y'are, lad, the whole sad story. How about a little old needle biopsy? Have a look at the old infection. Hurt you like hell, but it's fun for me. Give you an appetite. Make you dance and holler."

"Let it go," I said, and began dressing.

"No needle, huh?" Marvin said. "How am I supposed to know what's what? How about an X-ray, raise your bill a few bucks?"

"Drop the paper off any time after today," I said, accepting from Marvin another light for my cigar, which had gone out. "Please keep everything under your hat, Marv."

"I don't blame you," Marvin said, walking me to the door with his arm across my shoulders. "I'd be ashamed, too." We shook hands. "Well, hell, Toddy. it's been fun. Don't wait so long next time. And listen, by Christ, if the old prostate commences to hurt you, I'll cut it out. You ought to keep check, boy."

I smiled and shook my head.

"What do you say? Come on down to the hospital Monday for an X-ray, and I'll bet I can take her right out, clean as a whistle."

"Wait till Monday," I said. "But don't hold your breath."

We said goodbye, and Marvin went back to lie down on the examination table for a nap. He was (I'm late saying it) a beefy little man with sparse blond hair, flushed skin, and tiny red veins in his cheeks. His arms and hands were so full of meat that it seemed as if the skin of them were ready to burst, like overboiled frankfurters. It would be pleasant to be able to go on and say of Marvin's great hands that, awkward as they appeared, the moment they were slipped into surgeon's gloves they assumed the grace, deftness, and delicate strength of a violinist's. This is the sort of thing one usually hears. But the truth is that those clumsy-looking hands, once slipped into surgical gloves, remained rather clumsy, depending as they did from slightly clumsy arms and ultimately from a somewhat clumsy brain. The truth is that the magnificent Hopkins does not infallibly produce faultless medicine men; the truth, alas, is that in fact I should be markedly reluctant, even were I not opposed to it on principle, to allow my excellent friend Marvin to incise me with his not-altogether-unerring knives. The fact of affection needn't, I trust, entirely preclude objectivity?

XV. That puckered smile

One doesn't just move on without giving that tight smile, Betty June's puckered smile, some further attention. Mere drunkenness and pain are no excuse for my not having realized, until she was upon me with the bottle, that I had done to Betty June a thing warranting murder at her hands (I am, by the way, reasonably confident that it *was* Betty June in the Calvert Street whorehouse, although I was certainly drunk). She wanted to kill me, I see now, for having laughed that time in my bedroom.

Here's how I understand it: that Saturday morning in 1917 she had learned that Smitty Herrin, to whom she had unreservedly humbled herself, had all the while been married secretly to Mona Johnston, from Henry Street, and had made Mona pregnant. In desperation, Betty June had come to me and had attempted—unconsciously, I daresay—to reassert her wounded ego by humbling me with the great gift of her body, a lean receptacle for my innocence. But in the throes of intercourse I had laughed, so violently as to unman myself, and couldn't even stanch her shocked and injured tears for very helplessness. Quite understandably she had assumed that I was laughing at her, at some ridiculousness of her, although this was not *particularly* true. And then—what? Smitty and I both enlisted, he was killed, and she became a prostitute. Ordinarily, perhaps, it would have been possible for her to rationalize her behavior, first as a patriotic gesture and later as gaining a liveli-

hood from "the oldest profession"—but she had my
laughter in her ears to remind her, every time she un-
hooked her one-piece gown for a new customer, that
there was something ludicrous about her and about what
she was doing. For many sorts of people, and Betty June
is one of them, this suspicion would be nearly intol-
erable. So: seven years later, when she's doubtless so
deeply enmired in the business and all its attendant
vices that she can't very well escape (I think of pimps
and narcotics, for example), seven years later I show up
party-drunk at her whorehouse—looking prosperous and
smug to her, no doubt—accepting her as my whore without a word, and only later, after permitting her to mas-
sage my body, refer with vague regret to the time I
laughed at her.

Don't you agree that this is probably how it was? I
can't account otherwise for her murderousness (yet I
must say, though I can scarcely explain it, that if I hadn't
mentioned the matter, I believe Betty June would have
gone through with the intercourse I had paid for).
The remarkable thing, it seems to me, is not at all that
she wanted to kill me—even simple shame at being thus
discovered could account for that—but that I failed to
realize it at once; that I missed the obvious implication
of that puckered smile.

And this is what I wanted to say, because I consider
it fairly important (hell, even urgently important) to
the understanding of this whole story: quite frequently,
things that are obvious to other people aren't even apparent to me. The fact doesn't especially bother me, except of course when it leads to my not jumping clear
of dangerous animals like poor Betty. If I were called
upon to explain it, I should doubtless offend and an-
tagonize you, for the only likely explanation I can imagine is that out of any situation I can usually interpret
a number of possible significances, often conflicting,
sometimes contradictory. Why, for instance, could it not
have been that Betty June, after seven years of prostitution and various unfortunate experiences, had come at
last to see, as I did, the essential hilarious grotesque-

ness of the whole business—the very four-letter verb for which is wittily onomatopoeic—and upon encountering me had decided to demonstrate her agreement by a rousing good copulation, at which we'd both laugh long and loud? Or, less dramatically, why could it not have been that she'd forgotten the whole affair in my bedroom, and was smiling merely at my drunkenness, or in anticipation of scorching me with isopropyl alcohol? Or, less kindly, that observing my helplessness she was smiling at the thought of earning seven dollars for giving me nothing more voluptuous than a rubdown? Understand, I'm not especially defending myself: very possibly another person would have seen factors in the situation that would preclude all these alternatives; or, possibly, another person wouldn't have imagined these alternatives in the first place. I honestly believe that to most men (and to any woman) Betty June's intentions would have been obvious. To me they were not.

On the other hand, things that are clear to me are sometimes incomprehensible to others—which fact occasions this chapter, if not the whole book.

XVI. The Judge's lunch

I know of no *really* good restaurant in Cambridge;
I think there are none. Therefore, since a wide selec-
tion of excellent food is out of the question, one's
grounds for choosing a regular eating place are likely to
be rather gratuitous. Harrison and I were in the habit
of lunching at a confectionery store on Race Street, beside the old opera house. It was run by an Orphan's
Court judge, an engaging fellow who refused, for purely
aesthetic reasons, to serve hot platters: he disliked the
smells of cooking in his store. This integrity alone would
have attracted me to the place, but the proprietor had a
host of such opinions; like me, he was in the habit
of giving invariably sound, often unorthodox, and not
infrequently *post facto* reasons for his behavior, which
reasons he was wont to articulate at length to his regular customers in a loud voice, for he was slightly deaf.

It was to this place that I walked after leaving Marvin.
Race Street was afire with dry, dusty sunlight, and few
people were out. A number of unclean children were
playing violent tag on the wide cracked steps of the opera
house, swinging over and under the brown brass rail that
led up to the shuttered box office. On both inner walls
of the arcaded façade, crusty with weathered architectural
gingerbread, were plastered posters advertising *Adam's
Original & Unparalleled Floating Opera*.

May I say truly that it was not until I'd actually
entered the confectioner's—until the Judge, small, dap-

per, bald, and boutonniered, had greeted me and I'd remarked politely that he looked like a million dollars—that not until then did I remember that, should I choose, I was in a position to make my friend Harrison worth nearly three million? It may seem incredible that such a thing could simply slip one's mind, but it very nearly did. I believe that if the Judge hadn't prompted my remark, I'd have forgotten the matter entirely, perhaps until too late. And I was glad I'd remembered it.

You see, although Eustacia's information assured me that I could win the case (all that was necessary was to secure from Equity an order holding up the appeal until the missing portions of the estate—the bottles of pickled excrement—were accounted for. The thing could be complicated indefinitely, and after the coming elections, when Joe Singer had replaced Rollo Moore on the appellate court bench, I was confident that the Circuit Court judgment would be reversed)—although the thing was in my hands, by no means did it necessarily follow that I would do anything about it. Very possibly, I would decide to keep the new information secret, let it die that very day with me, instead of giving it to young Jimmy Andrews or Mr. Bishop to work with after my death. For one thing, you must remember that I was, after all, a fairly thoroughgoing cynic at the time, especially concerning money; also—and there is nothing cynical about this—I believed Harrison was undeserving of the money unless he overcame his former weakness. It was my opinion that in order for him to be worthy of the inheritance, he had to demonstrate a strength of character that would make the loss of it unimportant: a pretty lofty opinion for a cynic, I'd say. At any rate, I decided not to mention Eustacia's letter right away.

I was a few minutes late, and Harrison was waiting for me, talking to the Judge. We went back to our table.

"Janie dropped out to the plant just before I drove in," he said after greeting me. "What are you needling her for?"

"Needling her?"

"That note you sent her this morning," Harrison said mildly. "You know what I'm talking about."

"I do now," I smiled. "I swear I'd forgotten." I gave my order to the girl who came to our table then. Harrison had already ordered. "I wasn't entirely joking, Harrison. Cap'n Osborn's got a couple more years, at the most, before he dies. Suppose you were in his place: wouldn't you like a fine send-off like Janie? Hell, he couldn't do anything to her. Are you angry?"

"I wasn't before," Harrison grinned, "because I thought you were just being nasty. But if you're *serious* about her showing herself to the old buzzard, I probably ought to get mad."

I held a light for his cigar. He was doing fine so far.

"Well, if you want to," I laughed. "But Janie handled it pretty brightly, I think. Did she tell you about *her* note?"

"No."

"She said she'd do what I asked if I'd agree to let Marvin Rose look at me, to see why I'm such a pansy. Her very words."

Harrison chuckled, a little relieved. "Fair enough," he said. "What did she mean, *pansy?* Or shouldn't I ask?"

"You may ask, but ask a little more softly next time, please. The fact is, I spent most of last night looking out my window, and the rest of the time reading a book."

Harrison looked concerned. "What, Toddy, you getting senile?"

"Quitting while I'm still ahead, maybe," I smiled. "As a matter of fact, I don't think Marvin found anything especially wrong with me, at least not below the belt. I was just up there."

"You were!" Harrison's peace of mind vanished. "You actually did what she said?"

"Yep."

The girl brought our lunches: a bacon and tomato sandwich and iced tea for Harrison, and a chopped olive and Swiss cheese on rye for me, with iced coffee. The Judge's sandwiches are excellent.

"Well, what now?" Harrison asked. "I don't know what to say. You sure do change your mind about things."

I shrugged. "Don't worry about it, boy. It's not your problem; it's Jane's. Cap'n Osborn won't know the difference either way."

Harrison started to object, but then he changed his mind and bit into his sandwich instead.

"All right," he said, talking with his mouth full. "I won't worry about it."

"Good man," I grinned.

Harrison then changed the subject and talked idly about a possible strike of his cucumber picklers. His mouth was still full, and there were three little flecks of mayonnaise on his lower lip. As he spoke, an occasional crumb blew over to me. I admired two things: the casual bad manners that one often encounters in finely bred animals like Harrison (strict etiquette, I've long believed, is mostly Emily Post's wishful thinking; the aristocrats I've known generally have a fine disregard for it), and the fact that his description of the labor difficulties in his plant suggested neither a pro-union bias from his Marxist days nor an anti-union bias from his present position. He was interested in the situation, but rather cynical towards both the union leaders, who were making him out to be a slave driver, and his own administrative staff, who advocated firing the lot of them and hiring "new niggers" in their places. It seemed to me that cynicism, although he was not entirely at home with it yet, became him a great deal more than had his earlier attempt at saintliness. I listened with some interest, regarding his still-handsome face (he was forty-three, I guess, and Jane in her early thirties) and the little drops of mayonnaise, which he finally licked away.

We finished our sandwiches and smoked for a while, enjoying our drinks. The Judge's store wasn't air-conditioned, but he had three big old ceiling fans, and the place was fairly dark and cool.

"Oh, by the way," Harrison said, "Jane wasn't in when your secretary called this morning, but the maid took the message, and then apparently you were out when Jane called back. She says she'll drop Jeannine off at your office at three, if that's not too early. She's coming uptown to the hairdresser's around then."

"Swell," I said. As a matter of fact I was a little disturbed, not at the change of hours (I had planned to take little Jeannine to see the showboat at four), but because my instructions to Mrs. Lake—to call Jane— were the second thing I'd forgotten in a few hours. No, come to think of it, I'd had *three* lapses of memory: Eustacia's letter, my note to Jane, and my request to Mrs. Lake. This was a serious matter, for it could be taken as a sign of nervousness, of apprehension at my decision to destroy myself that day. I was of course not indifferent towards the resolution, but my feeling was more one of pleasure at having found the final solution to my problem than one of commonplace fear. And, pleasure or fear, I marked it an indication of imperfect control to be so touched by my feeling as to make unusual slips of memory on what I'd decided was to be a quite usual day.

"I thought I'd take her down to see the showboat when it pulls in," I said. "How's her tonsils?"

"All right, I guess. Anyhow it wasn't tonsillitis. Marvin came out and looked at her throat yesterday, and said it didn't look like he'd have to take them out, unless we wanted him to go ahead and get it over with. It was her throat that was infected, and her tonsils just swelled up on general principles. I don't know what Jane's decided. Both of us had tonsillitis when we were kids."

"Better leave them in," I suggested. "Mine used to swell up every now and then, whenever I had a sore throat, but it never amounted to anything."

Now there was a certain tactlessness in this remark, as I'll explain presently, and I made it for that reason, with great nonchalance. Harrison took the cigar from his mouth and studied its ash critically.

"I don't know," he said.

"Marvin's a little quick with the knife. Once when I was in law school and he was interning, he was all set to make a eunuch out of me."

Harrison replaced the cigar in his mouth and drew on it as we got up from the table.

"That would've been too bad," he observed, and put a quarter down for the girl. Then he fetched his straw and mine, and we walked through the front of the store. Have I described Harrison? Not being a writer by trade, I sometimes neglect these details. He was heavy —weighed perhaps two hundred pounds—and still well-built, though he showed slight signs of going to fat from lack of exercise. His features, which had been chiseled when I first knew him, had begun to round off a little, and his cheeks and belly no longer looked hard, as they had when he played much tennis and rode horses. He still had a good head of tightly curled blond hair, contrasting nicely with a complexion as much flushed as sunburned (I daresay his blood pressure registered somewhere between mine and Marvin's), and his eyes, teeth, and arms were excellent. Very wealthy-looking fellow, Harrison, and very clean and handsome. The thin, consumptive communist would justifiably loathe him, but the properly nourished parlour communist would be made uncomfortable by his charm. I am sometimes afraid that those particular aspects of Harrison relevant to this story have made him look less engaging than he really was—I can't dwell on him, of course, for it's not his story. Let me repeat, then, if I've mentioned it before, that he was by no means either a fool or a weakling. He was a reasonable, generous, affable, alert fellow. I might even say that if this were a rational universe and if I could be any person I chose, I should not choose to be Todd Andrews at all. I should choose to be very much like my friend Harrison Mack.

"How's the pickle business, Todd?" the Judge called to me as we stepped out on the sidewalk, where he spent much of his time watching the town. He referred, of course, to the disputed will, which case he had followed with great interest, he being an Orphan's Court judge himself. "You gentlemen in the money yet?"

Ordinarily I'd have enjoyed explaining the new development to him, for although he was not professionally trained, his mind was quick and sure, and he'd have appreciated the maneuver. But of course I could not.

"Nothing new, Judge," I said loudly. "Depends on how the war goes, maybe."

"Well, I doubt it'll go good for the Loyalists," he declared. "They've been holding their own lately, but it can't keep up. They've got the Russians, but Mr. Franco, he's got the Germans back of him, and like it or not, the German's a better soldier than the Russian is. The German might be dumb, but he's dumb like a smart dog. Old Russian, he's dumb like an ox."

Harrison was fidgeting to leave. For my part, I was interested enough in the Judge's prognostications, for though one might not care to accept his national characterizations (he, by the way, was of German stock), his predictions were usually accurate, for he knew how to read newspapers, and read five or six a day. Special abilities like this aren't infrequently found among intelligent, uneducated men, and where present they are often extremely reliable. It was, in fact, the Judge who had first predicted to me that Rollo Moore wouldn't be reelected, and I'd have gone ahead with my plans on the strength of his judgment even had I not been able to confirm it in certain Baltimore Republican circles.

"You think Franco's in, then?" I asked.

"I think it'll take him a couple of years yet to wind it up," the Judge said. "By that time the whole shebang might blow up."

"Well," Harrison fidgeted.

I said goodbye to the Judge—after all, I probably would never see him again, and he was one of my favorite citizens—and walked with Harrison as far as his car, which was parked on Poplar Street.

"Will you come for cocktails tonight?" he asked as he slipped behind the wheel.

I leaned down and talked to him through the window on my side. "Much obliged," I said.

Harrison put the Cadillac in gear.

"Don't feel obligated," he smiled ruefully. "Any time after four."

He slid away down the brick street, which shimmered now in the very hot sun. I walked toward the hotel for my nap, feeling fine about Harrison. There was no need for haste in making my decision, but the lunchtime had done his cause much good. Much good indeed.

XVII. The end of the outline

Climatologically, this day of which I write was rare for
Dorchester County, rare for the Eastern Shore, where
the same ubiquitous waters that moderate the tempera-
tures—the ocean, the Bay, the infinite estuaries, creeks,
coves, guts, marshes, and inlets—also make them quite
uncomfortable. This day, on the contrary, was exces-
sively warm (the temperature as I walked to the hotel
must have reached 95), but extremely dry. I was wearing shirt, suit, underwear, and hat, and there was no
shade on Poplar Street, but my body was as dry as a
white bone in the desert, and I was entirely comfortable.
It was a day when one would have liked to sit alone
on a high dune by the ocean—the Atlantic beach is
often just this dry, given a land breeze—in air as hot
and salty as Earth's commencement, the drought of
precreation before the damp of procreation; to sit a dried
and salted sterile saint, Saint Todd of the Beach, and
watch voracious gulls dissect the stranded carcasses of
sandy skates and sharks, bleached and brined to stench-
lessness. The locust trees by People's Trust were dusty,
and mast-truck high in the High Street poplars, locusts
rasped and whirred a parched dirge for my last high noon.
It was a lovely day for suicide. One felt that one would
hardly bleed into such aridity; more probably a knife
in the neck would be kissed with a desiccant hiss of
mere dry air.

Turning the corner of Poplar, High, and Locust Streets,
I found the loafer's bench empty: the old men were

doubtless home to nap. The Choptank sparkled at the foot of the boulevard. *Adam's Original & Unparalleled Floating Opera* posters graced every business window on the empty streets from the Judge's place to the hotel, red, white, and blue, as though the town had been set for Independence Day and then everyone—men, women, cats, and pallbearers—had gone to a parade somewhere else.

The hotel lobby was light and cool; a small chat with Jerry Hogey, and then I went to my room. Are you so curious as to follow me down the hall to the men's room? If you aren't—if your sensitivity is such as to leave you in my room while I go (I shall be only a minute), then read while you wait the story of my resumption of the affair with Jane Mack. Look back into Chapter III, and you'll find that near the end of that chapter I reproduced an outline of the events that I imagined led up to my pleasant, if unnerving, seduction by the Macks. In the final section of that outline I listed what I considered to be the four possible courses that my relationship with them could take after I'd broken it off by an act that, judged in the very terms that I objected to, they must regard as an insult. Now of these four courses, I must say that either I or IV (that is, either permanent disaffection or the resumption of a qualified affection, one of the qualifications being a suspension of the affair) seemed the most probable to me after the incident in my office with Dorothy Miner, which terminated the friendship.

However, I was reckoning without two things, neither of which I could reasonably have been expected to predict.

In the first place, just a few weeks after the Macks had severed relations with me, Jane learned, upon being examined by Marvin Rose for chronic nausea, that she was pregnant. Moreover, she was probably three months pregnant: it was possible for her not to guess it herself only because she had always been irregular. As soon as Marvin looked at her, he said, "You're pregnant," and it instantly seemed so obvious to her (she swore later that her tummy filled out the moment he spoke the word) that she became a little hysterical at not having recognized it herself. Marvin gave her a sedative. Jane hurried home and could scarcely wait to tell Harrison when he came in from work, she was so delighted. But when he walked into the house and she opened her mouth to tell him, it suddenly occurred to her that she was *three months* pregnant, not three weeks or three days; she remembered me, burst into tears, and nearly fainted. When finally she was able to explain things to Harrison, he couldn't say a word.

The pregnancy was pretty miserable for both of them (I learned this later, of course). It would have been simple enough to arrange an abortion, of course, but it happened that they really wanted a child, and had tried unsuccessfully for several years to have one. They both wished, too late, that Jane had been more diligent in using precautions with me, but the fact was that she hadn't; it is a mark of Harrison's saintliness that not once did he suggest a reproach for her carelessness, and a mark of Jane's that she owned up to it in the first place. Being intelligent people, they were able to talk about the matter quite frankly, and they tried hard to articulate their sentiments, to decide just how they really felt about it.

"Look at it this way," Harrison's most frequent argument ran; "suppose I was sterile—wouldn't we sooner or later probably adopt a kid? Or suppose you'd been married before and had a kid—wouldn't we still love it after you married me? Now, this is better than adoption, because you're going to be the real mother either way. And it's better than a previous marriage, because there's a good chance I'm the real father. After all, I slept with you more than Andrews did."

As a matter of fact, that was a pretty good argument, I thought, but Harrison just never could put enough conviction into his voice, and that last sentence, whether intended to do so or not, usually brought Jane to tears.

"That's all very true," was her typical reply, "but no amount of reasoning can get around the fact that if

I hadn't made love to Todd in the first place—or
if I'd only kept my stupid head and been careful—then
either I wouldn't be pregnant or we'd know you're the
father." This said with her fine head in her hands, her
excellent shoulders shaking.

Harrison then, quite calmly (but not kissing the sable
hair or stroking the shoulders): "What the hell, hon, a
fact's a fact. There's no use torturing yourself if you
can't go back and start over. Don't forget it was my
idea as much as yours. We shouldn't have taken the step
if we can't stand up to the consequences."

"But we didn't think of this!" Jane would wail.

And Harrison would shrug. "People get pregnant."

And so on. Oh, it was a lousy pregnancy. To make
it worse, Jane was ill for most of the remaining six
months; whether physiological or psychosomatic, her
nausea was serious. She could keep virtually nothing on
her stomach, and on several occasions required uncomfortable glucose injections to stave off malnutrition.
At the same time, though, her illness had the virtue of
keeping her weight down. I saw her just once, in her
ninth month, from a short distance away, and she was
so beautiful that I suffered a rare twinge of regret and
real longing, no less intense for its being short-lived. And
her moderate size eased her delivery: on October 2,
1933, in the Cambridge Memorial Hospital, after only
three hours of labor, she gave birth to a six-pound ten-
ounce girl, whom she named Jeannine Paulsen (Jane's
maiden name) Mack.

Harrison and Jane had, understandably, been not a
little fearful of the day when they must actually bring
their baby home; when it would be committed totally
into their hands and they would be expected to love and
care for it. The care was no problem—there were
bottles, formulas, and trained nurses—but they feared
that the love might simply not be forthcoming, might
not be in them. Jane especially feared this about Harrison, and Harrison about himself. But as it happened (I
shall be disappointed if you infer from this either a
natural law or divine intercession) they very quickly took

to their daughter—she was an engaging child, luckily, right from her infancy—and found it quite easy to be normally affectionate parents. Perhaps their knowledge of the very danger of any other reaction sufficed to open the buds of love in their hearts. They breathed much more easily (the baby, obviously doing her best to protect her own interests, contrived to resemble neither Harrison nor me to any embarrassing degree) and wondered what they'd worried so much about.

"I swear," Harrison volunteered, "if somebody should prove to me, right this minute, that Todd was Jeannine's father, I wouldn't love her a bit less for it."

"Oh, I'm sure he's not," Jane scoffed (you understand that I heard all this later). "But I don't think I would, either. She's beautiful."

But the important statement, for this story, Harrison made sometime in the spring of 1934, about a year after I'd insulted them.

"You know," he said, "you may not agree with this, because I know how much you dislike him, but I sometimes think that that business with Todd was partly our fault, too."

"Our fault!"

"I mean, what the hell, we put him on the spot, when you got in bed with him; he might not even have wanted to, you know—not because he didn't want you, but because he might have thought it would hurt our marriage. But if he'd refused, we'd have been insulted, wouldn't we? And, in fact, if he hadn't done it on our terms, we'd have been insulted, I think."

"Still, he had no business telling us he was a virgin," Jane insisted.

"But you can't deny we were pleased when he did," Harrison replied. "That proves we were expecting too much of him. And we certainly had no right to expect him not to make love to other women. What the hell, he's a bachelor."

"Yes, but he was supposed to be in love with me."

"You're in love with me, too," Harrison smiled, "but you made love to Toddy. You understand."

Jane sulked.

"We just plain expected too much. We should've known him better. We knew he gets foul moods on and likes to hurt people." (I don't entirely agree, by the way.)

"Well maybe you're right," Jane said. "But he certainly had no right to break it off like he did, with that damned colored girl!"

Harrison grinned. "I guess he's just unprejudiced. To tell the truth, the more I think about that, the more I believe he was just ad-libbing. That girl didn't know what was up any more than I did."

Jane grew exasperated. "You take up for him all you want to," she declared. "He didn't bite *your* ear and tell you he loved you."

"Whoa, now," Harrison reminded her gently.

"Well, you can't tell me he couldn't have just told us what was on his mind, without going out of his way to hurt us."

"I think two things about that," Harrison said calmly. "In the first place I'm not sure we wouldn't have been just as insulted no matter how he did it. What the hell, we wanted him to declare love for us, and he just didn't have it. We'd gone out on a limb."

"With his encouragement," Jane added sarcastically. "Don't forget the virgin and love stuff."

"That's the second thing. No matter how much we think of Toddy, or thought of him, he just isn't a saint, that's all. I think he said those things because he thought we expected them—and we did, God damn it—and I think when we got too demanding he broke it off the way he did either through cowardice or on account of his mean streak. What the hell, it might just be his mean streak."

Well, Jane sulked for a while, but after the ice had been broken they talked more freely about me, and less bitterly. Gradually it got to be assumed that they'd really been too demanding (a piece of objectivity that still appalls me), and that to some extent I'd been justified in showing my claws.

The next step was for Jane to say, "Hell, I forgive him; I just don't want anything to do with him any more. I don't want to get hurt again."

And for Harrison to say, "I still like Todd all right; it's just that I can't get enthusiastic about seeing him any more. I don't bear him any grudge."

Jeannine grew and grew, and discreetly began to look like her mother.

The second thing that I hadn't predicted was that on January 10, 1935, Harrison Mack Senior would die, leaving seventeen testamentary instruments for his wife, son, and nurses to play games with. But that he did, just as surely as sweet Janie got herself impregnated, and just as irremediably. No one needed to suggest to Harrison that he needed professional assistance, either; he consulted a lawyer a lot more quickly than Jane had consulted a physician, and the firm that he retained was Andrews, Bishop, & Andrews. The obvious necessity for legal counsel, the disturbance over his father's death, the excitement over the big estate—all these made his move seem quite natural, so that if there was anything in it of an overt act to reinstate our friendship, the overtness was effectively camouflaged, and one needn't even think of it.

There were, one can well imagine, dozens of details in the litigation that required discussion, strategies to be worked out, conferences to be held: many more than could be conveniently fitted into my rather leisurely office schedule. It was inevitable, then, that Harrison and I should occasionally utilize our lunch hours for the purpose; even that he should eventually invite me, with admirable aplomb, to come for late cocktails one evening, and that I, with commensurate grace, should accept. Of that evening—at first somewhat strained, since it was my first meeting with Jane in more than two years —just one incident will do here: the Macks had put Jeannine to bed early, thinking thereby to keep discomfort at a minimum, and with the assistance of Gilbey's gin and Sherbrook rye, the three of us had contrived to reach a condition of mellow, if tacit, mutual forgiveness. We all felt relieved that the nonsense of the past two years was done, though nothing was said about it directly; our good spirits were reflected in the unusual amount of liquor consumed, in the fact that whatever legal matters had provided the excuse for our meeting never got discussed, and (most significantly) by the fact that when Jeannine, who had a slight cold, began to fret in her crib, Jane, despite a private resolve to the contrary, said spontaneously: "Come on, Toddy, you haven't met this little Mack! Come upstairs with me and be introduced."

She realized her slip as soon as it was out, and added at once, without changing her tone or expression, "Harrison will do the honors, won't you, honey?"

The three of us went to the nursery, where Jeannine —a blond little charmer whom I must say I'd be delighted to learn I'd fathered—stood up sleepily in her crib and grinned at her parents, shyly, because I was there.

"Jeannine," Harrison said, "this is Toddy. Can you say *Toddy?*"

Jeannine could not, or would not.

"Would you like to kiss Toddy good night, honey?" Jane asked her. Jeannine hung her head, but looked up at me from under her eyebrows and chortled. When I kissed her hair—as soft as silk thread, and fragrant with baby soap—she dived headlong into the mattress and buried her giggles in the blanket.

Jane had crossed the room to adjust the window, and Harrison and I stood side by side at the crib, where Jeannine was already on the verge of sleep. A number of very obvious thoughts were in the air of the nursery— it was like a scene arranged by a heavy-handed Hollywood director—and I, for one, was terribly embarrassed when Jane, after her excellent and immediate good taste of a few minutes before, now came up behind us and simply grasped both our arms tightly while we looked at the little girl. *Our little girl,* the whole tableau simpered, underlining the pronoun, *and it doesn't matter which of you is the father, for she was conceived in the sweetness of all our love.* Ah, reader, the thing was so gross, so sentimental; and yet I was moved, in my uncomfortable fashion, for with the Macks these sentiments are always thoroughly sincere. They are simply full of love, for themselves, for each other, and for me.

We went back downstairs, soberly, but Harrison, sensitive by then to such solemnities, at once poured a round of inordinately alcoholic cocktails and we were soon gay again, like kids after communion—we were restored to grace. The evening was a success; I returned often; and soon, but for the two quiet years that sometimes hung heavy over our conversation, we spoke together as freely and easily as ever.

I will say honestly that had the friendship remained at exactly this stage of reconstruction, I should have asked for nothing more. I was content to see the Macks outgrow their earlier unbecoming and immature jealousy, which was as essentially dangerous to their own relationship as it was inconsistent with their previous behavior. Nor did I see how things could tactfully become any more intimate, after my rebuff of 1933. But on the night of July 31, 1935, while I was sitting at my window reading a book for my *Inquiry* (somebody's critique of Adam Smith's economics, I do believe), there was a small knock on my door, the knob rattled, and Jane stepped in, wearing shorts.

"Hi," she said, standing just inside the closed door.

"Hello," I answered. I closed my book, threw my cigar stub out the window, and got up to give her the chair. "Sit down."

"All right." She grinned quickly and came over to the window, where I was sitting on the sill, but she forgot to sit down. I didn't want any nonsense this time—for her sake, not because I objected to nonsense on principle —and so I kept my eyes on her face, not to make it any easier for her. She mostly looked down at the street.

"We've been for a boat ride," she said. "When I didn't answer, she looked at me irritably and began to fidget.

"I'm not going to grab you, Janie," I said, "or send you away either."

"You have to understand everything at once," she declared. "I'm not able to talk about anything just now."

"That's impossible," I said honestly. "I can understand everything at once in about three different ways."

"You're not helping me. You're not saying any of the right things." She laughed.

I didn't smile. "That's only because I don't know what you want to hear, Jane. You should know I'll say anything I think you want to hear."

Her smile disappeared, and she regarded the dark Post Office across the street and fiddled with the curtain pull.

"That was a hard lesson, Toddy."

"I wasn't teaching anybody anything," I said sharply. "What the hell do you think I am? I was just getting clear. I was concerned only with myself in that thing. Listen," I said, "don't fool yourself about me. You know how much I like you and Harrison—it's a lot, for me. But by now you ought to know about how far it goes, and what things it doesn't include for anybody."

She said nothing, just fiddled with the cord.

"Let me ask you," I said. "Do I love you?"

"No."

"Now damn it, let's get that straight. I don't want to hurt you all."

"You don't love me and I don't love you."

This was getting as theatrical as the other. I gave it up. For ten minutes more Jane stared at the Post Office. I honestly couldn't guess what would come of it. After a few minutes, though I didn't intend any such thing, my mind—never very impressed by this sort of dramatics —actually wandered to other things: to the seventeen wills, to Bill Froebel, to the critique of Adam Smith. And it startled me, for I'd honestly forgotten for an instant that she was there, when Jane spun around from the window and said, "Let's get in bed, Todd. Right now." Without looking at me, she walked to the bed,

unfastened her shorts and halter, and lay down, and very
shortly after that I joined her.

So. Nothing remains to be told of the affair, except
that after its resumption it was conducted in a manner
much more satisfactory to me. No schedules, no demands,
no jealousy, no fictions—all was spontaneity and can-
dor. I think that my increasingly frequent impotency
after that time (by 1936, about every fourth attempt at
intercourse was a failure; by 1937, about every other
attempt) would have led me to call off the thing for
good in time anyway, even had I not resolved on this
day to kill myself. But by 1937 I could contemplate with
equanimity the prospect of terminating our affair, for
it left, from my point of view nothing to be desired.
Jane Mack is the finest woman I've ever slept with.
Literally, I repeat, she left nothing to be desired; since
that last morning, the morning of the day at hand, when
she last left my rented bed, I have desired nothing from
women. She satisfied me.

Now, if you'll excuse me, I shall sleep.

XVIII. A matter of life or death

Although it was my custom to nap for at least an hour every day, on the day I intended to be my last I was waked almost as soon as my eyes were closed, by an urgent knock on my door.

"Come on in," I called, and pulled a bathrobe on over my underwear.

There was no response for several moments, and I had begun to decide that my unknown caller had gone away, when I heard two or three footsteps in the hall and then another knock.

"Yes, come on in," I repeated, still tying my robe.

Another pause. I started toward the door, but it opened just before I reached it, and Mr. Haecker, taut as a piano wire, stepped stiffly inside.

"Sit down, Mr. Haecker!" I exclaimed, for he looked ready to faint. His smile was thin and broken like the smiles of army recruits hearing heavy artillery for the first time, and his face was white. I took his arm firmly and led him to the chair. "Let me get you a drop of rye, Mr. Haecker." My first thought was that the old fellow was ill and had come to me for help.

"No thank you, Todd," he managed to say. His voice I can describe only as a prim croak, if that makes sense at all. He perched on the edge of the chair as daintily as a canary on its swing, and his hands clutched his knees tightly for support.

"Is anything wrong, sir?" I asked. He looked a bit better now, but still none too stable.

"No," he said shortly, closing his eyes and shaking his head slightly. "No. I just—came in to talk to you, Todd." He looked directly at me then for the first time, and gave me a quick, sick smile. I can recall smiling at my father in just that way once at some amusement park—Tolchester, perhaps—when he put me on a carousel much too large, loud, and rapid for my tastes, and expected me to enjoy it as everyone else did. "Are you busy?"

"Busy loafing," I said, and sat on the edge of the bed. "What's on your mind, sir?" I offered him a cigarette, which he refused with a quick shake of his head, and then I lit one myself for a change.

"I daresay you'll think me very foolish, son," he began, in a tone that I at once recognized as false— an unnaturally deep, head-of-the-clan tone. "A garrulous old man, like many another."

"Not unless what you say is foolish," I said flatly, for his pose annoyed me.

Mr. Haecker blushed—a surprising thing in a man seventy-nine years old. "It may well be," he laughed nervously.

"You don't talk nonsense as a rule," I smiled.

Mr. Haecker sighed, but his sigh was not spontaneous as his blush had been. And he glanced at me sharply.

"It's a not uncommon thing for quite old men—men my age—to lose their perspective," he observed judiciously. "I'm quite aware of that fact, and I often wonder whether we are always being fair when we call it simply senility."

He paused, but I said nothing: I was waiting for him to finish tuning his piano.

"What I mean is, there are conditions of most people's old age, other than mental failure, that could lead to the same crankiness, if you like. Disease, for example, or poverty, or isolation. Don't you think?"

"It certainly sounds reasonable to me," I agreed mildly.

Mr. Haecker looked relieved. "Now, then," he said, "the thing I actually came down here for was this—" He clenched his lean fists on his knees and stared at them. "You must tell me quite frankly—I think you'll be honest with me—did you think the things I told Captain Osborn this morning were entirely silly? You said you didn't agree with me, I remember."

To myself I said "Ah," and regarded my visitor's face more carefully, for the first note on the piano had been sounded. To him I said, "This morning? Oh, you mean the 'growing old' business."

I'd hoped his question was merely rhetorical, an attempt to get himself going; but apparently he expected an answer, for he remained silent, a distracted look on his really quite distinguished face.

"Well, yes and no," I answered. "If the idea you're referring to is the one I'm thinking of, that old age is the glorious finale of life—the last of life for which the first was made, and all that—then I'd say yes, it's possible that Cicero wasn't just whistling in the graveyard. After all, with no church to stop him, a good Roman fell on his sword when things got too miserable; Cicero, remember, was famous and pretty well off in his old age, and probably got a toot out of being a public figure."

"I believe he deeply loved life," Mr. Haecker remarked in another false tone, a ministerial one delivered with chin thrust out and head nodding gravely. "Every stage of it for its own peculiar virtues."

"And I think the notion probably works for a good number of people who are either devoutly religious and actually believe in a blessed hereafter, or who are honestly content with their careers, or who are temperamentally stoical."

"I quite agree," Mr. Haecker said. "But you said *yes* and *no*."

"That's right. I think it's silly to talk about what a man's attitude *should* be, toward a thing like old age and death. Even if you start with *If he wants to die content,* you'd find that different people are content with different things. Cap'n Osborn, for example, will die content, I think; he'll be having the time of his life cussing around his deathbed, and whipping his legs for turning cold."

Mr. Haecker clucked his tongue. "And what about me? I quite respect your opinion, Todd, as you should know. I've often wished I were your age"—he smiled ruefully—"or you were mine, so we could discuss things more freely. Intellectual discussion, after all, is the real joy of the winter of life, when other pleasures have flown, as it were."

I spoke as gently as I could without defeating my purpose. "If I were used to feeling pity for people," I said, "I think I'd feel sorrier for you than for anyone in this hotel, sir."

Mr. Haecker's eyes grew panicky—their first really honest expression. "Indeed?" he snickered sharply.

"Don't assault me when I say this," I smiled. "I'm not by any means the truth-at-any-price sort, I swear. But since you asked, I'll admit I consider your position the least enviable of anyone's in the Explorers' Club. Miss Holiday Hopkinson has been ready to die for so long, with her daily vitamins and crossed hands, that when death actually gets to her it'll be an anticlimax. That could lead to hysteria, like the kid who studies diving from books all winter and then gets out on the high board and forgets everything he learned, but probably it won't. She'll die in her sleep, I'll bet. And Cap'n Osborn has known how he honestly feels about it too, for a long time, whenever he bothers to think about it, which is damned seldom. He'll just put up a whale of a holler and tussle when the time comes. But the trouble with you, sir, if I may say so, is that you've tried to pretend you're enjoying yourself and looking forward to death as a grand finale, when actually you're not."

"Oh, that's not so!" Mr. Haecker protested.

"There's nothing wrong with fooling yourself," I said soothingly. "Lots of times it's that or the insane asylum. But it just doesn't work if it doesn't work. The whole trouble is that you're *not* fooling yourself, as maybe Cap'n Osborn is; you're just *trying* to fool your-self, and you know very well it's all an act. What the hell's glorious about your old age? What's wrong with facing the fact that things are pretty bleak, and com-plaining like hell about it?"

When Mr. Haecker slipped anger onto his face then, I began to weary of the colloquy and wish I were alone. Had he been sincerely angry I'd not have objected, but his anger was another of his wardrobe masks.

"You're being quite frank, young man!" he cried.

"Forget I said anything, then." I sighed, and stretched out on the bed in my robe and slippers. "All's for the best in the best of all possible worlds."

"I'm not angry at your impertinence," he went on, "but I must say I'm disappointed in your values. They're pretty commonplace, for you."

I said nothing, and wished I'd said nothing from the beginning. After all, he was seventy-nine; even with his excellent health, he couldn't be expected to live much more than ten short years, and it was no special con-cern of mine whether he enjoyed them or not.

"Of course my career in the public schools wasn't spectacular, if you judge it purely by promotions and the like," he pouted. "And I shan't deny that I'd be happier if my wife were alive, or if we'd had children—" He was watching himself being strong. He even paused before continuing in a firm voice, "—but she's not, and we didn't. Do you want me to go around in mourning, begging for pity? My friend Cicero has something to say about that, too: *'In times like these, theirs is far from being the worst fate to whom it has been given to ex-change life for a painless death.'* And this: *'If she had not died now, she would yet have had to die a few years hence, for she was mortal born.'* What has happened has happened."

Was there any reason to bother pointing out to him how directly his first quotation contradicted his whole position? I flipped my cigarette out the open window.

"Of all my acquaintances," Mr. Haecker went on determinedly, "I'd have expected you to be the first to recognize the happiness a mature man can get from a solitary old age, if he doesn't act childish about it. After all the hustle and bustle, one is finally able to live in the company of his thoughts, and contemplate the beauty of God's works. Isn't that what all the philosophers wanted? I can understand Captain Osborn not realizing it; good a chap as he is, the poor fellow hasn't had the opportunity to educate himself. But *you* certainly must be aware that the life of solitary contemplation is the best—after all, you're alone, too."

"I do precious little contemplating," I said. "And if I wanted to, I could chuck the whole thing tomorrow and get married. The point is, I'm here by choice. Also, I can't quote you the lines," I added, "but your pal Cicero wasn't so enthusiastic about the contemplative life. He said somewhere that if a man could ascend into heaven all by himself and see the workings of the universe and so forth, the sight wouldn't give him much pleasure; but it would be the finest thing in the world if he had somebody to describe it to. I'm not saying I believe any of this nonsense—I think all these generalizations are asinine. But you're changing texts every few minutes."

Another mask: Mr. Haecker got up from the chair and assumed an injured tone. "I see I'm keeping you from your nap," he said. "It took some courage for one my age to discuss these things with a young man. I thought you'd be interested in them, though."

"You're begging the question with that attitude," I said, sitting up. "If there *was* any question. You asked me how I felt about it."

"Well how *do* you feel?" he cried vehemently. "What do you want a man to do who doesn't have anything to live for? It's either pretend to be content, like a man, or go around wailing and weeping like a child."

"I don't care what anyone does," I said. "It makes no difference to me, on principle, whether you're happy or not. I'm no humanitarian. I only said I pitied you; I just wouldn't want to be in your shoes. But I don't agree that the two alternatives you just mentioned are the only ones."

"What else is there?" Mr. Haecker cried. He was getting quite worked up again, and his eyes, honest now, showed despair through any mask he donned. "Maybe you recommend suicide?" He laughed explosively. "Is that the other alternative?"

"It was for Cicero's crowd," I said. "Let me tell you something. Unless a man subscribes to some religion that doesn't allow it, then the question of whether or not to commit suicide is the very first question he has to answer before he can work things out for himself. This applies only to people who want to live rationally, of course—who want to work out an ethics for themselves. Most people never realize that there is such a problem in the first place, and I don't see any particular reason why they should have it pointed out to them. I'm telling you only because you asked me."

"Well, I'm not a religious man," Mr. Haecker declared, "but I think that's reason enough not to kill myself. If death is the absolute end, then you're better off alive under any circumstances."

"That doesn't follow. If death is the end, then it's neutral. Which is better, to be unhappy or to be neutral? It would be different if you could look forward to something better in the near future. I wouldn't commit suicide, for instance, just because the Yankees lost a ball game."

Mr. Haecker stood rigid and pale, refusing to be entertained by my remark.

"You advise me to kill myself," he said stiffly.

"Not at all. I didn't say everybody *should* work out a rationale. But if you do, then you must answer the suicide question for yourself before you start, obviously. If you want to make sense, then I've learned that you should never use the word *should* or *ought* until after you've used the word *if*."

"Then if I want to live rationally, I should kill myself?" he asked, his voice a thin laugh.

"You should only think about the question," I repeated. "Hamlet's question, whether 'tis better in the mind to suffer . . ."

"Of course, Hamlet was either insane or pretending to be," Mr. Haecker remembered triumphantly.

"You're evading the question," I said.

"How about you?" he snickered. "Have you thought about it? I see you're still alive. Why is that?"

I smiled. "I promise I'll think about it after supper tonight, and let you know tomorrow what I decide. You do the same, and we'll compare notes and chip in for either a box of cigars or a pistol, as the case may be. Okay? But don't forget," I added seriously, "to consider every objection to suicide that you can think of. If you decide *not* to kill yourself, you can always change your mind later, but the other decision is hard to correct."

Again Mr. Haecker refused to be entertained. "It's a question of values," he observed, "and life itself has a value, under any circumstances. There is an absolute value to human life that won't be denied."

"I deny it," I said. "There's no reason why you shouldn't believe that, but you can't prove it. If you want to accept it on faith, okay, but then there's no argument."

Mr. Haecker smiled grimly and went to the door. His eyes were still honest; he could do nothing with the fear in them, although he covered the rest of his features with a visionary falseface when he turned at the door and said, "Life, the simple fact of life, is good, young man. Life has an intrinsic value."

I was licking a cigar.

"Nothing has any intrinsic value," I remarked, as coolly as though I'd known it for years, when in fact that fundamental notion had just occurred to me, between licks. Mr. Haecker closed the door, and I wondered why he'd come to see me; what exactly he'd had on his mind. If it had been some sort of confession, my reaction had driven him behind his masks. No matter: if now in protest against my ideas he actually began to believe his own, that was no concern of mine.

XIX. A premise to swallow

Quantitative changes suddenly become qualitative changes. From all of Marxism, which I once thought attractive enough, I find only this dictum remaining in the realm of my opinions. Water grows colder and colder and colder, and suddenly it's ice. The day grows darker and darker, and suddenly it's night. Man ages and ages, and suddenly he's dead. Quantitative changes suddenly become qualitative changes; differences in degree lead to differences in kind.

When Mr. Haecker had gone (Where? Up to his room, for another day of solitary confinement in the contemplative life), I donned my trousers, shirt, coat, and straw, and walked back through the great dry heat to the office. The sky was brilliant blue, the water likewise—a darker shade. Everything was still: only a few cars moved along High Street; no boats were visible on the river; the flag at Long Wharf hung limply against its staff. Everything was baking in the enormous heat, which nevertheless drew not a bead of perspiration from my skin.

What was on my mind, as I walked, was this grand proposition that had occurred to me while I was licking my cigar: that nothing, absolutely nothing, has any intrinsic value. Now that the idea was articulated in my head, it seemed to me ridiculous that I hadn't seen it years ago. It seemed to me that all my life I'd been deciding that specific things had no intrinsic value—that things like money, honesty, strength, love, information, wisdom, even life, are not valuable in themselves, but only with reference to certain ends—and yet I'd never considered generalizing from those specific instances, had never looked beyond whatever single tree happened to be before my eyes. But again: one instance was added to another, and another to that, and suddenly the total realization was effected—*nothing* is intrinsically valuable; the value of everything is attributed to it, assigned to it, from outside the thing itself, by people.

In my tranquil way, I must confess to feeling some real excitement at the idea. Need I repeat that I am not a thinker? That technical philosophy is not my cup of tea? Doubtless (as I later learned) this idea was not original with me, but it was completely new to me, and I delighted in it like a child turned loose for the first time in the endless out-of-doors, full of scornful pity for those still inside. *Nothing is valuable in itself.* Not even truth; even this truth. I am not a philosopher, except after the fact; but I am a mean rationalizer, and once the world has impinged forcefully upon my consciousness, has, as it were, grabbed me by the throat and forced me into a new position, once there has been in my world a sufficient accumulation of quantitative change to effect in my attitudes toward it a qualitative change, then I can philosophize (or rationalize) like two Kants, like seven Philadelphia lawyers. In short, beginning with my new conclusions, I can work out magnificent premises.

On this morning, for example, I had opened my eyes with the knowledge that this day would be my last; that I would this day destroy myself (a conclusion in itself demonstrating Marx's dictum); here the day was but half spent, and already premises were springing to my mind, to justify on philosophical grounds what had been a purely personal decision. The argument was staggering. Enough now to establish this first premise: nothing is intrinsically valuable; the values that things are said to have—good or bad or whatever—are attributed to them by people.

If you are no philosopher either, reader, then take a

good comfortable time to swallow that proposition—I daresay it will stick in not a few throats. Consider it, and its ramifications. If you can stomach it, why then you've done quite enough for one chapter, and so have I.

XX. Calliope music

As you doubtless decided long ago yourself, not only am I
not a philosopher; I'm not a prose stylist, either. At best,
my prose is a plodding, graceless thing: I've no com-
prehension of stylistic tricks, nor can I stick to the
straight highway of the plot, when there's half a
world on either side. Just now, for example, it's time
for me to tell you about my brief afternoon's activities in
my office—which to many people will seem altogether
irrelevant to the story in the first place, though I can't be
expected to agree—and I find myself faced with the necessity of introducing this chapter twice. How is it to be
done? My first thought is to deliver the two introductions simultaneously, in double columns,

one to be read with the left
eye, and one with the right,
so; but I daresay the more
crochety among you would
be annoyed by such an un-
orthodox expedient.

one to be read with the left
eye, and one with the right,
so; but I daresay the more
crochety among you would
be annoyed by such an un-
orthodox expedient.

My second thought is to deliver them consecutively, or
else by recourse to interlineation; but it occurs to me that
no matter how the thing is done, I shan't escape the
reckless charge of disorganization from those who would
prefer our world to be a rational one, in which single
chapters have single introductions and all chapters are
relevant. And it is, without question, those people, among
others, whom I'm trying to please as much as is
convenient.

For one thing, I have more to say about Prince Hamlet. You'll recall that chapter before last I declared to Mr. Haecker that anyone who wishes to order his life in terms of a rationale—anyone, then, who wishes to live reasonably—must first of all answer for himself Hamlet's question, the question of suicide. I would add further that if he wants my respect, his choice to live must be based on firmer ground than Hamlet's—that "conscience does make cowards of us all": that to choose suicide is to choose unknown evils for known ones. This position (quite like Montaigne's argument against revolution and reform) is, as the Prince admits, simply cowardly, not reasonable. On the other hand, if one chooses to die, for mercy's sake let this choice be more reasonably founded than Hamlet's, too—merely escaping the "slings and arrows of outrageous fortune" is as cowardly as is fearing dreams beyond the grave. Don't think I'm an indiscriminating promoter of suicides; such an oversimplification makes objections too easy. I merely hold that those who would live reasonably should have reasons for remaining alive or else kill themselves. This, I think, is reasonable enough?

But I cannot accept bad luck as sufficient reason for anyone's suicide, including my father's. Indeed, it was the absence, in my opinion, of any valid reason for his hanging himself that turned me quite suddenly into a cynic after his death, though I had, of course, the seeds of cynicism in me all along. It was a sudden qualitative change, the impingement of the world onto my philosophy. I'll say more presently about my reaction to Dad's death, and about the charming little adventure that followed it, but I want first to review very briefly the case on which I spent my afternoon hour's work—what I meant to be my final hour's work as a lawyer. It will serve as an introduction to Col. Henry Morton, who plays a role in the little adventure, and at the same time keep you from assuming that I simply loafed all afternoon.

When I re-entered my office (this is the second introduction), the clock in the tower of the Municipal

Building was just striking two, and as if by a prearranged
signal, at the same moment the raucous voice of a steam
calliope came whistling in off the river: *Adam's Original
& Unparalleled Floating Opera,* one could guess, had
just passed Hambrooks Bar Light and was heading up the
channel to the bell buoy and thence to Long Wharf. For
the thousandth time I blushed at the clumsy ironies of
coincidence, for it happened that just as I drew from my
files the nearly completed brief of a litigation involving
a slight injury to the left foot of perhaps the richest man
in Cambridge—who stood to be some fifteen thousand
dollars richer if my client lost the case—the calliope
broke into "Oh, Dem Golden Slippers," and a few minutes later, when I was reflecting on the difficulties my
client would have in scraping together that sum, the
melody changed to "What You Gon' Do When De
Rent Comes 'Round?"

In fact, even to think of the name *Adam's Original &
Unparalleled Floating Opera*—its completely unsubtle
significance—when I had before me the extraordinary
case of *Morton* v. *Butler,* was the greatest of accidental
ironies: never did there exist such an unparalleled floating opera as the law in its less efficient moments, and
seldom had the law such inefficient moments as those during which it involved itself—nay, diffused, dissipated,
lost itself—in *Morton* v. *Butler.* Hamlet listed "the
law's delay" as one of the things that could drive a man
to suicide. That I don't accept the Prince's list, you've
already observed; that neither Morton nor Butler accepted this particular annoyance as suicidal is evidenced
by their both still walking the earth. Let me review the
case very briefly. If you are incapable of discerning in it
any greater relevance, simply regard it as a curious
bump on the knotty log of my story:

Morton v. *Butler,* by June of 1937, was already a
litigation almost six years old, and at the time of this
story the litigants hadn't yet even begun to try the case
on its merits, but were still enmeshed, via their attorneys, in procedural disputes. Col. Henry Morton, the
packer of Morton's Marvelous Tomatoes, along with his

wife, was the plaintiff, and was represented by Charley
Parks, my neighbor and poker partner. I represented the
defendant, Mr. William T. Butler, a wealthy invest-
ment broker who happened to run the New-Deal wing
of the local Democratic machine, the other, conservative,
wing of which was run by Col. Morton.

What happened was quite simple. On October 31, 1931,
Mr. Butler was driving his Cadillac sedan down Court
Lane, just outside my office, and Col. Morton's only son,
Allan (for whom the Colonel had a great, if overprotec-
tive, affection), was driving *his* Cadillac sedan down Gay
Street, which meets Court Lane at the creek. Col. and
Mrs. Morton were passengers in their son's car. The two
cars met at the bottom of the hill. Butler had to make a
right turn up Gay Street, and young Morton a left
turn up Court Lane. Both drivers signaled their turns,
and each saw the other's signal. Then (from what I
gather privately) both drivers executed poor turns simultaneously, Butler turning too wide and Allan Morton too
short. The automobiles collided, and both were damaged
slightly. Also, Mrs. Morton broke her spectacles and
scratched her face on the lenses, and the Colonel
wrenched the tendons of his left foot rather severely. The
drivers got out; Butler and the limping Colonel shook
hands, as rival candidates for the same office might.

"Well, Bill!" the Colonel bellowed heartily. "Can't
you drive that machine?"

"Not on the same street with that boy of yours!" Butler guffawed back. The two men chortled and chuckled,
slapped each other on the shoulders, and then parted,
having tacitly agreed that the injuries didn't seem
serious, and that among responsible gentlemen such
private affairs didn't go to court. Next day, Butler sent
Mrs. Morton a fifteen-dollar spray of mixed flowers, and
the Colonel sent Butler a quart of Haig & Haig.

Had it not been for Franklin Roosevelt, the affair might
have ended there. But Roosevelt was elected in 1932,
initiated the New Deal just afterwards, and in the summer of 1933 actually sailed up the Choptank to Cambridge, to dedicate the just-completed Harrington Bridge

across that river. Both factions of the party were
feverishly enthusiastic: when it was announced that the
President would not come ashore, but would broadcast
his dedication from the presidential yacht *Potomac*, an-
chored out by the bell buoy, Col. Morton took it upon
himself to have razed the old freight house that stood on
Long Wharf, declaring it to be a natural place of conceal-
ment for assassins with high-powered rifles. The city
council nodded, and the old structure came down. The
Colonel then declared that no private vessels should be
permitted to leave the creek or the yacht basin while
the *Potomac* was at anchor—the scene otherwise would
be disrespectfully cluttered. The mayor made such a
resolution, and the yacht club followed suit. Surely a
magnanimous solicitude for an anti-New-Dealer! But of
the citizens of Cambridge, thousands of whom respectfully lined the bulkheads to see the *Potomac* and listen
to the President's amplified voice, only one was invited
aboard: "Old Bill" Butler, of the Butler Democrats.

One month later, for no stated reason, Mr. Butler
dropped into my office and described to me his automobile accident of nearly two years before.

"I'll want you to handle it if anything comes up,
honey," he chuckled (it was his habit always to speak
with a chuckle, whether the thing he said was funny
or not).

And not long after that (it was, in fact, on October
13, 1933, just two weeks before the statute of limitations
would have run out), Charley Parks called me to say
that he was filing suit against Butler for Col. and Mrs.
Morton, who claimed personal injuries, and for Allan
Morton, who claimed damages of $75.00 for repairs to
and $600 for alleged depreciation in the value of his
Cadillac. The injury claims of the Colonel and his wife
totaled nearly $15,000: their hospital and medical ex-
penses amounted to a total of $854.26, and in addition
they claimed $14,000 for pain and suffering (in the case
of the Colonel) and mental anguish (resulting from
Evelyn Morton's permanent, if faint, disfigurement and
the Colonel's perpetual limp). I guessed at once that

even had Mr. Roosevelt remained in Washington, Butler's retaining me as his counsel would have been sufficient reason for the Colonel to decide, belatedly, to press the case, for as you shall see directly, between the Mortons and myself there was small love lost. I worked out my strategy at once.

Now, although Charley and I have on occasion enjoyed long sessions of legal hair-splitting over beer and seven-card stud, at no time did we ever say in so many words that we were making game out of *Morton* v. *Butler*. Nevertheless, here is what happened in the remaining two months of 1933: On November 20, the three plaintiffs filed their official complaint, charging that the collision had been due to Butler's negligence in that he took the corner at an excessive rate of speed; that he failed to have his car under proper and adequate control; and that he was guilty of other acts of commission and omission. On December 15, I filed for Butler a petition for severance of Allan Morton's action from that of the other plaintiffs. On December 29, the Circuit Court dismissed the petition. I went to Butler's New Year's Eve party and drank sloe gin.

1934: On January 9, I filed a petition to set aside the court order of December 29, which had dismissed my original petition. On April 26 the court set aside that order and granted the severance we wanted. Then, on May 4, I obtained a writ to join Allan Morton as an additional defendant, along with Butler, in the severed suit of Col. and Mrs. Morton, and filed a complaint against him—substantially identical to his complaint against Butler. On June 18, Charley Parks answered for Allan, pleading in new matter the statute of limitations, which of course had run out nearly eight months ago. On August 8, Butler replied to the new matter. On October 26, Charley filed a motion, in Allan's name, for a judgment on the proceedings relative to Butler's complaint. On December 29, exactly a year since the dismissal of my original petition for severance, the court dismissed my complaint against young Morton, and on New Year's Eve, far from committing suicide (as Hamlet would have done by this time), I got drunk at Butler's party, on vodka sours.

1935: On January 10 (while Harrison Mack, Sr., by the way, was dying in his bed in Ruxton), I petitioned for permission to file an amended complaint for Butler. On January 18, the court granted its permission, and I filed an amended complaint against Allan Morton, averring that his parents, in their complaint against Butler, had charged that their $15,000 injuries were due solely to Butler's negligence; that Butler was prepared to serve a copy of that very complaint against their son; that Butler admitted neither in whole nor in part their charges; that Allan had been negligent in the operation of *his* Cadillac; that only the actual trial would determine whether Allan's own negligence had been the sole or a major contributing cause of the accident, but that it was one or the other; that Butler desired to be able to protect his right of contribution in the event the court found him to have been jointly or concurrently negligent with Allan; and that therefore Allan was jointly liable with Butler upon the causes of action declared upon by Col. and Mrs. Morton. On February 6, Allan—or rather, Charley—filed his answer along with new matter again pleading the statute of limitations. On April 8, the court, while not ruling on the accuracy of Butler's charges, dismissed my amended complaint on five grounds, all as sensible and exceptionable as are the grounds for any such ruling. Charley and I played poker a few times in March and April, and then on May 1 a stipulation of counsel was filed, agreeing to my filing a second amended complaint for Butler against Allan, and I filed the new complaint, a document differing from its predecessors only in its rhetoric. On May 21, Charley filed Allan's answer, with new matter as before. On October 21, the court dismissed the second amended complaint on the same grounds as before, and on November 12 entered orders in each of the two cases separately to the same effect. By this time I was well enmeshed in the Mack will case, but nevertheless, as Charley grinned and Butler chuckled, I took the Circuit Court's

order to the Court of Appeals on November 13. That
New Year's Eve I drank Sherbrook rye, first with the
Macks in their club cellar, then with Butler in his club
cellar, and finally with Jane in my room, but did not
get drunk.

1936: The Mack will case was now involved in its
own glorious intricacies, but I found time on March 17
to argue in the Maryland Court of Appeals for reversal
of the Circuit Court's order. The question, for both
courts, was whether, since the statute of limitations pre-
vented our joining young Morton as an additional defendant on grounds of sole liability, we had averred in
our amended complaint facts sufficient to warrant a finding of joint or concurrent liability, and the Court of Appeals agreed (on December 4) that we did not. But
they quite reasonably allowed me to appeal to the Maryland Supreme Court their affirmation of the Circuit
Court's order, so that the procedural question might be
finally determined. That New Year's Eve, as I recall, I
drank alone in my room.

1937: Now I had never agreed with the two lower
courts that what they thought was the question was
really the question. And so, on April 26, I argued to the
Supreme Court that the *real* issue was whether a defendant
in a tort action who, like Butler, was barred by the
statute of limitations from joining an additional defendant (to whom he was also liable, you see) on the
grounds of sole liability, might yet preserve his right
of contribution by pleading joint or several liability
without alleging facts admitting his own liability to the
plaintiff (Col. and Mrs. Morton). My position was that
if Butler, in order to establish Allan's joint liability,
were obliged, in addition to averring facts showing Allan's
negligence, to admit his *own* negligence, it amounted to
denying Butler's right to bring Allan on the record at all,
since any such admissions could be placed in evidence
and exploited by Col. Morton when the case came to trial.
Now, since in our amended complaint we alleged facts
establishing Allan's negligence, all we were pleading,

actually, was that if, when the thing ever came to trial, the jury should find Butler to be negligent as the plaintiffs charged, then Allan's negligence, as described in our complaint, was also a contributing cause of the collision. The Supreme Bench, reasonable fellows all, saw no justification for not allowing such a plea, especially in the case of an automobile collision, where it is always possible that both drivers were at fault. On May 24, they rendered their opinion, which reversed the order of the Court of Appeals affirming the order of the Circuit Court dismissing our second amended complaint against the additional defendant, and remanded the record to the Circuit Court with a procedendo.

There was no appealing this judgment. Charley set me up to a drink, and the suit was ready to be tried, Col. Morton in effect suing his only-begotten son. Bill Butler chuckled happily, for with Roosevelt so firmly entrenched in the White House and in public popularity as he was in 1937, the Morton wing of the local Democratic party could ill afford any bad publicity.

I wish, reader, that I could at this point announce some stratagem, some *colpo mortale*, some trump that I'd saved to play on this last day of my career, when already I'd been able to settle, as far as I was concerned, the Mack will case in favor of Harrison. But the truth is that my interest in *Morton* v. *Butler* ended with the Supreme Court's ruling, for that terminated the procedural dispute. I didn't mind missing the actual trial, which would be dull enough whoever won. I had got out the record of the case on this last afternoon only because Bill Butler, according to a note Mrs. Lake had left on my desk, was coming to see me at two-fifteen.

At two-thirty he strode in, chuckling, a bald, beefy fellow with good eyes and bad teeth, carrying a shoe box.

"What do I owe you, Todd old cod?" he sang out. "What's my bill, hon?"

"You owe me your skin," I smiled. "Charley would have hanged you. You better wait till after the trial to pay me the rest of your bill, though."

"Ain't going to be any trial," Butler chuckled.

"Does the Colonel know that?"

"Oh hell yes indeed," Butler chuckled. "He's the one thought of calling it off, honey. Called me yesterday, day before, gives me the old family squabble routine, old party harmony song-and-dance. Haw! Told me if I'd let some of his boys run on my ticket next year in the primary, he'd call off the suit."

"You didn't have to take any conditions."

Butler chuckled grandly. "I told him he could have sheriff and one county commissioner if he'd call his damn state cop off my ass. You know that cop Yarberry, that the Colonel got him his job? Every time I go over the new bridge that lousy Yarberry is after me—Colonel's got him looking for me. I could tell you plenty on Yarberry and the Colonel, hon! Old Colonel don't much care about one lousy county commissioner, but he sure did want sheriff, so he promises to curb his cop and drop the suit. I already sent Evelyn another bunch of flowers."

"Hell, you didn't have to give him a thing, Bill," I said again. "He'd never sue his boy."

"Haw!" Butler chuckled. "Tell you the facts, Todd old clod, I didn't have a sonofabitch in the stable to put up for them jobs, that I would walk on the same side of the street with, so old Colonel would of got them anyhow. Oh hell yes indeed! That's *principles*, buddy boy! Give old Roosevelt another go-round in '40, honey, and I'll elect you governor. How 'bout that?"

"No trial, then?" I grinned.

"No trial," Butler chuckled. "Fetch in old Charleyhorse from next door, hon, and we'll try the Colonel's whiskey."

He opened the shoe box and took out a fifth of Park & Tilford.

"Call up old Charleyhorse Parks, Julia," he chuckled to Mrs. Lake. "Come on, there, Harry Bishop; come on, here, Jimmy boy. We're drinking up the Colonel's whiskey!"

The calliope down at the wharf broke into "Out of the Wilderness." I blushed, replaced the bulky brief of *Morton* v. *Butler* in the file, and accepted a good pull of Park & Tilford.

XXI. Coals to Newcastle

When, as I said earlier, I came home from the office on the afternoon of February 2, 1930, and after searching the house for my father, finally found him dead in the cellar, one end of his belt spiked to a floor joist and the other fastened around his neck, there was not a smudge of dirt anywhere on him, though the cellar was quite dusty. His clothes were perfectly creased and free of wrinkles, and although his face was black and his eyes were popped, his hair was neatly and correctly combed. Except that the chair upon which Dad had stood was kicked over, everything in the cellar was in order.

The same could not be said of his estate. Indeed, as soon became apparent, there was no estate. It is such a commonplace story that I hesitate to tell it—and yet nothing was ever less true or pitiful for its being commonplace. Dad had had a sizable savings account; between the years 1925 and 1927 he increased it by investing in stocks. He didn't expect the boom to last, and so decided to make one big splash and quit. To make the splash he mortgaged all his property—a summer cottage and lot at Fenwick Island, Delaware, and one or two timber lots down the county—for as much as he could, and sank the whole wad on the market. In early 1929, when the whole speculative structure began to quiver, and every public official in the country began to assure us that the economy was fundamentally sound, Dad mortgaged the house and lot, borrowed on his life insurance, and contracted private notes from what few of his many friends were willing and able to lend him money. All this, too, went on the market. No, not quite all: five thousand dollars he persuaded Harry Bishop to put in his safe-deposit box, in my name—suspecting, perhaps, that otherwise he'd not be able to resist plunging that, too.

Then the market collapsed. People were anxious enough to hire lawyers, all right, to collect debts, but they had no money to pay the lawyers with, and most debts had suddenly become uncollectable. Dad had payments falling due on at least four mortgages and countless loans, and no money to meet them with. Foreclosures threatened from all sides, lawsuits from every quarter. He would, it appeared, lose his summer cottage, his timber lots, the family home, the car, and virtually everything else he owned. His debts amounted to perhaps $35,000. He would have to sleep in the office, walk to court, wear his suits threadbare. Very possibly he would never reach again his former security, never regain all his former respect. It was a hard pill to swallow. Instead of swallowing it anyway, or at least trying to, he hanged himself.

Does one's father hang himself for a simple, stupid lack of money? And is one expected to set up again the chair one's father has kicked over in his strangling frenzies? Can one actually, with a kitchen knife, saw through the choking belt? Carry one's father's body up to the bed whereon one was conceived, and laying him on it, dig one's fingers into the black and ruptured flesh to release the dead neck from its leather collar? Reader, I still recall with shudders a summer day when I was five years old. My father (dressed, of course, in good clothes) for some reason or other was killing chickens in the back yard. He caught one, and holding it by the feet, laid it on the chopping block, a sawn stump; unruffled by the flailing wings, he raised the old axe, which he held choked close to the head, and with a soft stroke beheaded the hen. The head still lay on the stump, the little red eyes staring, the beak opening and shutting in soundless squawks. The body, once my father released it, flailed

madly about the yard for a full thirty seconds and then
died. I watched everything with great, uneasy absorption.

Dad picked up the chicken by its feet again and extended it toward me.

"Will you take this in to Bessie, please?"

I was shocked, and held out my hand dumbly. Dad
put the feet in my hand—cold, hard, dirty, stringy,
scaly, dead yellow feet. I was ill then, reader, and if I
think of those feet a minute longer I shall be ill as
heartily now. But of this matter one *can* think, if queas-
ily. Is one, then, expected to close the popping eyes of
his father's corpse? Eyes the very veins of which are
burst? Surely the dirt of the planet would scream the
overwhelming reason for it, the justification that would
brook no questioning. I waited.

Of course there were debts. The Fenwick place; take
it. The timber lots? To be sure. The house? The car?
The insurance? Take them, take them. One doesn't
concern oneself with trifles at one's father's grave. One is
concerned only with reasons. I waited.

Back at the office, Harry Bishop gave me the envelope
from Dad. I took it eagerly, hoping it would contain the
answer, but instead it merely had five thousand dollars
in it. There was a note, too, which I must have suppressed
—it's honestly, completely gone from my mind—because it said all the things I certainly didn't want to
hear, in just the wrong language. Is five thousand dollars
enough to pay for digging my fingers under that belt?
It's not enough payment even for thinking about it! His
debt to me was the last, but hardly the least debt my
father had escaped.

If I was demoralized by Dad's death, I was paralyzed
by the five thousand dollars and the note. Certainly I
sat in the office for thirty minutes with my jaw actually
slack, staring as incredulously at the bills as if I'd
opened that precious last envelope and discovered inside
a handful of dung, the color of a hanged man's cheeks.
Five thousand dollars! After some time I replaced the
crisp new thousand-dollar bills in their envelope, which

was, after all, unstamped and unaddressed, and thought of all the people I knew.

The question became very simple: Who was the richest man in Cambridge? Col. Henry Morton. I wrote on the envelope *Col. Henry Morton, c/o Morton's Marvelous Tomatoes, Inc., Cambridge, Maryland,* put a three-cent stamp in place, and snuffling like a hobbled race horse, dropped the envelope into a mailbox on my way to lunch. Next day I moved into the Dorset Hotel.

This was, I believe, in early March, 1930. Very soon afterwards I received a call from the Colonel, whom I knew only slightly.

"Hello? Hello?" he shouted, as though it were not his custom to speak on telephones. "Is this Todd Andrews?"

"Yes, sir."

"Hello? Andrews? Andrews, what's this money I got from you in the mail?"

"It's a gift from me to you," I said.

"Andrews? You there, Andrews? What's going on, eh?"

"It's a gift," I repeated; "a gift."

"Huh? What? *Hello?* Andrews! Gift! Hello?"

"It's a gift," I repeated.

The day after that, the Colonel came in personally to see me, striding unappointed into my office.

"Andrews? You Andrews? See here, young man, I don't know what you've got up your sleeve—"

"It was a gift," I explained; "that's all."

"A gift? You're crazy, son! Here, take it back, and no more foolishness!"

He did not wave anything at me—no bills under my nose.

"Of course not," I said. "It was just a gift."

"Gift? Well! Gift? What's up your sleeve, young man? What do you think I'm supposed to do?"

"Not a blessed thing, sir," I repeated. "It was a gift."

"I won't stand for tricks," the Colonel warned. "Here, take it back. No more!"

Again, he extended nothing toward me.

"I've never been obligated to any man," the Colonel said then, more calmly. "I shan't begin now."

"No obligation, sir," I insisted.

"Hmph! Whatever's on your mind, you might as well forget it. I can't be bought! If anybody was to ask me the secret of my success, I'd tell them I was never obligated to any man."

"I'd never try to obligate you, sir. It was just a gift."

"I'll teach you a lesson, son." The Colonel smiled, as though the idea had just dawned on him. "I'm going to keep half your money, and you shan't get a thing out of me in return."

"You must keep it all," I said. "I don't take back gifts."

"Hmph! You've got a lot to learn, boy. A lot to learn! Never obligate yourself to anybody."

"I shan't, sir."

"Hard times, Andrews!" the Colonel sputtered. "Bad times! Plant's laying off! A man doesn't throw his money away! What's on your mind? Eh? Eh?"

I shook my head. "Nothing, sir. No explanation."

The Colonel stood up suddenly to leave, looking grimly around my office and chewing his cigar.

"I'll teach you, boy," he said. "You'll wish you had it back!"

"No, sir."

He started out and then grinned back into the doorway.

"You'd've been better off using it to square some of your Dad's debts!" he declared and, satisfied that he'd demonstrated his independence, left. Mrs. Lake gasped at his remark.

Some time afterwards a letter came.

Dear Mr. Andrews:
    By this time you are doubtless of a different
mind concerning the transaction of some days
ago. I am, however, a man of my word, and

intend to carry out my resolution for your instruction.
>   Yours truly,
>   Henry W. Morton

I replied at once:

Dear Col. Morton:
    I have not changed my mind at all. The mat-
ter to which you refer was not any sort of
transaction, and you are not obliged to me in
any way. It was a gift.
>   Yours truly,
>   Todd Andrews

Within the month, Morton's Marvelous Tomatoes,
Inc., became involved in a contractual dispute with a
small shipping concern that ferried some of the Colonel's canned goods to Baltimore. The evidence was all
in favor of the shipping company (the suit was an
intricate one, and I shan't describe it here), but the
Colonel had never lost a litigation before, and so he
determined to spend his way to justice. An executive
from MMT, Inc., called on me and announced that the
Colonel wanted Andrews, Bishop, & Andrews to handle
his defense.

"Sure," I said. "I'm personally not interested, but Mr.
Bishop can take the case."

"I believe the Colonel is anxious for you to handle it
personally," the executive said (he was Wingate Collins,
a kind of vice-president); "in fact, I'm sure he is. I
heard him say so."

But I declined. The Colonel took his business to
Charley Parks, and ultimately obtained justice in the
Court of Appeals.

Then the drivers of the Morton Trucking Company,
a subsidiary of the packing house, went on strike when
the Colonel refused to allow the company union to
affiliate with the CIO, and Norbert Adkins, of the union, asked our firm for legal counsel. Jimmy Andrews,
who had just joined us, was itching for the job, and

Mr. Bishop and I saw no reason why he shouldn't take it. But Wingate Collins gave us a reason.

"I'll tell you frankly," he said, "the Colonel doesn't want any of his friends to take that job. Your outfit would be pretty unpopular if you fellows took it. You know what I mean?"

"Cut it out, Wingate," I smiled. "You've been going to the movies too much."

"I'll tell you what," he said. "You stand to come into a good thing if you don't stick up for those strikers. The Colonel's been unhappy with Matson & Parks lately— just between us, of course—and he's looking around for another law firm to represent MMT officially. That's between six and eight thousand a year extra for the firm that gets it. The Colonel's taken a liking to you, Todd, I don't mind saying. He thinks you're a very promising fellow. And I'd bet my bottom dollar you'd get that job if you'll lay off these strikers. Hell, I know you would— off the record, now—I heard him say as much yesterday."

"I guess Jim wants to handle it, Wingate," I said. "You'd better talk to him."

"I already did," Wingate sniffed. "He says he wants the union thing, but it's up to you and Harry. Harry says he don't care one way or the other."

"I don't either," I said.

"Well, I frankly think you're a damn fool, if you'll excuse me for saying so!" Wingate said heatedly. "The Colonel'll have a tough time swallowing this, I declare!"

But apparently he swallowed it. Jimmy counseled the union in the arbitration that followed, and Matson & Parks, next door, counseled the company. It was finally decided that the union would remain "independent," and, solemnly, that the strikers would pay from their treasury for the damage to six trucks that they'd overturned during the strike.

During the next year or so, the Colonel approached me, either directly or through his vice-presidents, on ten different occasions with offers of business. I declined to handle any of them personally (they were routine affairs, if lucrative); some he took elsewhere, others he rather reluctantly allowed Mr. Bishop to handle. Whenever I encountered him on the street (he rarely walked), he clapped me on the shoulder, took my arm, invited me for dinner, invited me for cruises on his yacht, invited me to membership in the Cambridge Yacht Club, the Elks, the Rotary, the Masons, the Odd Fellows (the Colonel was a joiner), and the country club (because I sometimes played golf, I was already a member). I declined his invitations politely. He fumed and stewed.

More offers for legal business came in from Morton's Marvelous Tomatoes.

"I'll say quite frankly," Wingate Collins said, quite frankly, "I think you're a damn fool. What you got against us? You fellows are passing up the chance of a lifetime. You got more money than you can use? That's it? I'll tell you the Christ truth, Todd, the Colonel's got ants in his pants about that money you sent him—off the cuff, now, understand. I told him you're just a damn fool, frankly, but he don't know you like I do. He can't understand it. He's got ants in his pants because he says he don't want to be obligated to any man. Now, then. You'd make him a lot easier to live with if you'd take some of this business he's throwing your way."

"The firm's not turning it down," I reminded him. "I'm just not interested personally."

"Hell, man, it's not like it's an outright gift to you!" Wingate cried. "He just wants to hire you, like anybody else might do. What you want to hold him by the tail for? Nobody else ever got him so het up before!"

"He's being childish," I said. "He knows he's not obligated to me. He even took the trouble to get it in writing."

Wingate told me frankly I was a damn fool.

Word got around town somehow (I suspect through either Wingate or Mrs. Lake or Jimmy) about the five thousand dollars, and I was asked about it by a few extra-curious people.

"It was just a gift," I shrugged.

Most people, though, had already regarded me as

rather eccentric, and so were pleased enough to have their suspicions confirmed. I heard through friends that one or two of Dad's creditors were disgruntled, but of course the money was mine, not Dad's, and so they could do nothing. Some cynics wondered what I was after.

On Christmas the Colonel sent me, via his chauffeur, a case of Harvey's Scotch, excellent stuff. When he got it back two days later, via the Cambridge Cab Company, he came again in person to my office.

"Good morning, sir," I said. "What can I do for you?"

"You can quit this damn nonsense!" the Colonel said heartily. I offered him a cigar, which he refused almost violently. I waited for him to continue.

"Do you still mean to sit there and swear to God you gave me five thousand dollars out of a clear blue sky for nothing? With times as hard as they are?"

"It was a gift," I said.

"Don't think I don't know why your father committed suicide, young man," the Colonel said. "No offense intended; you know how these things get around."

"That's right."

The Colonel sighed impatiently and tapped his cane on the floor. "I don't get it," he said.

"There's nothing to get."

"Listen," he said, rather quietly. "This needn't go beyond the two of us. Wingate Collins—you know him? Good. Wingate Collins is my vice-president unofficially in charge of labor relations. Good man, Wingate, but he's doing a lousy job. Makes everybody mad, and he's supposed to make everybody happy. Union doesn't like him, office people don't like him, I don't like him. Great fellow, you know, but just makes folks mad. Well, then. Wingate's going to retire soon—he don't know it yet—and I'm going to hire a labor relations man. Want a lawyer, somebody knows people. Take you half a day, five days. Five thousand a year, and you can keep your law practice on the side."

"Nope."

"Listen," the Colonel said. "This isn't any gift. I

don't know anybody else I'd rather hire. I'm just glad I
got to know you."

"Thanks," I said. "I don't want the job, sir, thank
you just the same."

"Don't want it!" the Colonel cried. "Men are begging for work! Don't you want it!"

"No, sir."

"*Yes!*" the Colonel shouted, forgetting himself. His
face was red.

"Nope," I said again.

"Take your damn money back!" the Colonel cried,
but waved no bills under my nose.

"Of course not."

The Colonel actually mopped his forehead with his
handkerchief.

"How about the Scotch?"

"No thank you, sir," I said.

He rose to leave, quite shaken.

"I shall have a great many guests in on New Year's
Eve," he said softly. "You'll get an invitation; Mrs.
Morton has already sent them out. It's her first big
affair, and she's heard of you but hasn't met you."
The Colonel had remarried perhaps a year before, his
first wife having died in 1926.

"Thank you," I said.

"You needn't take the trouble to send it back, as
you did the Scotch. There's no need to insult Evelyn.
Just throw it in your wastebasket."

I did indeed get the engraved invitation next day, and
on New Year's Eve, having drunk four double highballs
in my room after supper, I impulsively decided to drop
in on the Colonel's party, thinking it consistent with
my policy of incomplete consistency. At eleven o'clock I
took a cab out to the Morton estate on Hambrooks Bay.

The party was in full swing when I arrived. Both
wings of the great brick house were ablaze with lights,
and perhaps a hundred and fifty people milled around inside, in tuxedos and gowns. I wouldn't have thought that
there were that many tuxedos in Dorchester County. A
champagne fountain had been rigged up in the main liv-

ing room, and a sparkling burgundy fountain in the
library. The women were drinking mostly from these.
On the summer porch three white-coated Negroes tended
bar, and male guests stood two deep before them. A small
orchestra was playing in the club cellar.

The butler took my coat and my invitation at the
door, but before he could do anything with the latter, the Colonel caught sight of me from across the room,
where he stood laughing with some vice-presidential-
looking friends. He stared incredulously for a moment,
took the cigar from his mouth, and then broke into a
great smile.

"Well, well, *well!*" he roared, charging toward me
with hand extended. "Andrews!" He could think of
nothing to say, and so pumped my arm for half a minute.

"Well, well, *well!*" he roared again.

"Looks like a pleasant party," I declared.

"Well!" the Colonel said. "Ha! Say, you must meet
Evelyn. *Evelyn! Evelyn!*"

Evelyn appeared from the library, near at hand. She
was perhaps forty—slightly more than half the Colonel's
age—and, perhaps because she'd borne no children, her
figure was still quite slender, and the skin on her face
fairly tight. She was no beauty, but much better-looking
than her husband.

"Evelyn, this is young Andrews, Todd Andrews; the
young lawyer, you know."

"How do you do, Mr. Andrews."

"Good evening," I said.

"My husband had doubted that you'd do us the
honor," Mrs. Morton smiled. I guessed that she was
thoroughly enjoying her first big affair: her smile was
just a trifle liquorish.

"Ha!" the Colonel exclaimed, a bit nervously, and
still held fast to my arm, as though afraid I'd bolt for
freedom. "He's an independent young man, all right!
Yes, sir! Well, what say to a drink, Andrews? A little
Scotch, eh? Ha!"

"I thank you," I said.

"I'll be seeing you in a moment, Mr. Andrews," Mrs.

Morton said—rather coquettishly, I thought. "I certainly must get to know you while we've got you. Toodleoo!"

"Toodleoo," I said.

"You've made her very pleased by coming tonight, young man," the Colonel confided as he marched me through the crowd to the summer porch. Many people turned to watch us go by.

Well, it was the first party of any size that I'd been to since my saintly days prior to Dad's suicide, and I found myself reverting almost unconsciously to that pose. As soon as I could escape the Colonel's endless introductions to people I already knew—there were only ten or twelve strangers at the party—I garnered two double Scotches from one of the Negroes (whom I also knew well) and retreated to the darkened club cellar, which had been cleared out for dancing. An auxiliary, one-tender bar had been set up across from the orchestra, and so I was able to drink uninterruptedly for some time, watching the players and the dancers. And, truth to tell, I got really drunk, splendidly drunk, on the Colonel's unparalleled Scotch.

What followed I must tell in broken sequences, for that is how I remember it:

At midnight the place went absolutely to hell, as though every guest—there must have been more than two hundred then, or else all were in the club cellar—had decided simply to throw back his head and holler at the top of his lungs for several hours. The orchestra played on, but without audible effect, and people danced brokenly to no music. For a while someone was kissing me, and I proposed to whoever it was that we fling our glasses into the fireplace, as one should.

"There isn't any fireplace."

"Well, into the noise, then."

"You can't hit noise, silly."

"*Regardez*," I said, and threw mine at the drummer.

I did indeed dance a tango with Evelyn Morton. Nay, ten, a dozen tangos, without the encumbrances of music or prior experience. And in every ill-lit corner, as his wife clung to me, I saw the Colonel smiling redly,

benignly, nodding his great head, flashing his gold
teeth, his gold-headed cane.

Certainly there was a floor show of drunken wives of
vice-presidents, to the horror of some husbands. A can-
can line, so to speak. Remarkable. I recall vividly the
upflung leg, the fat veined thighs of the wife of Wingate
Collins, that marked man. The roaring went on and on,
no matter how many glasses one threw at the orchestra, who played in terror. There is a picture of the
drummer shielding himself behind a great cymbal, apparently carried for that purpose; of my thin, elegant
highball glass glittering through the air to splinter against
the wall just off his starboard ear. No matter whom one
attempted to dance with, it was Mrs. Morton—slender,
graceful, unattractive, drunk—and the Colonel nodded.

Then there was a tendency afoot to take cold showers
in several of the upstairs bathrooms. These showers were
taken by gluts of singing men. My group sang various
verses of "Mademoiselle from Armentières," and I recall even now the ringing vibrancy of my baritone, but
I don't remember getting wet at all until the entrance
of wet Mrs. Morton. Standing outside the shower, we
had sung the line declaring that Mademoiselle had not
enjoyed herself for forty years, and then somewhere between the *hinkey* and the *dinkey* my whole choir vanished, just as in a movie, and shimmering, dripping
Mrs. Morton leaped like a damp naiad from behind
the shower curtain, into my arms. Her dewy bosoms,
none too firm, crushed into my shirt front; her dripping
hair fell over her eyes; her teeth sank into my lapel,
into my boutonniere; she ground herself against my
trousers. We danced a magnificent *parley-voo*, stopping
with a dip that dropped us both to the tiles, tapped by
the tip of the Colonel's cane. Mrs. Morton caught sight
of the gold teeth glinting in the light from the bathroom
bulb and swooned or died, sprawling pink and sprinkled
like a blushing dugong hoisted from the deep.

I picked myself up meticulously and straightened my
wet bow tie. The Colonel grinned feverishly and tapped

his cane (seven inches from his wife's wet head) as though conversing with her spirit by Morse code.

"Mrs. Morton dances excellently," I said, bowing slightly to the Colonel as I stepped over Evelyn en route to the door. And then, parting, with what seemed to me a glorious conjunction of wit and *savoir-faire:* "One is tempted to call her Morton's Most Marvelous Tomato, isn't one? Good night, sir."

One was, in fact, tempted to add that it was indeed a pity to see such a fresh tomato stewed, as it were, if not altogether canned—but one knew well the delicate line beyond which the prick of wit becomes the sting of insult, and so one held one's tongue and exited gracefully.

In the new year that followed, the firm of Andrews, Bishop, & Andrews was not pressed to render its services to the Colonel, nor was I dunned with invitations to join clubs or lodges, nor confronted at every turn with invitations to parties and dinners at the Morton manor. Indeed, if there have been any parties at the Mortons' since that New Year's Eve, I've not heard of them. Jacob Matson, of Matson & Parks, became vice-president in charge of personnel for MMT, Inc., when Wingate Collins suddenly retired.

And on the extremely rare occasions when I met Col. Morton on Race Street and tipped my hat in greeting, he flushed red, bared his gold teeth, and ignored me with the grim smile of one who is obligated in no way to any man.

XXII. A tour of the opera

At three o'clock, just after Bill Butler and Charley Parks
had left my office to have another small drink in Charley's, Jane Mack came in with her daughter. I heard
Jane exchange greetings with Mrs. Lake, and then little
Jeannine—three and a half years old now, and brown and
lovely like her mother—came up to my desk and
watched me shyly.

"Hi, Toddy," she said.

"Hi, baby."

"Honey, may I fix your pencil?"

"Sure." It was Jeannine's habit to sharpen everyone's
pencils. I gave her a good long one, and she went happily to the sharpener and proceeded to grind away on it.

"Oh, my," Jane said, coming into my office, "she's
happy now. How do you feel, Toddy? Any better?"

"Hello, Jane. I wasn't sick."

"Then why did you act so silly last night?" she asked,
more softly, so that Mrs. Lake couldn't hear. She
perched on the corner of my desk. She was wearing khaki
shorts—unusual for that year—and a blue cotton blouse,
and looked quite fresh and desirable.

"I guess I just wasn't in the mood," I smiled.

She smiled back and patted me on the head. "That's
a stupid way to be," she said. "*I* was in the mood."

"*I* was, too," Jeannine declared from the pencil
sharpener.

"Maybe I'm getting senile," I proposed. "Stamina was never my strong point, as you know."

"I know your strong point," Jane said. "Did you get my note?"

"I did indeed."

"You sent me a dumb one, so I thought I'd send you a dumb one."

I smiled. "I don't know what Marvin found wrong with me. He'll bring the report around tonight, and we'll look at it next time you're up."

I had certainly expected some astonishment at this news, but Jane, unlike Harrison, didn't bat an eye.

"God knows it's time you went to a doctor," she said. "Well—" She jumped off the desk. "I'll be seeing you later at the house, won't I? For a Manhattan? Try not to keep Jeannine right in the sun for too long, if you can help it. She's got that bonnet, but it's awfully hot out, and she might not be all finished being sick yet."

"All right."

"I'll be done at the hairdresser's in an hour, if you want me to drop in and pick her up. If you're finished before then and she gets on your nerves, pop her in a cab and send her home. She likes that. And for God's sake buy her an ice-cream cone."

"All right."

" 'Bye, now, honey." Jane kissed her daughter. "So long, Toddy."

" 'Bye, Mommy," Jeannine said.

"So long," I said, and she left. I was mightily impressed: between the time in 1933 when I insulted her and the time in 1935 when we resumed our affair, Jane's personality had strengthened in some ways; for one thing, she was unpredictable. I wondered with really quite sharp interest what she intended to do about my note, now that I'd fulfilled the conditions of hers—and when it occurred to me that I'd not be alive to find out, I experienced a small sensation of regret; the only such sensation I felt that day.

"Let's go see the showboat, honey," I suggested to

Jeannine, who by this time was pushing the last frag-
ment of the pencil into the sharpener.

"All right, honey," she said, and very politely took
my hand.

We went out into the bright sun and walked the dry
block to Long Wharf, where the showboat lay immensely
along the bulkhead. Unlike its Mississippi counterparts,
Adam's Original & Unparalleled Floating Opera was no
architectural extravaganza of gilt and gingerbread. It was,
by comparison with them, severely unadorned, for it had
been built to withstand the sometimes tempestuous
moods of Tangier Sound and the lower Bay, and even
ventured into the Atlantic on occasion. The *Opera* itself
was a long, narrow clapboard box mounted on a massive
barge. On the bow was lettered *S. S. Thespian*, the vessel's registered name, but down both sides of the clap-
boards, in red letters three feet tall, was emblazoned its
less modest trade name. A simple balcony affair graced
either end of the theater, appparently for the employees'
benefit, and lifelines ran down both sides. On the roof
were ventilators, stovepipes, clotheslines, lifeboats, a trim
little shed with window boxes and curtained windows,
an improvised bandstand, and the steam calliope, now
silent. The whole structure was braced against humping
or buckling by a trusswork of piers and cables on both
sides. Two tugboats moored alongside, the *Pamlico* and
the *Albemarle*, provided the showboat's motive power.

"What's that, Toddy?" Jeannine asked excitedly.

"That's a showboat," I said. "Can you say showboat?"

"*Showboat.*"

"Would you like to go up close and see it?"

"All right."

Fortunately, for I'd forgotten my promise, some entre-
preneur had set up a refreshment stand near the bulkhead, and so I was able to buy two vanilla ice-cream
cones before we went up for a close look at the showboat. Not many people were curious enough to come out
in the terrific heat; we had the spectacle pretty much
to ourselves, and I set Jeannine up on a piling to get a
good view.

As was her habit when excited, Jeannine slipped into the "Why?" routine, which never annoyed me.

"What's it for, Toddy honey?" she shouted, awed at the *Opera's* size.

"It's a showboat, hon. People go on it and listen to music and watch the actors dance and act funny."

"Why?"

"Why what?" I asked. "Why do the actors act funny or why do the people like to watch them?"

"Why do the people?"

"The people like to go to the show because it makes them laugh. They like to laugh at the actors."

"Why?"

"They like to laugh because laughing makes them happy. They like being happy, just like you."

"Why?"

You understand, of course, that she wasn't the least bit interested in either her questions or my answers, as questions or answers; she was simply excited over the monstrous showboat, and wanted to hear me talk. I could have recited the alphabet in a knowing tone, and she'd have been satisfied.

"Why do they like being happy? That's the end of the line."

"Why do the actors?"

"Why do the actors act funny? They do that so the people will pay to come see them. They want to earn money."

"Why?"

"So they can eat. They like eating."

"Why?"

"You have to eat to stay alive. They like staying alive."

"Why?"

"That's the end of the line again," I said.

"Hey there!" cried a little man on the aft balcony. "Want to look 'er over?"

"Sure would," I called back. "Thanks."

"Go on up forrard, I'll show ye round," he invited.

"Want to go on the showboat?" I asked Jeannine.

"All right."

The little man met us at the gangplank and waved us aboard. He was tough-looking, wiry, and leather-faced, with knotted hands and the eyes of a starling, and was dressed in wrinkled black trousers, an immaculate white shirt, and a yachting cap. Jeannine regarded him soberly while I shook hands.

"Are you Captain Adam?"

"That's a fact, sir, I am. Jacob Adam. Bring yer little girl along now, and I'll show ye the boat. Quite a boat, ain't she?"

"She is indeed," I agreed.

"Quite a boat, sir," Capt. Adam agreed. "Thirty-one years old, she is, and she's still sound as a dollar, if you know what I mean—" He tugged my arm and chortled. "Dollar ain't worth what it was in 1906!"

"Quite a boat," he said again. "Had 'er built in Little Washington, North Carolina, in 1906, sir, and I had 'er built strong. Why, you set one o' them Miss'ssippi showboats down in the ocean for a minute, there wouldn't be a stick left fit to pick yer teeth with."

"Why?" Jeannine demanded, gaining courage.

"Did you use to run boats on the Mississippi?" I asked.

"No, sir, I don't mind tellin' ye," the Captain declared, "I never set foot on a boat in my life till I built the *Op'ry*. Not even a row-skiff; now, then. I run a two-car ten-cent vaudeville show all over the country, sir, from 1895 till 1905, and did so good I had to quit, 'cause ever'body I hired cut out to start a ten-cent show hisself. Next thing I knew there was so much competition I couldn't make the nut. I figured I'd set me up in something that takes a big wad to start with, so ever' Tom, Dick, and Harry with ten bucks and a lot o' brass can't squeeze in. I don't mind tellin' ye, I sunk sixty thousand dollars in this showboat, sir, in a time when dollars was dollars, I mean. But I wanted 'er tough, and I still got 'er."

"She looks plenty sturdy," I admitted. So far we hadn't moved from the gangplank: there is that in me which brings out old men's garrulity.

"She *is* sturdy, sir. Ye see them strakes along the sides there?" He pointed to the barge's side planking. "First time I saw them boards, they was trees. I walked around the Carolina woods for a year, sir, pickin' out my timber where it stood. Hundred-and-twenty-two-foot long and four inches thick, them strakes, and not a splice in 'em from stem to stern, nor a knot, either. And I got 'em drift-bolted ever' two feet with twenty-seven-inch bolts. That's for the ocean, sir! Thirty-two-foot planks across the bottom, beam to beam; not a splice. Cost me plenty, sir, but it was money well spent, let me tell *you*. One time in 1920 we was caught in a squall in Tangier Sound, and they couldn't get a boat to us. I'm not lyin', sir, for fourteen hours the waves was breakin' over the *Op'ry's* roof. Took Mrs. Adam's pansies right out o' the window box up there, but the *Op'ry* didn't spring a plank. That's what plannin' does, sir!"

Jeannine was jumping up and down; I moved toward the shuttered box office.

"Come on inside," the Captain invited, taking the hint. We entered the theater, dark and cool, and Capt. Adam provided us with a running commentary on what we were observing.

"Seats seven hundred," he said. "White folks down here and in the boxes, colored folks in the balcony."

Jeannine, happily, didn't ask why.

"Used to be, couldn't get a darkie on board," he went on. "Word got around we was baitin' 'em on to send back to Africa. (That there stage is nineteen foot across; the hall's eighty foot long.) Used to carry a car on board, but the salt water ruined 'er, seemed like."

"Where's *your* house?" Jeannine demanded.

"Well, little lady, I live up on the roof."

"Why?"

"*Why?* Heh! She's a fresh one, ain't she? Well, sir, come on back here with me, and I'll show ye the dressin' rooms and all."

We followed the Captain behind the stage, where a row of numbered doors ran along a short hallway.

"Good big dressin' rooms," Capt. Adam said proudly.

"The actors live in 'em, too. Most ever'body's into town just now, sir."

"Why?" Jeannine murmured.

"Now come on down here." We were led down a companionway. "Here's the cook's quarters and the dinin' room—we're right under the stage now—and over there's the galley. Bottle-gas stove and a nine-hundred-pound icebox. That there door leads right out to the orchestra pit. What do ye think of 'er?"

"Very impressive," I said.

"Whole shebang don't draw but fourteen inch o' water, by golly. I always say, 'You give me a good-size mud puddle, I'll give you a show!' Yes, sir. Six big ventilators up on the roof. Runnin' water in all the dressin' rooms. Plenty o' heat in the wintertime. See them pipes runnin' under the stage? Heat pipes, water pipes, acetylene pipes for the footlights."

"You don't use electricity?"

"I use it for the ventilators and lights too, when I can, but ye can't depend on it. Lots o' landings ain't electrified. Ye can give a show without ventilators, but not without lights. I carry two banks o' footlights, one electric and one acetylene."

I remarked that acetylene seemed a dangerous shipmate to me.

"No sirree!" Capt. Adam denied. "Never had a speck o' trouble. I got the tanks rigged outside, where a leak won't cause no trouble, and I just run it in through this little copper line here"—he indicated with his finger a small pipe leading through a valve, from which hung a sign reading *Do Not Open Until Ready To Light Footlights*—"and out to the foots. That there valve sends the gas out to the footlights, sir. The rig works fine. Don't ye worry, sir; there ain't nothin' about this boat that ain't been thought out plenty careful. Got a tug bow and stern, so she rides steady in a seaway. Got our circuit figured out so we hit fresh water twice a year, to kill off all the moss and barnacles on the bottom. Start out from Elizabeth City, North Carolina (fresh-water town), soon's it gets warm, and play up along Albemarle Sound,

Pamlico Sound, through the Dismal Swamp Canal, and up the Chesapeake as far as Port Deposit, hittin' all the best landings on the way. That's fresh water up by Port Deposit, so we head back home with a clean bottom again. Saves me a haulin' out."

Jeannine had begun to fidget with impatience, and to swing back and forth on my hand. I thanked Capt. Adam for showing us around his craft, and he ushered us through a side door that led from the dining room, where we'd been standing, to the starboard quarter of the barge.

"Did you like the showboat?" I asked Jeannine.

"All right." Her face was flushed, and I thought it best to get her out of the sun.

We passed the refreshment stand, unoccupied except for the vendor himself.

"Toddy honey, will you buy me another ice-cream cone?" Jeannine asked.

"Why?"

"I want one, honey."

"Why?"

"I want one."

"*Why* do you want one?"

"I want one."

"But why? Tell me *why*."

"I want one."

She got one, and we strolled back to the office in all the heat and light.

XXIII. Another premise to swallow

A little girl with her one little question can, like Socrates, bring any man to either anger, pique, or stalemate, depending on his temperament.

Consider: A man attends the *Floating Opera*. *Why?* Excellent reason: a change from the old routine, a chance to laugh. *Why is it better to laugh than not to?* Easy: because a laughing man is happy, and it's better to be happy than sad. *Why?* Well, without happiness, or the hope of it, a man might as well be dead, and surely it's better to be alive than dead. *Why?*

The actors entertain the man. *Why?* So that he'll like them; they want him to like them. *Why?* They want him to tell all his friends. *Why?* So that there'll be a good gate; they want a good gate. *Why?* Why? For heaven's sake! So that they'll make money to live on, of course! Certainly it's better to eat than to starve. *Why?* Because to starve is to die; it's better to live. *Why?*

If one is wise, he will, confronted with a child like Jeannine, either rebuff her at once (while she's still a baby) or else take refuge in the "if" clause, which in itself can be invulnerable: *If* the actors want to eat, it's better for them to please their audiences than to displease them. *If* you want to live, you should eat. This is no more than what I observed to Mr. Haecker: that *if* one is interested in intelligibility, then one should never use the words *should* or *ought* except after the word *if*.

It is merely a corollary to the premise I offered you four chapters ago—that the values of things are not intrinsic, but are attributed to the things by people. The corollary is that things are valuable only with reference to certain ends, as illustrated above. This is not anything new to philosophy—in fact, after some research I found such a statement in my lecture notes from Johns Hopkins, 1922—but it is one thing to give it "notional" assent, quite another really to swallow and digest it. But if, like me, you are a child of the twentieth century (I barely made it, to be sure), then digesting the premise should be impossible, even if we don't find it palatable, and we might even throw down the corollary for good measure, as a chaser.

But here, I think, in Jeannine's questions, lies a real hogchoker: *the reasons that people have for attributing value to things are always ultimately arbitrary;* that is, if the question *Why?* is asked often enough, it will be discovered that the ultimate end (which, remember, gives the whole chain its value) is rationally indefensible, logically unjustifiable. Suppose Harrison were to say that he gave the Loyalists four thousand dollars because he prefers Marxism to either fascism or capitalism. *Why?* He answers, "If your end is social justice, Marxism is the best means." *Granting your hypothesis, why is justice better than injustice?* (Here he might say "It just *is*," as Mr. Haecker said "The simple fact of life is good," in which case we're dealing with beatific visions and cannot ask further questions.) "Because justice is the optimum condition for civilization: if you desire civilization, you must desire justice." *Why is civilization better than savagery?* "You shouldn't ask that: all the things you probably value are possible only in a civilized society." End of argument, for we're back where we began. The point is that the *if* device, excellent for making value statements intelligible, is defensible only so long as the *if's* aren't questioned. The reasons for which people assign value to things are always ultimately (though not necessarily immediately) arbitrary, irrational.

In short, there is no ultimate reason for calling anything important or valuable; no ultimate reason for preferring one thing to another.

Well, chew on that for a while, and I'll get on with
the story.

XXIV. So long, so long

Long before we reached Court Lane, Jeannine's second ice-cream cone had melted all over her arm, was dripping from brown chin and dimpled elbow, all down her sundress and onto her sneakers. I paused under a great poplar tree to scrub her up a bit with my handkerchief. My head felt a little dizzy—whether from the sun or from my new premise, I couldn't say.

"Toddy, honey, I got to sit on the potty," Jeannine remarked.

"Can you hold on a minute?" I grinned, hoping she wouldn't start asking *why*.

I picked her up and strode quickly up the sidewalk, expecting at any moment to have my coat sleeve moistened, but Jeannine chuckled distractedly and clung tightly to my neck, her fat little arm over my mouth.

"Mmm, you smell like your mommy," I said.

This amused her. "You smell like my daddy," she countered glibly.

"Ah."

We reached port safely, and Mrs. Lake took Jeannine to the lavatory. I spent the time writing a note to Jimmy Andrews, who stood not ten feet from me, and thinking about Jeannine, whose opinion it was that I smelled like her daddy. Very possibly, of course, she was right: *I* could certainly smell some Andrews in her infant curiosity.

I finished the note (which informed Jimmy of the letter from Eustacia Callader and instructed him to institute proceedings against Harrison's mother for recovery of that part of the estate which she'd disposed of) and put it in my inside coat pocket. A few minutes later Jane came in, her hair cropped short, and we left to go to her place for cocktails. I didn't bother to straighten out my desk, to say a last goodbye to Mr. Bishop, Jimmy, or Mrs. Lake, or even to take a final look at my office, at my wonderful staring-wall. Why should I?

On the drive to East Cambridge, although I chatted amiably with Jane and Jeannine, I was filled with myself and my plan, which had crystallized by then into its final form. If out of my meager vocabulary only the term *unenthusiastic excitement* comes anywhere near to describing the feeling with which all my thoughts were suffused, you must resolve my meaning from that term's dissonance. There remained still no small measure of the excitement which had attended my first realization that I was ready to destroy myself; but, like all my major decisions of policy, that resolution had been a rapid one, the effect of external impingement upon whatever was my current mask—and as in those other cases, the resolution itself was only afterwards rationalized into some kind of coherent and arguable position. Though it is too much to expect that I should become solemn about it, certainly the direction of this day's rationalizing was an awesome one—yet full of the attractiveness of desolation, the charm of the abyss. Such a simple fact— that there are no ultimate reasons—and how chilling! I heard beyond it the whistling of the black winds of Chaos; my hackles rose at the thought, as if I had been breathed upon by a cold sigh from the pit.

It was four o'clock; the heat lingered at its greatest intensity. What Jane's car filled with as we drove over the creek bridge was not the black wind of Chaos, but the stench of the crabhouses, steaming up from small mountains of red carapaces and other nonedible parts of the crab thrown out in the sun by the pickers. It is a smell that grabs you by the nose—I've seen many a visitor retch while crossing the creek in summer—but like many another thing, it can be lived with: most of the natives aren't even aware of it, and I, for one, have learned to relish it, to inhale it deeply and savor its every rank ingredient in my nostrils. I did so as we drove off the bridge, and composed a mental note for my *Inquiry,* as follows:

> Olfactory pleasures being no more absolute than any other kinds of pleasures, one would do well to outgrow conventional odor-judgments, for a vast number of worth-while smells await the unbiased nose. It is a meager standard that will call perverse that seeker of wisdom who, his toenails picked, must sniff his fingers in secret joy.

A meditation worthy of a man's last day! It took its place beside my early morning's reflection on Plato and the crabbers—a good day for my *Inquiry!*—and I continued without interruption my conversation with Jane, who was as a matter of fact talking quite animatedly. She had announced, to my surprise, that she and Harrison were planning a trip to Italy for the fall.

"It's Harrison's idea," she said, "and I'm tickled to death with it. He wants to stay till Christmas, but I'm holding out for Easter. I was there one summer when I was a kid, and it's all beautiful! I wish we could live there."

I believe she kept glancing at me to judge my reaction, but that belief might be simple vanity. At any rate, I showed no reaction at all.

"Are you counting on the inheritance to travel on?" I asked. "It's probably wiser not to."

She looked surprised. "I thought that was out of the question. Isn't it? I'd given up hoping for that."

"I suspect you're doing the right thing."

"We're going on Harrison's salary. Hell, we can afford it." She glanced at me again. "We might even consider selling the house—if you don't mind."

"Why should I mind?"

"Well—" She shrugged her shoulders.

"Do you think Harrison will be able to swallow Mussolini's boys?"

"Oh, this isn't a political tour," Jane smiled. "I'm not even interested in politics, are you? I don't think Harrison is any more, either, the way the Spanish thing's going. He's getting cynical about political movements, I believe. He's cynical about everything nowadays, in fact, but in a sweet way. I think he got it from you."

"Not the sweetness, certainly."

"Certainly not," Jane said, and patted my leg. There was still some nervousness in her exuberance, or so I thought at least: I smelled a plan in the air, now that the crabhouses were out of range.

"When did you decide all this?" I asked cheerfully. "About the trip and the house?"

"Oh, it was Harrison's idea," she said. "About the trip. The house was my idea, because I want us to be independent. I guess it sort of popped up about a week ago. We haven't worked out any details. You don't mind, do you, if we go? I mean—" She looked at Jeannine, who was staring listlessly out the window. "You know what I mean."

"Of course I don't mind."

"I'd love it! With the money from the house we could stay there a year. Harrison can fix it with his job. God, just think—*Italy!*"

"When did you get so hot on Italy?" I smiled.

"I've always been hot on Italy. Didn't I tell you? Are you mad at me, Toddy?"

"No."

"You kind of acted like it."

We pulled up in front of the Mack house, and I lifted Jeannine down to run to Harrison, who waved from the porch.

"Were you offended by my note this morning?" Jane persisted as we walked up the lawn. "I certainly didn't think you'd take me up on going to Marvin, but I'm glad you did."

"How about *my* note?" I asked. "Harrison seemed a

little concerned when I told him lunchtime I'd been
to see Marvin, but you don't seem alarmed at all."

"Should I be alarmed? What about?"

By that time we were at the porch, and Jane skipped
up the steps, kissed Harrison lightly on the forehead,
and disappeared inside.

Usually we drank our Manhattans on the porch, but
on this day it was much cooler in the living room. Harrison and I chatted for a few minutes about the weather,
agreeing that the dull haze over the Bay prophesied a
squall, and then we went inside.

"So you're going to Italy?" I remarked.

"Yes, it looks like it," Harrison confessed, fumbling
at once for a cigarette in his shirt. "Did Janie tell
you?"

"A minute ago. I think it's a fine idea, of course."

"Do you really? Well, I wasn't so sure. It means
selling the house and all—but you know how crazy Jane
is about Italy, Fascists or not, and I'd like to see the
place myself while there's still time. I suspect things are
going to blow up over there sooner or later. Frankly,
I wasn't sure how you'd feel about it," he added carefully.

"How *I'd* feel? What possible difference could it make
if I objected? And I don't, at all."

"Well—"

Jane reappeared from the kitchen, and behind her
came the maid with our cocktails. Jane sat down beside
Harrison, on the couch; I was in an easy chair across
the room, facing them.

"Well," Jane said brightly, smiling at her cocktail.

We all sipped intently.

"Will you be going to the showboat tonight?" Harrison asked me, laughing.

"Maybe so. I hadn't thought much about it."

"Jeannine was crazy about it this afternoon," Jane
told Harrison, for my benefit. "She got two ice-cream
cones, and the man took her and Todd all over the
boat."

"Oh? Well," Harrison said.

"In fact, she got too excited—she's a little feverish. I called Marvin, and he says don't worry."

We sipped some more.

"Why not have supper with us?" Jane asked me. "It's just cold platters—sliced ham and potato salad."

I shrugged. "Sure, if you want."

"I'll tell Louise." She jumped up and went into the kitchen again. Harrison and I sipped and sipped, and after a while I lit a cigar.

"Don't be offended by what I'm going to say now, Toddy," Harrison began, and immediately, involuntarily, I smiled around my cigar: the pressure was off.

"You can't offend me," I declared.

"Well, here's the thing. You know very well we'd like to have you come along with us to Italy"—I made a quick gesture of negation—"but I figured you had your work, and besides, the fact is, I think Jane sort of planned this thing just for the two of us. Three, counting Jeannine. You know."

"Sure, man; don't even speak of it."

"Well, that's not the thing. The thing is, of course Janie won't be around here for a year, maybe two years, you never can tell. Now—I don't know how I can say this without hurting you, Toddy—the truth is, I kind of think when we come back (I don't know when that'll be) what with Jeannine getting older and all—well, it might not look too good, you know what I mean, if Janie kept on going up to the hotel."

"I agree completely," I said at once.

"Hell, I guess you're insulted, Toddy. I don't want you to take it the wrong way. You know what I think of you, and how much I've approved of the whole thing. But hell, you know—"

"Sure, man. No explanation."

"Well, I want to make certain you take it right," Harrison persisted, examining his empty glass closely. "It's not that we like you any less—"

Jane came in, glanced quickly at me, then at Harrison, and took a seat midway between us. She absorbed herself in rubbing her brown knee.

"You don't need to explain anything," I insisted firmly. "As a matter of fact—"

"I'll tell you the honest truth, Toddy," Jane broke in (I believe it was the very first time she'd ever interrupted me). "If it's all right with you, I'd like to call the thing off as of now. Do you mind?"

"I was just going to suggest it," I said. Jane smiled briefly at her knee. "I'd been thinking about it for some time."

"Well, let me see if I can explain it right, Toddy," Jane said, looking at me directly and pleasantly. "I'm not too good at expressing things."

"There's no need to say a word," I declared.

"Oh, yes there is," she smiled. "I don't want to break it off unless you can understand everything."

"I understand everything."

"No, you don't," Jane said sweetly. I looked up in surprise. "If you'd understood everything, there wouldn't have been that trouble a few years ago."

"Whoa, now—" I protested.

"Let me see if I can say what I want to say, and then you can take it apart," she proposed. I grinned shortly at Harrison, who, however, didn't see me, engrossed as he was in his empty glass. "When Harrison and I got married we were as prudish as they come about extracurricular sex," Jane began. "I swore I could never look at another man, and Harrison swore he never even thought of another woman in a sexual way. Then as we got more sense we saw how dishonest that was —is that the right word?—yes, *dishonest;* and stupid, too. I won't go into all that; you understand, I think. Well, we decided there was nothing wrong with either of us making love to somebody else just for fun, because we were absolutely sure of each other. There could never be any jealousy between us. I was very attracted to you as Harrison's friend, and as soon as we didn't have to be stupid or dishonest any more, I realized I'd like to make love to you. And except for the one bad spell, it worked out fine. It was mostly our fault, we realize, about that bad time. We had no right to expect so much."

"Oh, I don't know." I shrugged. This was all very embarrassing for Harrison and me.

"Well, anyhow, neither one of us has any regrets that I made love to you."

"Or that you're calling it off," I smiled.

"Aw, hell, man, don't be bitter," Harrison complained.

"I didn't mean it that way."

"You're right," Jane said. "We don't have to have any regrets about that either, if you can try to understand why I'm doing it."

"Is it because of that note this morning?" I asked.

"The note? Oh, that stupid thing! I never did pay any attention to that. I just assumed you were upset about last night, for some reason or other. I sent you my note as a joke, to get even. Heavens no, that's silly! I hadn't even considered it. Here's the thing: I don't want you to think that Harrison and I are retreating in any way to our old standards, just because we're calling this off."

I raised my eyebrows.

"Hell, I can't find the damned words—what I mean is, we were kind of unsure of ourselves when we decided to try this extracurricular business. I guess that's why we were so demanding, come to think of it. We wanted reassurance that we hadn't made a mistake. God knows that's understandable enough!"

"I think that's probably why Janie thought she was in love with you," Harrison put in, "and why I thought that was a good thing."

I pursed my lips.

"That's right," Janie agreed, looking at her husband. "Then after we started up again, after Jeannine was born, everything was just fine. We all understood each other perfectly, and nobody was kidding himself. Now, then. What I want to say is that it was kind of *necessary* before to be actually carrying on an affair, to prove to ourselves that we meant what we were talking about. But now I don't feel like it's necessary any more. I feel

I have enough—what the hell, *self-confidence,* I guess;
that I'm sure enough of our attitudes toward this business that I don't have to be demonstrating it all the
time, or ever again, for that matter. I just feel stronger,
is all. Harrison does, too. Do you understand anything
I've said, Toddy?"

"I told you before, I understood everything before
you said a word. I exude understanding. Didn't I say
that the same thing exactly was on *my* mind? I was
going to broach the subject this evening."

"He doesn't understand," Harrison observed to Jane.
I turned to him at once, startled, but said nothing.

Jane sighed. "I can't make it any clearer."

The maid signaled silently from the dining room.

"Dinner's almost ready, if you want to wash up,"
Jane said. She got up and headed for the kitchen,
paused, and came over and kissed me lightly on the
mouth.

"You were wonderful a great many times," she said.
"I hope this doesn't leave you with a bad taste."

I licked my lips appreciatively. "It tasted fine," I
said. Jane laughed and went to help the maid, and Harrison and I went upstairs to wash.

"Did you find a buyer for the house yet?" I asked
him.

"No, not yet," Harrison said. "Matter of fact, the
whole thing's been sort of tentative. All we knew for
sure is that we wanted to go to Italy for a while. It's
kind of crazy, I guess, but a small town can be right
stultifying."

We talked for a while in the bathroom, but there
was a coolness between us that made all the conversation a bit forced. The friendship, in fact, was over—
at least on any intimate level, and that's the only level
I cared for, though I've never quite attained it with
anyone. And at dinner afterwards, the talk, though pleasant (even relieved), was devoid of warmth. Harrison
and Jane seemed fused into one person, alienated from
me by their own doing instead of mine, entirely self-
sufficient. They should, it occurred to me, be perma-

nently locked together, like the doubler crab or Plato's proto-humans. I caught myself smiling inadvertently at my cold cuts all through the meal, as I thought of Jane's speech. And, I am obliged to add, I noticed several times that Harrison and Jane smiled at their cold cuts as well: for what reasons, I shan't presume to say.

A final observation: When, after dinner, I went up-stairs to the bathroom before leaving the house; when, indeed, I stood there comfortably reflecting, an entirely unexpected emotion gripped me: I suddenly wavered in my resolution to die—was shaken, in fact, by re-luctance. The reason was simply that my suicide would be interpreted by the Macks as evidence that their move had crushed me; that I was unable to endure life after their rebuff. And this interpretation would fill them with a proud pity that I loathed. But, happily, this faltering lasted only a moment. By the time I'd washed my hands, I had come to my senses; my new premises reasserted themselves with a force that brooked no quibbling. What difference did it make to me how they interpreted my death? Nothing, absolutely, makes any difference. Nothing is ultimately important. And, sane again, I was able to see a nice attraction in the idea that, at least partly by my own choosing, that last act would be robbed of its real significance, would be inter-preted in every way but the way I intended. This fact once realized, it seemed likely to me that here was a new significance, if possible even more genuine.

Passing down the hallway from the bathroom to the stairs, I happened to glance into my old bedroom, now a guest room, and my eye fell on a large mirror near the bed. I chuckled so hard that my eyes watered, and I walked jauntily down the stairs, more ready than ever to carry out my plan.

"I'll be seeing you around," Harrison called from the porch as I left; and Jane, too, added most cheerful goodbyes.

"So long, so long," I called back, just as cheerfully. Looking over my shoulder as I walked down the road, I saw them standing close beside each other, talking together as they watched me leave. Perhaps—I clucked my tongue—their arms were even encircling each other's waists. I waved, but they didn't see me.

I turned and went on, headed back toward the hotel. I believe I might even have whistled something or other, for I was as unburdened at that moment as must have been Socrates when, Xanthippe at last departed, he was free to face without distraction the hemlock that lay at the end of his reasoning.

XXV. Three million dollars

No, wait: that Socrates metaphor, that really quite admirable sentence I just wrote—that doesn't apply quite yet. There was one final matter to be settled before I could call myself really free from distracting encumbrances: I had to decide what to do about Harrison's three million dollars.

I paused halfway across the creek bridge to think about it. In order to focus the problem sharply, I took from my billfold the letter from Eustacia Callader, and from my coat pocket the note to Jimmy Andrews, and laid them both before me on the bridge railing. Either I must put Eustacia's letter in my writing desk, where Jimmy was instructed to find it, and drop the note to Jimmy in the mailbox, or else I must drop both documents into the creek below, where fat gray seagulls fed lazily on white perch killed by the pollution from the packing houses. The first course would result in Jimmy's filing suit for Harrison against Elizabeth Sweetman Mack, charging that, by allowing her gardener, R. J. Collier, to spread the contents of the seventy-two pickle jars on the ailing zinnias, she had disposed of a portion of the Mack estate which was no more hers to dispose of than the three million dollars. This suit would, of course, serve to postpone the hearing of my appeal of the Circuit Court's order (to execute the will in favor of Mrs. Mack) until after Joseph Singer had replaced Rollo Moore on the Court of Appeals bench. Then Jimmy would drop the suit and argue our appeal: for the reasons explained in Chapter X, the lower-court order would almost certainly be reversed, and Harrison would get the inheritance. If, on the other hand, I decided to drop both letters into the creek, then there was little chance that the appellate court would do anything except affirm the court order.

Now, you'll recall that in the morning I had decided that the basis for my decision was to be Harrison's and Jane's strength; specifically, whether they had the strength not to care, except superficially, whether they got the money or the manure. And I must say that the morning's note from Jane and my luncheon conversation with Harrison had both prejudiced me in their favor. By afternoon I had, although I didn't clearly realize it at the time, more or less resolved to let the deciding factor be Jane's response to my note of the early morning, now that I'd fulfilled the conditions of hers by going to see Marvin Rose. If she chose to make Capt. Osborn the happiest old satyr in the county, I'd make her the richest woman in the county; if she was as angry and insulted by my proposal as Harrison had been by the incident in my office in 1933, then I'd destroy the letters.

But Jane had nullified this basis by choosing a third course, one difficult to evaluate. She'd been neither angry nor insulted, nor had she felt obliged to carry out her end of the bargain. She'd simply laughed at the whole thing. Was this evidence of obtuseness, insincerity, or a real and formidable strength? In fact, I no longer knew how to feel about the Macks at all, whether their new resolutions were manifestations of a commonplace sentimentality or a strange integrity. I had no feeling about them at all.

Consequently, after inhaling deeply the fetid air of the creek for several minutes, I chose a new basis for judgment: taking a nickel from my pocket, I flipped it, caught it, and slapped it down on the letters. Heads, I preserve them; tails, they go in the creek.

My hand uncovered the skinny-assed, curly-tailed old buffalo.

—Despite which fact, I gathered up the letters, dropped one in the mailbox on the corner of Academy, Market, and Muse Streets, just off the creek bridge, and put the other in my desk when I reached the hotel. Harrison, you see, had survived a double chance: that the coin would demand the destruction of the letters, and that I would allow myself, a free agent, to be dictated to by a lousy nickel.

Then, let us say, I doubtless whistled some tune or other, for I was as unburdened at that moment as must have been Socrates when, Xanthippe at last departed, he was free to face without distraction the hemlock that lay at the end of his reasoning.

XXVI. The Inquiry

It was a few minutes after six o'clock when I reached my room, set my straw hat on the dresser top, and prepared to put in a last evening's work on my *Inquiry*. I gathered around my writing desk the three peach baskets and one cardboard box of notes and data, put in a convenient place the empty beef-stew can that functioned as my ashtray, and began my night's work by transcribing from memory the two mental notes I'd made that day (concerning the doubler crabs and the smell of the creek) and filing them at an appropriate depth in one of the peach baskets. Then I sat back in the chair and stared at the window for a while, deciding which aspect of the project should receive my attention.

When the clock on the People's Trust Company chimed six-thirty (the Macks, as usual, had eaten early), I sat up, took a long ruled sheet of yellow legal paper from one of the dozens of pads stacked on the desk, and wrote on the top:

I. Nothing has intrinsic value.

Because I regarded this sentence for some minutes before adding to it, and because so much staring and regarding is much duller to describe than it is to do, let me use the time to explain as clearly as I can the nature and history of my *Inquiry* (any such summary of so intricate and vast a subject will, of course, be over-simple) and of the great project of which the *Inquiry* itself is only one part.

The full title of the *Inquiry*, if it ever should reach the stage of completion where a title would be appropriate, will, I suppose, be *An Inquiry into the Circumstances Surrounding the Self-Destruction of Thomas T. Andrews, of Cambridge, Maryland, on Ground-Hog Day, 1930 (More Especially into the Causes Therefor)*, or something of the sort. It is simply an attempt to learn why my father hanged himself, no more.

And no less—for it became apparent to me after a mere two years of questioning, searching, reading, and staring, that there is no will-o'-the-wisp so elusive as is the cause of any human act. Easy enough to spend weeks poring over bank statements, budget books, letters from stockbrokers; to spend months examining newspaper files, stock-market reports, volumes on the theory and the history of economics; to spend years in careful, unhurried, apparently casual questioning of every person who had more than a superficial acquaintanceship with my father. All this is just more or less laborious research. But it is quite another thing to examine this mass of information and see in it, so clearly that to question is out of the question, the *cause* of a human act.

In fact, it's impossible, for as David Hume pointed out, causation is never more than an inference: we never *see* causes. And any inference, of course, involves at some point the leap from what we see to what we can't see. Very well. It is the purpose of my *Inquiry*, then, to shorten as much as is humanly possible the distance over which I must leap; to gather every scrap of information that a human being might gather concerning the circumstances of my father's suicide. Say, if you wish, that the true reason for this investigation is my reluctance to admit that Dad hanged himself because he was afraid to face his creditors. Perhaps so (much noble work has been accomplished for more questionable reasons), although consciously, at least, I have a different reason. At any rate, I am certainly prepared to admit that my

observation of the data I collect is biased, and it is
partly for that reason, as I'll explain further presently,
that even in 1937 I kept one peach basket reserved for
notes on myself—it was into this basket that my two
thoughts of the day, for example, were filed. It would,
perhaps, be more accurate to say that my rejection of
the stock-market losses as the cause of his suicide was the
hypothesis with which I approached the *Inquiry,* the
thesis that oriented my investigations.

You understand, do you, that the nature of my purpose—to make as short as possible the gap between
fact and opinion—necessarily renders the *Inquiry* in-
terminable? Because, you see, one can never know for
sure that every last scrap of information has been discovered, and so one must be perpetually searching for
another scrap. One could, of course, stop at some point
and declare, "I have sufficient information to warrant
the inference that the cause of Thomas T. Andrews'
suicide was such-and-such." But my purpose is not
really to leap the gap (which can be abysmally deep,
however narrow), only to shorten it. So, the task is endless; I've never fooled myself about that. But the fact
that it's endless doesn't mean that I can't work on
other things, other aspects of the grand project, even
though the *completion* of those aspects depends ultimately on the leaping of the gap in my *Inquiry.* It
doesn't follow that because a goal is unattainable, one
shouldn't work toward its attainment. Besides, as I
have observed elsewhere, processes continued for long
enough tend to become ends in themselves, and if for
no other reason, I should continue my researches simply
in order to occupy pleasantly the two hours after dinner.

But let's suppose that by some miracle, by some divine revelation, it were given to me to know the un-
knowable, to *know* the cause or causes of Dad's suicide.
My *Inquiry* would then be complete. But my researches
would not, for after supper on the day of that revelation
I should simply draw to my desk a different peach basket
—that one beside the lamp there—and after some minutes of wall staring, resume work on a larger *Inquiry,*

of which the above-mentioned *Inquiry* is at most a relevant chapter. And this *Inquiry*, had I world enough and time, might someday be entitled *An Inquiry into the Life of Thomas T. Andrews, of Cambridge, Maryland (1867-1930), Giving Especial Consideration to His Relations with His Son, Todd Andrews, (1900-   ).* In other words, a complete study of my father's mind and life from his birth in the front bedroom of the Andrews house to his death in its cellar; from the umbilicus that tied him to his mother to the belt that hanged him from the floor joist.

Truly a monumental task: it is my aim to learn all that can be learned of my father's life; to get the best possible insight into the workings of his mind. To do this I must, in addition to carrying out on a larger scale all the researches described in connection with the other *Inquiry*, perform extra labors as well—I must read, for example, all the books that I know my father read, looking for possible influences on his character, his way of thinking. If one can compare infinities, this task is even more endless than the other.

I said a moment ago that the death-*Inquiry* was but a chapter in the life-*Inquiry;* this is not entirely true. For in another sense, the study of Dad's life is only a necessary preliminary to the study of his death. And ultimately, I should say, they stand side by side, for they share a common purpose: what I really want to discover is the nature and extent of my father's contribution to the imperfect communication that existed between us.

Imperfect communication, that is the problem: the imperfect communication that existed between my father and myself. If you understand that (for to go into greater detail would enmesh us beyond all hope of ever returning to the story), then I think it is time to pass on to the last document of all—the document of which my two colossal *Inquiries* combined are no more than important studies for one aspect: the *Letter to My Father.*

This document dates from the fall of 1920, when after my unsuccessful attempts to tell Dad about my uncertain heart, I enrolled in Johns Hopkins University. I had resolved, you'll remember, not to tell him at all while I lived, because I believed that my death was imminent and that therefore I'd as well humor him during what remained of my life. Nevertheless I worried that I'd been unable to tell him when I wanted to, and (I was no cynic then) that the both of us would go to our graves without ever having understood each other.

And so I began to write a letter to my father, working on it in snatches during my four exhausting years at Hopkins. The letter was to be found by him after my death, and its original purpose was to explain to him what Dr. John Frisbee had told me about my heart. But this purpose, though I never lost sight of it, was soon subsumed into a larger one. Naïvely ignorant of the fact that there never exists between people—especially between fathers and sons—the sort of communication I seem always to have longed for, I set out to study myself, to discover why my communication with Dad had always been imperfect. I reviewed my whole life carefully, selecting and rejecting incidents for use in the letter. I spent a month, at least, attempting to explain to Dad why I'd never finished building my boat in the back yard. More than a year went to searching my muddy embrace with the German sergeant (with whom my communication had been pitifully imperfect) and to analyzing the effects on me of a certain particular popping noise. I worked, of course, irregularly, completing perhaps twenty pages of notes and one page of letter every month; seldom more than that. By the time I was installed in law school, the letter was perhaps fifty pages long, and I had a respectable stack of notes. I did not shy away from mentioning Betty June Gunter, even, although I realize now that those early attempts to understand our liaison were shallow. Especially between 1925 and 1927—the first of my saintly years—I worked with some diligence on the letter.

Then in 1927, when I set up practice in Cambridge, the letter and notes were packed into my trunk. I moved in with Dad and to my great pleasure found myself—or so I believed—closer to him than I'd ever been before. He was still garrulous and gruff by turns, but I thought I was beginning to understand him somewhat; at least I had hope that our communication was becoming less imperfect, and in this hope I abandoned the letter. I had, you see, always assumed that the source of the imperfection was in myself, and it seemed to me that perhaps as I matured (although I was twenty-seven then) my difficulty would vanish.

But Dad hanged himself, and rack my memory as I might until sleep was a red-eyed wish, I could find no adequate reason for his act. I realized then that I had been pursuing an impossible task since 1920: to understand an imperfect communication requires perfect knowledge of the party at each end, and I'd been studying only myself. When, in the course of moving into the Dorset Hotel, my letter and notes came to light, I put the pages of the letter on my new writing desk, dumped the notes into an empty suitcase (not until later did I begin to use peach baskets), and began to work on it again. I saw at once that the next step was to open an inquiry into Dad's life, in order to understand the nature and extent of his contribution to our imperfect communication; and at the same time I saw the necessity of a special and separate inquiry into the circumstances surrounding his death, this inquiry to be in the nature of a control (for unless the suicide were explained, nothing was explained) and also perhaps a key (for should I find the answer to the question of his death, the whole problem might be solved by the same solution). Thus my two *Inquiries* were initiated; but they did not close off my work on the letter and the notes on myself.

You see, then, the purposes of the three peach baskets beside my desk in 1937: one represented the life-*Inquiry*, one the death-*Inquiry*, the third the less organized self-*Inquiry*. And the cardboard box (MORTON'S MARVELOUS TOMATOES) contained the drafts of the letter to my father. To be sure, he can never now receive it, since I outlived him. If you don't see that this fact only demon-

strates further the imperfection of my communication
with him, and hence only intensifies the need for the
letter, instead of eliminating it, then between you and
me, too, the communication is less than perfect. But
you shall have to investigate it: I've quite enough to do
with the three baskets and the box beside me—four
parallel projects which, like parallel lines, will meet
only in infinity.

On this particular evening, to be sure, their progress
would cease, for the notes I took then I intended to be
my last.

> *I. Nothing has intrinsic value. Things assume value
> only in terms of certain ends.*
> *II. The reasons for which people attribute value to
> things are always ultimately arbitrary. That is, the
> ends in terms of which things assume value are
> themselves ultimately irrational.*
> *III. There is, therefore, no ultimate "reason" for
> valuing anything.*

By seven o'clock, these were the things I had written
on my piece of paper, not knowing exactly which file
would finally receive them. But I felt very strongly that
this sequence of ideas, which represented my day's rationalizing, was of supreme importance to my *Inquiries*
and my letter. In fact, when in the same list I entered the
Roman numeral *IV*, without yet writing anything after
it, I had a nostril-flaring sensation of the chase; I felt
that some sort of answer was on the verge of being treed.

I called these ideas rationalizings, and so they were:
the *post facto* justification, on philosophical grounds, of
what had been an entirely personal, unphilosophical resolve. Such, you remember, has been the case with all
my major mind-changes. My masks were each first assumed, and then justified.

My heart, reader! My heart! You must comprehend
quickly, if you are to comprehend at all, that those masks
were not assumed to hide my face, but to hide my
heart from my mind, and my mind from my heart. Un-

derstand it now, because I may not live to end the chapter! To be sure, each mask doubtless hid other things as well, as a falseface hides identity and personality as well as nose and mouth; but it was to hide my enigmatic heart that I became a rake, a saint, and then a cynic. For when one mask no longer served its purpose of disguise, another had perforce to take its place at once. I had been a not-very-extraordinary boy; then one day in 1919 while standing retreat I collapsed on the parade grounds at Fort Meade, Dr. Frisbee looked up from his stethoscope, and I began to eat, drink, and be merry at Johns Hopkins—my first mask. In 1924 Betty June Gunter slashed me with a broken bottle, a man named Cozy rabbit-punched me and threw me out of a Calvert Street brothel, Marvin Rose found a wicked infection in my prostate, and I became a saint—my second mask. In 1930 my father, with whom (thinking my saintliness was bringing on maturity) I had thought I was beginning to communicate, *inexplicably* hanged himself; I took the belt from his neck, mailed my legacy to Col. Morton, and became a cynic—my third mask. And each time, it did not take me long to come to believe that my current attitude was not only best for me, because it put me on some kind of terms with my heart, but best in itself, absolutely. Then, on the night of June 22 or 23, 1937—

But now you must know my last secret. In my life I have experienced emotion intensely on only five occasions, each time a different emotion. With Betty June in my bedroom I learned *mirth;* with myself in the Argonne I learned *fear;* with my father in the basement of our house I learned *frustration;* with Jane Mack in her summer cottage I learned *surprise;* with my heart, in my hotel room on the night before this last day, I learned *despair,* utter despair, a despair beyond wailing.

My despair began, not with my heart, but with two other parts of my body. Jane Mack was in my room for the night, as you know. She had come in at perhaps ten o'clock; we'd had a drink and retired shortly afterwards. Jane had sat Turk-fashion on the bed for some time, plucking her eyebrows before we turned out the light, and I had stroked her idly while I lay beside her reading a book. We hadn't been talking at all. Then, taking my hand in hers to examine it, she said, "I love your body, Todd—all but your fingers. Did you ever ask Marvin about them? My, they're ugly."

Involuntarily I jerked my hand away, blushing hotly. Had you forgotten that my fingers were clubbed? Ah, and so had I, reader, and Jane's remark, though offered in a mild enough tone, stung me all out of proportion to my actual sensitivity about my fingers—perhaps because I'd been caressing her.

"Oh, I'm awfully sorry, honey!" she said at once, alarmed. "I didn't mean to insult you at all." She tried to kiss my fingers then, but I couldn't bear the thought. I kept them out of sight.

My subsequent failure at love-making no doubt grew out of that. For one thing, in her efforts to redeem herself Jane made all the advances, immediately, and I have rarely responded well in such situations. For another, the remark about my fingers made me irrationally disgusted with my whole skinny body, and disgust is a cold bedfellow for desire.

"Please tell me what's wrong, Toddy," Jane pleaded. "I really don't want to hurt you." (There was more to this than ordinary solicitude, as I realized next day when she announced the Italian trip.)

I assured her that I wasn't offended—after the first few minutes I really wasn't—but both her curiosity and her desire had to go unsatisfied. I got up, smoked a cigarette, went to bed, tossed and turned, sat up and read, drank another drink, and tossed and turned some more. Jane finally fell asleep, annoyance and injured pride still pouting from her lips. I kissed her very lightly on her frowning brow and got out of bed, resolved, since sleep was impossible, to work on the *Inquiry*.

My mood was black; I had little patience with my work. It is only in very weak moments like this that I call my project silly; I sat for an hour in the window, looking down at the Post Office and thinking how incomparably silly my thirteen years' work was. How silly, for that matter, was my whole life during those thirteen years—one feeble mask after another!

Ah, there was a symptomatic thought: it was, I think, the first time I'd ever used the term *masks* in referring to what I'd always considered to be the stages of my intellectual development. Moreover, it was not the thought of a cynic, for as soon as it lodged in my consciousness it sent out quick rootlets of despair to all corners of my mind. Indeed, as I vaguely recognized at the time, it was a sign that the mask of my cynicism—I saw then that it was a mask—was wearing thin, was no longer doing its job. If it were, would I even have thought of my heart?

And suddenly my heart filled my entire body, even my head; it was not my heart that would burst, but my body, so full was it of my heart, and every beat was sick. Surely it would fail! I clapped my hand quickly to my chest, feeling for the beat; clutched at the window frame to keep from falling in my dizziness; stared at *nothing*, my mouth open, like a fish on the beach. And this not in pain, but in despair!

Here is what I saw: that all my masks were half-conscious attempts to master the fact with which I had to live; that none had made me master of that fact; that where cynicism had failed, no future mask could succeed; that, in short, my heart was the master of all the rest of me, even of my will. It was my heart that had dictated my masks, not my will.

Don't be so shallow as to suggest that I should have seen a doctor at once to verify my ailment: even this night, when I was far less reasonable than I was next day, I sensed, although not articulately, that to do so was to evade the question. The dilemma was a genuine one either way, and as I've said earlier, it is my bad luck that I tend to attribute to abstract ideas a life-or-death significance. And the conclusion that swallowed me in its overwhelmimg despair was this: *There is no way to master the fact with which I live.* Futility gripped me by the throat; my head was tight. The impulse to raise my arms and eyes to heaven was almost overpowering—but there was no one for me to raise them to. It was a draining, grinding flood, this feeling; all I could do was clench my jaw, squint my eyes as though in pain, and shake my head from side to side. But every motion made only pierced me with its own futility, every new feeling with its private hopelessness, until a battery of little agonies attacked me from all sides, each drawing its strength from the great agony within me.

I can't say for how long I sat paralyzed by my despair before the more dramatic of its manifestations appeared. What finally happened, when I had become sufficiently demoralized, was that my nerves, fatigued already, succumbed to the unusual strain imposed on them. My body was suddenly quite soaked in icy perspiration, and I trembled from head to foot. So deteriorated was my moral and intellectual strength that I came closer than I'd come for fifteen years to invoking the aid of a God whose nonexistence I'd long ago assumed, for mine was a despair that drives men to temples, churches, and messiahs, to any crutch within their grasp.

Indeed, I can't find it in me to deny that, had no other crutch been available, I should very possibly have ended that night on my knees, laying my integrity on the altar of the word *God*. But another crutch was within reach: Jane, now sleeping soundly. And the embarrassment that I feel at telling you how I went shocked and trembling to the bed; how I buried my head blindly, desperately, against her; how I lay there until sleep found me, shuddering, my knees clasped to my chest, fighting despair as one fights appendicitis—this embarrassment is not different from that I'd feel at having to confess that I'd buried myself in God. I am in truth embarrassed, reader, but in good faith I recommend this refuge to your attention. There is nothing in it of the foolish ostrich, because the enemy you flee is not exterior to yourself. And you will be safe.

I have no idea whether Jane was aware of any of this. At the tick of six I popped awake; my head was on the pillow, Jane's on my right shoulder. In great wisdom I inhaled deeply the smell of her hair, always sunshine and salt; there have been no women in my bed since that morning, and yet still at 6:00 A.M. I can summon to my nostrils the smell of Jane Mack. I sat up and looked around me, bursting with incipient wisdom. What had been the problem I'd buried? As was my habit, before I got up I reached to the window sill for my Sherbrook, took a good pull, and shuddered all over, but no answer came. I rose carefully from the bed, so as not to wake Jane, donned my seersucker suit, splashed cold water on my face—and realized that on this day I would destroy myself.

"Of course!"

I grinned at my dripping face in the mirror—dumb, stunned surprise. There was the end of masks!

"Of course!"

There was no mastering the fact with which I lived; but I could master the fact of my living with it by destroying myself, and the result was the same—I was the dictator. I choked back a snicker.

"For crying out loud!"

III. There is, therefore, no ultimate "reason" for valuing anything.

Now I added *including life,* and at once the next proposition was clear:

IV. Living is action in some form. There is no reason for action in any form.
V. There is, then, no "reason" for living.

This last statement merited some minutes of expressionless contemplation, after which I capped my pen and clipped it in my pocket, put Eustacia's letter where Jimmy could easily find it, fetched my straw, and left my room without a shred of regret.

My *Inquiry* was closed.

XXVII. Will you smile at
my rowboat?

Ideally, a new philosophical position, like a new rowboat, should be allowed to sit for a day or two at the dock, to let the seams swell tight, before it is put to any strenuous application. But not always is it possible to arrange such a period. It was close to eight o'clock when I left my room, and the boat-show was due to begin at eight-thirty.

Let me say this: For a man's actions, particularly his important ones, there are always, doubtless, a complexity of reasons, some conscious and some unconscious. And so with my decision to end my life. Smile if you will at the notion that a man can commit suicide on philosophical grounds—I've no objection to anyone's smiling at a floating opera! Point, if you've a psychoanalytic bent, to my motherless boyhood, my murder of the German sergeant, my father's hanging himself, my isolated adulthood, my ailing heart, my growing sexual impotency, injured vanity, frustrated ambition, boredom —the analyst always has causes aplenty!—and say, "These (or some combination thereof) are the *real* causes." They're all there; take your pick. Even I began by deciding to destroy myself as a last means of coming to terms with my heart, and I shan't deny that any one of the items in that shabby catalogue above may have played its special little secret role. But by the time I closed my *Inquiry,* I was interested in only one reason for dying, and that was the philosophical one; other reasons, even my heart, were by that time no longer conscious reasons.

"So what?" smiles the analyst. "Nonetheless they're the *real* ones."

But I say that a man's conscious reasons, the causes he *thinks* lie behind his acts, are not without importance, and I don't mean symptomatic importance. In fact, when you begin to speak of what a man *should* or *shouldn't* do, they're the only ones that count. Ethics can necessarily concern itself only with conscious motivation. Psychic determinism rules out choice, and with choice goes ethics: a man can't be held responsible for acts for which he's not responsible, in other words. When you speak of ethics, only conscious reasons are valid reasons (validity and truth, to be sure, do not necessarily attach to the same statement). And because since my conversation with Mr. Haecker I was interested only in whether a man (in this case myself) *should* or *shouldn't* commit suicide, not whether he *would* or *wouldn't* (an analyst's interest), I was interested only in the abstract ideas involved, not in any more personal, biographical considerations.

So while it may be foolish to assert that anyone, even Socrates, ever killed himself for *purely* philosophical reasons (perhaps he was too timid or vain, subconsciously, to go along with Crito's plan to spring him?), nevertheless I should call it equally foolish to deny that a man's *interest* in his own suicide can be purely philosophical; that so far as he is concerned, the philosophical reasons are the only important ones. Do you see what I mean? Psychoanalyze a man as you will, but don't hold it against him if he is merely bored by your analysis. And tell him, smiling, that his philosophy is no more than a rationalization of the truth; he can reply, with equal claim to God's ear, that your psychoanalysis is no less a rationalization of the truth. The truth is multiform.

Capt. Osborn hobbled from his room, gave a grunt or two, and hocked some vagrant phlegm into one of his handkerchiefs.

"Are ye goin' to the boat-show, Toddy?"

"Yes, sir."

"I'll jest walk along with ye, if ye don't mind. Ain't seen a boat-show for years." He chuckled. "Young Haecker—I call 'im Young Haecker now—haw! Young Haecker's been gloomin' around so much lately I figured I better have me some fun while I can. All set, boy?"

"Where is Young Haecker?"

"Oh, he ain't goin'," Capt. Osborn sniffed. "He's too old for such carryin'-on! I ain't seen 'im since this mornin'. Here, look, I got somethin' for ye."

Smiling broadly, he withdrew from his pocket a pint of Southern Comfort, which he presented to me.

"There, now!"

"What's this for?" I laughed, breaking the seal and sniffing appreciatively.

The old man blushed slightly. "I owe it to ye," he said, "for a couple o' things. That little business we was talkin' about this mornin', for one."

"Come on, then, let's drink it up," I said. "You'll need it as badly as I will, because that particular show's all over with."

"Shucks, it would o' been all over anyhow, far's I'm concerned," Capt. Osborn declared righteously.

"How about Young Haecker?" I suggested. "Suppose we cut him in on it, too? And maybe I can talk him into seeing the boat-show."

I went up to the top floor to Mr. Haecker's little dormer room and knocked, but he didn't reply.

"Mr. Haecker?" I turned the knob, for it was doubtful that a man of his age and circumstances would be either out or asleep at eight o'clock.

The door opened onto a strange scene. A single tall white candle burned in a brass holder on the writing desk beside the bed, though it was not yet dark, and flickered slightly in the small breeze from the window. Also upon the writing desk, as I saw on approaching it, were an alarm clock stopped at seven forty-five; a volume of Shakespeare opened to Act Three, Scene One, of *Hamlet* (with, believe it or not, the words *not all* noted in the margin opposite the line *Thus conscience does make cowards of us all*); a stack of thirteen fat notebooks each labeled *Diary, 19*—(I never had the nerve to examine those); and a glass bottle with two sleeping pills left in it. On the bed Mr. Haecker lay dressed in heavy black silk pajamas, his eyes closed, his arms crossed in the funereal manner of Miss Holiday Hopkinson, next door, his features calm (*composed* is a more accurate adjective), his pulse and respiration—as I discovered upon quickly snatching up his wrist and putting my ear to his chest—almost imperceptible. It was marvelous!

As far as I could see, there was nothing to be done in the way of first aid, and so I simply hurried downstairs and notified Hurley Binder, the night clerk, who in turn very sensibly telephoned the hospital for an ambulance. Then the two of us returned to Mr. Haecker's room with Capt. Osborn, who pleaded with us to help him up the stairs so that he wouldn't miss the excitement, and waited for the ambulance to arrive. Hurley Binder and Capt. Osborn clucked their tongues and shook their heads and took generous drinks of the Southern Comfort, mightily impressed by Mr. Haecker's elaborate preparations for departure.

"What d'ye think o' that?" Capt. Osborn exclaimed several times. "And him such a educated feller, too!"

From time to time I felt Mr. Haecker's pulse. He seemed to be losing no ground—but then there was little to lose, for pulses do not beat much more slowly. After a few minutes the ambulance wailed up past Spring Valley, and Mr. Haecker was carted off to the hospital, black silk pajamas and all.

"It makes a man stop and think, now, don't it?" Capt. Osborn said—confident, I doubt not, that he had uttered a meaningful statement.

"It does indeed," I agreed mildly. What I thought, at least officially, was that should he live through this foolishness, Mr. Haecker would find the remaining years of his life less burdensome than the ones recently past, because both his former enthusiasm for old age and his apparent present despair of it were, if one judges from exterior appearances, more calculated than thought out, more elaborate than sincere. (I should enjoy saying that history proved me correct—but in fact Mr. Haecker, upon recovering from his generous dose of barbiturates, went from the hospital to a sanitorium in western Maryland, it having been discovered that he was incipiently tubercular, and there, in 1940, attempted once again to take his life, by the same means and with as much flourish as before. This time he was successful.)

"Well," Capt. Osborne sniffed reverently, "ain't in our hands now, I guess. Do ye still want to see the show?"

"Why not?" I shrugged, thinking still of Mr. Haecker: it is always something of a shock to learn that someone has taken your ideas with literally deadly seriousness.

"I'll jest take yer arm, sir, if ye don't mind."

"Of course." I led him down the steps.

My rowboat, then, for better or worse, was afloat.

XXVIII. The Floating Opera

Plain enough by daylight, the *Original & Unparalleled Floating Opera* was somewhat more ornamented as Capt. Osborn and I approached it across Long Wharf in the hot twilight. Power lines had been run from a utility pole near the dock, and the showboat was outlined in vari-colored electric lights, which, however, needed greater darkness for their best effect. On the roof of the theater Prof. Eisen and the thirteen members of his $7,500 Challenge Atlantic & Chesapeake Maritime Band were installed in their bandstand, rendering, as I recall, "I'm a Yankee Doodle Dandy" to the crowd of several hundred onlookers gathered around—many of whom, particularly among the Negroes, came only to hear the free concert and regard the "Op'ry Barge" with amazement, not having money to spare for admission to the show. The box office was open (it was nearly showtime), and a line was queued up from the ticket window down the gangplank to the bulkheads. Capt. Osborn grew excited and used his cane to nudge small running urchins out of his path, which led unswervingly to the ticket line.

The band wound up George M. Cohan and began, not surprisingly, a Stephen Foster medley. When we reached the top of the gangplank I looked around at the crowd and saw Harrison, Jane, and Jeannine just taking a place in line. Apparently Jeannine was better, or, more probably, Jane hadn't had the heart to disappoint her. They were occupied with opening Jeannine's popcorn bag, and didn't notice me.

The auditorium was already nearly half filled with the citizens of Cambridge. Capt. Osborn and I took seats about seven rows from the rear, on the extreme starboard side of the theater—he complaining that we hadn't arrived earlier to get really good seats and at the same time looking around for any of his colleagues to whom he could break the news about Mr. Haecker. The hall was illuminated with electric lights, each built into a double fixture along with a gas mantle for use at less progressive landings. Scanning the audience, I saw almost no unfamiliar faces. Col. Morton and his wife sat in the front row on the aisle, the best seats in the house. Marvin Rose, a showboat *aficionado,* sat a few rows behind. Bill Butler waved cheerily to me from across the theater. My partner Mr. Bishop was there with his wife, whom one seldom saw in public. Harrison, Jane, and Jeannine came in—if they saw me, they made no sign, although I waved to them—and sat on the other side of the theater. Jimmy Andrews, as I'd anticipated, was absent—doubtless out sailing with his fiancée, for a mild but usable breeze had sprung up earlier in the evening.

Above our heads the $7,500 Challenge Band concluded its free concert with "The Star-Spangled Banner." There was some uncertainty in the house as to whether it was necessary to stand, since the band was outside. Some men made a half-hearted motion to rise, hesitated, and sat down embarrassed, laughing explanations at their wives with much pointing of fingers toward the roof. Finally Col. Morton stood unfalteringly, without a backward look, and the rest of us followed suit, relieved to have a ruling on the matter. When the anthem ended there was applause from the free-loaders outside, and much discussion inside about whether it had really been necessary for us to stand. Soon, however, everyone's attention was focused on the small door under the stage, from which the members of the orchestra, resplendent in gold-braided red uniforms, began filing into the pit. When all were in their places, and instruments had been tootled cacophoniously, Prof. Eisen himself—lean, hollow-cheeked van-Dyked, intense—stepped to the podium amid generous applause from orchestra and balcony, rapped for attention, and raised his baton, on the tip of which the whole house hung. The lights dimmed slightly, the baton fell, and the band crashed into "The Star-Spangled Banner." An instant's murmur and then we sprang to our feet again, none more quickly than the Colonel—although Evelyn was a trifle flustered.

No sooner had the final cymbal clashed than the house lights went out completely and the electric footlights rose, playing on the mauve velvet stage curtain. Prof. Eisen's baton fell again, and the sprightly overture was commenced: a *potpourri* of martial airs, ragtime, a touch of some sentimental love ballad, a flourish of buck-and-wing, and a military finale. We applauded eagerly.

Captain Jacob Adam himself stepped from behind the curtain, bowed to our ovation, and smilingly bade us listen.

"Good evenin', good evenin', friends!" he cried cheerily. "I can't say how happy I am to see ye all here tonight. It does my heart good when the *Floatin' Op'ry* comes round Hambrook Light, I'll tell ye, 'cause I know that means it's Cambridge ahead, and I tell John Strudge, my calliope man, I say to him, 'John,' I say, 'get up a good head o' steam, boy, and let's have 'Dem Golden Slippers,' 'cause that there's Cambridge yonder,' I says, 'and ye'll sail a lot o' water 'fore ye meet finer folks than ye'll see aplenty in Cambridge!' Now, then!"

We cheered enthusiastically.

"Well, sir, folks, I'm glad so many of ye got out tonight, 'cause we got such a fine new show this year I was anxious for all my friends and even my enemies in Cambridge to see it." He squinted over the footlights. "Guess my friends'll be in later," he mumbled loudly, and grinned at once lest we miss the jest—but we were alert, and laughed especially loud to reassure him.

"Yes, sir, a brand-new line-up this year, folks, from a crackerjack start to a whiz-bang finish! But before we haul back the curtain and get on with the fun, I'm afraid I'll have to disappoint ye just a wee, wee bit."

We murmured sympathy for ourselves.

"Now I know ye was just pinin' to see Miss Clara Mulloy, the Mary Pickford of the Chesapeake, do her stuff in *The Parachute Girl*. So was I, I got to admit, 'cause no matter how many times in a row I watch Miss Clara jump down in that there par'chute, them legs o' hers is so durn pretty I can't see my fill!"

We laughed more raucously, Capt. Osborn jabbing me in the ribs and exploding with mirthful phlegm.

"But I'm sorry to say Miss Clara Mulloy has caught a germ from someplace—must have been Crisfield, couldn't of been Cambridge [applause!]—and I swear if she ain't got the laryngitis so bad she can't say a durn word!"

We voiced our disappointment, some of us resentfully.

"I know, I know," Capt. Adam sympathized. "I feel like walkin' out myself—hey, Miss Clara," he shouted into the wings, "come on out here and show the people yer—ah—yer *laryngitis!*" He winked at us, we roared, and then Miss Clara Mulloy—brown-haired, brown-eyed, trimly corseted—curtsied onto the stage, the sequins flashing on her black gown, a red flannel scarf tied incongruously around her white neck. She curtsied again to our ovation, pointed to her throat, and moved her lips in silent explanation, while Captain Adam looked on adoringly.

"What do ye say?" he cried to us. "Shall we call the whole thing off? I'm willin'!"

"NO!" we shouted, almost as one man—two or three rowdies cried "*Yes!*" but we glared them down.

"Do I hear *yes?*" the Captain asked.

"NO!" we roared again, our stares defying contradiction from the one or two hoodlums who are forever spoiling honest folks' fun. "No!" we pleaded, hoping Capt. Adam wouldn't judge us citizens of Cambridge by our most unfortunate element.

"*Yes!*" one of the incorrigibles snickered.

"That man should be thrown out!" I heard the Colonel declare in exasperation.

"Well, I say let's be fair and square," Capt. Adam said. "Any man, woman, or child that wants to leave can get up right now and go, and John Strudge'll give ye yer full admission money back at the box office, despite ye already heard the overture!"

We laughed at this last and applauded his generosity. The house lights came up for a moment, but no one dared move.

"All right, then, let's get on with the show!"

The house lights were extinguished, Miss Clara Mulloy rewarded our applause with a blown kiss (her eyes dewy), Prof. Eisen struck up a lively tune, and we relaxed again.

"Now, then," the Captain announced. "Instead o' *The Parachute Girl* I'm proud to present the great T. Wallace Whittaker, one o' the finest singers and actors that ever trod the boards, yes sirree! Ye all know T. Wallace Whittaker as the great Southern tenor—got a voice sweet as a honeycomb in a sweet-gum stump, by Joe! But what ye probably don't know is that T. Wallace Whittaker is one o' the best Shakespearian actors in the U.S.A., or England too, for that matter! Ladies and gentlemen, I have the *great* honor to present T. Wallace Whittaker, the eminent tragedian, in scenes from the Bard!"

Uncertain applause. The band played some heavy chords in a minor key, the curtain opened, and we looked into a Victorian parlor (first set for *The Parachute Girl*), in the center of which stood T. Wallace Whittaker, bowing low. He was a clean-cut, slightly broad-beamed, rather Sunday-schooly young man, and he wore a tight black Hamlet-looking outfit. From the tone of his very first words—a lofty "I shall begin by reciting the famous speech of the duke Jacques, from Act Two of *As You Like It*"—he lost the sympathy of us men, although some wives nodded knowingly.

T. Wallace walked to the footlights, struck a declamatory pose, and closed his eyes for a moment. He did not clear his throat, but some of us cleared ours.

"*All the world's a stage,*" he declared, "*and all the men and women merely players. They have their exits and their entrances, and one man in his time plays many parts. . . .*"

Already Capt. Osborn had the fidgets, and began ticking his cane against his high-top shoe. The rest of us sat uncomfortably as T. Wallace ran through the seven ages of man.

"... *Last scene of all* ... *mere oblivion, sans teeth, sans eyes, sans taste, sans everything!*"

Polite applause, especially from the ladies. I thought I heard Jeannine ask shrilly for more popcorn, but it could have been some other child. One of the rowdies made a sneering remark that I couldn't catch, but that set his neighbors chuckling, no longer so hostile to him as before, and rewarded him with a scornful flash of T. Wallace Whittaker's eyes.

"Mark Antony's funeral oration, from Act Three of *Julius Caesar*," he announced. "*Friends, Romans, countrymen, lend me your ears.* ..."

"Ye can have mine, boy," the hoodlum said loudly. "I've took enough!" He stalked out of the theater, and the rest of us, instead of being angry, were shamefully amused. Even some wives stifled smiles, but T. Wallace Whittaker went on, blushing furiously, to inflame an imaginary mob against Brutus and company. The oration was long, for T. Wallace went through the whole routine of reading Caesar's will. By the time he insinuated his desire to move the stones of Rome to rise and mutiny, his audience was on the verge of doing likewise; we were tapping our feet, sneezing, and whispering among ourselves. When he cried at the end, "*Mischief, thou art afoot; take thou what course thou wilt!*" someone whistled shrilly and flung a handful of pennies onto the stage.

T. Wallace ignored the insult; rather, he acknowledged it with a defiant glare at us, but refused to be bowed.

"What I shall recite now," he said grimly, "is the most magnificent thing in the whole English language. I shan't expect a noisy rabble to appreciate its beauty, but perhaps a respectful silence will be granted, if not to me, at least to Shakespeare!"

"Where's the minstrels?" someone yelled. "Bring

on the minstrels!" More pennies sailed over the foot-lights.

"The soliloquy from *Hamlet*," T. Wallace Whittaker almost whispered.

"Go home!"

"Take 'im away!"

"Come on, minstrels!"

"*To be, or not to be: that is the question. . . .*"

"Ya—a—a—ah!"

The audience was really quite out of hand now. Several young men stood on their chairs to take better aim with their pennies, which no longer merely fell at T. Wallace's feet, but struck his face, chest, and gesticulating arms until he was forced to turn half around; but he would not be vanquished.

"*To die, to sleep: to sleep: perchance to dream: ay, there's the rub. . . .*"

One pimply-faced lad, standing in a front-row seat, began aping T. Wallace's gestures, to our great delight, until Col. Morton struck at him with his gold-headed cane.

"*For who would bear the whips and scorns of time, the oppressor's wrong . . .*" T. Wallace Whittaker was determined, come what might, that we should have our culture. I greatly admired him.

"*. . . the proud man's contumely, the pangs of dispriz'd love, the law's delay . . .*"

"Yahoo! Boo! H—s—s—s—s—s!"

It was open warfare now; T. Wallace could no longer be heard, but nevertheless he continued undaunted. Capt. Adam appeared from the wings, greatly disturbed lest we begin taking the vessel apart, but we greeted his conciliatory wavings with more boos. He went to T. Wallace, doubtless to ask him to call it a day, but T. Wallace paid him no heed, and declaimed right in his face. Capt. Adam grew panicky, then angry, and tried to drag him off by force, but T. Wallace shoved him roughly away, still gesticulating with the other hand. Capt. Adam shook his finger at the young man, shouted, "Yer fired!" and signaled to Prof. Eisen to strike up the band. The $7,500 Challenge Maritime Band waltzed into "Over the Waves." T. Wallace Whittaker stepped through the closing curtains, and shaking both fists at us through a copper shower (to which I, too, contributed, standing up and flinging all my change at him), in blind defiance he screamed: *"Thus conscience does make cowards of us all; and thus the native hue of resolution is sicklied o'er with the pale cast of thought!"* Finished at last, he scooped a handful of pennies from the stage, flung them back at us with all his strength, and disappeared behind the curtain.

A few more late-thrown pennies sailed after him, hitting the curtain and clicking onto the stage. We were all laughing and comparing notes, a little sheepish, but exhilarated for all that—none more so than I, for it is often pleasant to stone a martyr, no matter how much we may admire him. For my part, as I believe I've mentioned elsewhere in this book, I'm seldom reluctant to assist in my small way in the persecution of people who defy the crowd with their principles, especially when I'm prejudiced in favor of the principles. After all, the test of one's principles is his willingness to suffer for them, and the test of this willingness—the only test—is actual suffering. What was I doing, then, but assisting T. Wallace Whittaker in the realization of his principles? For now, surely, having been hooted from the stage and fired from his job in the cause of Shakespeare, he would either abandon his principles, in which case they weren't integrated very strongly into his personality, or else cling to them more strongly than ever, in which case he has us to thank for giving him the means to strength.

Capt. Adam appeared next from the wings, smiling thinly, and raised his hands. We were willing enough now to be silent, having made our point.

"Oh, well, who likes Shakespeare anyhow?" He shrugged cravenly, kicking a few pennies around the footlights. "If ye think yer gittin' any o' these pennies back, though, yer crazy!"

We laughed, as relieved as wayward children who learn that they won't be punished after all.

"Now, then, see if ye can't be a little nicer to the next folks," Capt. Adam grinned. "At least pitch quarters at 'em. Ladies and gents: those knights of the burnt cork, the U.S.A.'s greatest sable humorists, the chaste and inimitable Ethiopian Tidewater Minstrels!"

We applauded complacently, for this was what we'd come to see. Prof. Eisen ripped into "I'm Alabammy Bound" at an express-train tempo, and the curtains parted. The set for *The Parachute Girl* had been replaced by a solid blue backdrop, against which stood out shockingly the bright uniforms of a small semicircle of minstrels. There were six in all: three on each side of Capt. Adam, who took his place as interlocutor. All wore fuzzy black wigs, orange clawhammer coats, bright checkered vests and trousers, tall paper collars, and enormous shoes, and sang in raucous unison the words of the song. The two minstrels on either side of the interlocutor assisted the effort with banjos and guitars, while Tambo and Bones, the end men, played the instruments from which their names are derived. With a great rattling and crashing the tune shuddered to its end.

"Gentle-*men-n-n-n* . . ." cried Capt. Adam, raising his arms to heaven, "BE . . . SEATED!"

Tambo and Bones, to be sure, missed their chairs and fell sprawling on the floor, accompanied by thumps from the bass drum. Knees were slapped, ribs elbowed. Capt. Osborn, beside me, strangled rapturously. Col. Morton's cane banged approval. In his new role as Mr. Interlocutor, Capt. Adam was suddenly transformed into an entirely different person—grammatical, florid, effusive—so that one doubted the authenticity of his original character. When the end men, great eyeballs rolling, had regained their seats, the classical repartee ensued, the interlocutor being tripped up in his pomposity again and again—to our delight, for our sympathies were all with the impish Tambo, the irrepressible Bones.

("*Good evening, Mr. Tambo; you look a little down in the mouth tonight.*"

"*Mist' Interlocutor, ah ain't down in de mouf; ah's down in de pocketbook. New hat fo' de wife, new shoes fo' de baby. Now dat no-good boy ob mine is done pesterin' me to buy him a 'cyclopedia. Say he needs 'em fo' de school."*

"An encyclopedia! Ah, there's a wise lad, Tambo! No schoolboy should be without a good encyclopedia. I trust you'll purchase one for the lad?"

"No, sah!"

"No!"

"No, sah! Ah say to dat boy, ah say, ''Cyclopedia nuffin'! Y'all gwine walk like de other chillun!'"

We were led by the nose, step by step, through the most rudimentary of jokes, clubbed on the head with long-anticipated punch lines, titillated—despite the minstrels' alleged chastity—by an occasional *double-entendre* as ponderous as it was mild. Joke followed elephantine joke: Negroes were shiftless and ignorant; foreigners were suspect; the WPA was a refuge for loafers; mothers-in-law were shrewish; women were poor drivers; drunkenness was an amusing but unquestioned vice; churchgoing a soporific but unquestioned virtue. Tambo and Bones, being uneducated and lazy and dark, deserved their poverty, but their rascality won our hearts, and we nodded to one another as their native wit led the overeducated, pontifical interlocutor into one trap after another. Tambo and Bones vindicated our ordinariness; made us secure, even smug, in the face of mere book learning; their every triumph over Mr. Interlocutor was a pat on our backs, a reassurance. Indeed, a double reassurance: for were not Tambo and Bones, our champions against intellectuality, but irresponsible Negroes? Superior to the interlocutor, to be sure, but we solid, responsible citizens (down here in the orchestra)—*we* were superior to all. Good is good, bad is bad; and the good wins out in the end. Virtue is rewarded, vice is punished; and we are so agreed on the obvious meanings of those terms that to question us about them would be impertinent, sir!

We were sung to of heart, hearth, and home by Sweet Sally Starbuck, the singing soubrette, she of the moist eyes, corn-silk hair, and flushed cheeks. What did she

sing us? "I Had a Dream, Dear." "After the Ball
Is Over." "A Mother's Prayer for Her Son." "Harvest
Moon."

("*Y'all so smaht, Mist' Interlocutor, ansah me dis,
sah: whut got twenty-nine legs, six arms, twelve ears,
three tails, twenty feet, and a passle ob faucets, and say
cockadoodledoo?*"

"*Great heavens, Tambo! What does have twenty-nine
legs, six arms, twelve ears, three tails, twenty feet, and a
passle of faucets, and says cockadoodledoo?*"

"*Three farmers, three milkin' stools, three Jersey
cows, and a loudmouf roostah! Ha!*")

We were preached to by J. Strudge, calliopist, ticket
collector, and banjo player extraordinary, the Magnificent Ethiopian Delineator, the Black Demosthenes:

"Ladies, gemmen, houn' dawgs, bullfrawgs, an' pole-
cats: de tex' fer today come from de forty-leben chaptah,
umpteen verse—borry fo', carry three, give or take a
couple, chunk in one fer good measure—ob de Book ob
Zephaniah, whar de two Jedges, name ob First an'
Secon' Samuel, done take de Axe ob de Romans an' cut
de 'Pistles off from de 'Postles fer playin' de Numbahs!
Hyar how she go, bredren: *Blessed am dem dat 'specks
nuffin', 'caze dey ain't gwine git nuffin'!*"

We were serenaded by banjo and fiddle, bones and
tambourine.

("*Mr. Bones, I spoke to your wife today, and she tells
me your mammy's been living with you all for three
years now.*"

"*Mah mammy! Ah been thinkin' all dis time dat was
her mammy!*"

"*No! How can you be so consistently stupid, Mr.
Bones?*"

"*Well, Mist' Interlocutor, dat ain't easy fo' a dahkie
like me dat's neber been to one ob dem fancy colleges!*")

We were supposed to hear pastoral lays of the corn and
cotton fields from the vibrant throat of T. Wallace
Whittaker, famous Southern tenor, but we did not, much
to the disappointment of the ladies. We heard instead
Sweet Sally Starbuck once more, and she sang to us this

time "Just a Song at Twilight," "Beautiful Dreamer," "It's a Sin to Tell a Lie."

And Mr. Tambo! And Mr. Bones! Did they pat us the Juba? They did. Did they cut us the Pidgin's Wing? They did. Did they scratch us the Long Dog Scratch? They did.

> ("*Mistah Tambo, Mistah Tambo! Ah fails to unner-*
> *stan'*
> *How a wuthless, shif'less dahkie such as you, sah,*
> *Kin conglomerate de money fo' a Caddylac sedan,*
> *Jest to keep yo' yaller gal fren' sweet and true,*
>   *sah. . . ."*)

There were banjo exhibitions, comic dances, novelty songs, more jokes.

"And now, ladies and gents," Capt. Adam announced, "for the last feature on our program: the world-renowned imitator Burley Joe Wells, all the way from New Orleans, Louisiana!"

The dead-pan banjoist seated next to Tambo stepped forward, a great black hulk, and held his arms out from his sides. Tambo and Bones stumbled up, and after some pantomimed horseplay, commenced working the arms up and down like pump handles. Burley Joe rolled his eyes and puffed out his cheeks, as though a pressure were building up inside him, and when at last he opened his mouth, the blast of a steam calliope rocked the hall with "Oh, Dem Golden Slippers," the *Floating Opera's* musical signature. A full chorus he tootled, and came whistling to the end accompanied by Prof. Eisen and our applause.

"Looziana sawmill, down in de bayou," Burley Joe grunted next. He took up a stance at one side of the stage, his back against the exit, and after some preliminary coughing, produced a hum like that of an idling buzz saw. Tambo and Bones disappeared into the opposite wing and reappeared a moment later carrying a yellow-pine plank, perhaps eight feet long and a foot wide. They tripped, they stumbled, they pulled and tugged, and finally they fed the plank in under Burley Joe's left arm. The saw whined and screamed, and the

board disappeared into the wings, followed by the end
men. The saw hummed on. Tambo and Bones reappeared
ten seconds later with two pine planks, each six inches
wide. The process was repeated again and again, the
saw chunging against knots and squealing in pine resin,
until at last the end men appeared with enormous satisfied smiles on their faces, each holding a single tiny tooth-
pick in his hand; little Bones strode up to big Burley Joe
and wrenched his nose as though turning a switch, and
the saw's buzz slowly died away.

"Steamboat race," growled Burley Joe, who wasted
none of his art on elaborate introductions. "De *Natchez*
soun' like dis [*A high-pitched chugging, pumping, swish-
ing sound. A shrill whistle*], an' de *Robert E. Lee* soun'
like dis [*A low, throaty throb. A resonant bass whistle*].
Har dey goes, now."

It was amazing! Ship's bells clanged. Orders were
shouted, soundings called. The great pumps thundered.
The great stern wheel spun. A deep blast of the whistle
announced the *Lee's* departure. Some moments later a
deck hand cried "Steamboat round de bend!" and a faint
shrill whistle identified the *Natchez* ahead. Prof. Eisen
insinuated soft, excited music under the sound of the
throbbing engines. *Toot toot!* The *Lee* flung down the
gauntlet. *Peep peep!* The *Natchez* accepted the chal-
lenge. A race was on! More orders, excited cries, signal
bells. The engines accelerated, and the music likewise.

I glanced at Capt. Osborn: he was entranced. At the
house in general: enthralled. At my wrist watch: ten
o'clock. A spotlight directed at Burley Joe was the only
illumination in the house at the moment. Quietly, but
with no particular attempt at secrecy, I left my seat,
slipped down the aisle next to the starboard wall, and
stepped out through a side exit, attracting very little
attention. Inside, the *Lee* was gaining slowly on the
Natchez.

It was, of course, entirely dark outside except for the
Opera's lights. I found myself, as I'd planned, on the out-
board side of the theatre. I walked swiftly down the
starboard rail to that small companionway in the stern

which I'd fixed in my mind during the afternoon's tour of the vessel, and let myself cautiously into the dining room, under the stage, closing the door behind me. Over my head the *Lee* and the *Natchez* were side by side. The music was louder and faster; the minstrels called encouragement to one or the other of the ships; an occasional excited cry broke from the audience. I went at once to the darkened galley and without hesitation turned all four burners of the bottled-gas stove full on. I opened the oven door and turned the gas on there, too, and then, after closing the galley door and checking the one window to make sure it was tight shut, I sat in the cook's chair and waited for the gas, now hissing quietly from every burner, to fill the tiny room. Already its smell was conspicuous—a slightly nauseous smell, but nothing compared to that of a crabhouse on a summer afternoon.

Upstairs the audience broke into cheers. I was without emotion—entirely so, because just then my whole self was the subject of my rationality, and what emotion logically follows from any situation? I waited calmly for the first sign of dizziness, my mind as clear as it had ever been in my life. Certainly it would have been quicker for me to have acquired a pistol somewhere and put it to my temple, but one of the several things that made me decide, during my afternoon's tour of the showboat, to use this particular means to my end, so to speak, was precisely this opportunity to wait out the minutes between my act and its consequence in utter calm. If it failed, no matter: there would always be time for pistols.

The *Natchez* threatened to overtake the valiant *Lee*. I contemplated lighting a cigarette, but the thought of possible explosion—which would certainly burn me, but probably wouldn't kill me—changed my mind. I blinked my eyes, or rather closed them with the intention of blinking, and when it occurred to me upon opening them that they'd been shut at least thirty seconds, I guessed that the gas was commencing its work. Indeed, my head suddenly developed an ache, and my breath came differently. It made me smile when some part of myself observed to some other part, "Todd Andrews is killing himself." Smile, because this observation (which thinly veiled the question, "Do you *really* want to do this? All this philosophical crap aside, boy, do you *really* want to kill yourself?") died in the womb, itself asphyxiated by the demon "Why not?"—that overwhelming genie I'd released from his bottle earlier in the evening, having struggled unknowingly with the cork for most of my life, and who now filled my mind as completely and lethally as the gas was filling the room. There was no escaping this genie; my suicide could be called many things, perhaps, but no man could call it unreasonable.

I smiled again (I was reelingly dizzy now, and remember being pleased that my last reflections were without solemnity): there was piquancy in a lawyer's dying, as he had lived, by sophistry. . . . I leaned back and closed my eyes for good, no longer able to follow the sounds above my head.

But—*deus ex machina!*—someone came into the room outside. I heard, uncomprehendingly, people enter the dining room and mumble excitedly. Then the galley door burst open behind me, and the light was turned on.

"Hey, there!"

I was grabbed roughly by the shoulders and shaken.

"Hey, now, what the hell you think you're doing?"

Very reluctantly I opened my eyes. The intruder, a young man dressed in overalls, apparently a crew member, had left me and was turning off the gas, cursing and fumbling. His back was toward me; he quickly shoved open the window to air out the galley and then, turning and seeing me awake, began to abuse me loudly, standing with his hands on his hips.

"Crazy damn fool! What you want to do, blow us to hell? What you doing down here anyhow? I swear, everything at once!"

Well, I was supposed to say something, make some apology or explanation, but the fellow ran out of the galley into the dining room. And anyhow a strange thing had happened, a very strange thing. I was unable to open my mouth to speak at all! This, I think, has to do with my genie that I mentioned a moment ago: it was *futile* to say anything—I mean ultimately futile—even though the situation demanded explanation, and ordinarily I could have talked my way out of it easily enough (I can, as I've said before in connection with Betty June's puckered smile, almost always explain an act in three or four different ways). But why explain at all? Why move at all? I could be handled roughly, perhaps arrested. So what? Embarrassed. So what? There was no reason to open my mouth, as there was no reason to do anything, and I will say that the realization of this worked upon me involuntarily. This is important: it was not that I decided not to speak, but that, aware in every part of me of the unjustifiable nature of action, and completely subject as I was then to the operation of my reasoning, I simply could not open my mouth; my arms and legs would not move. An amazing helplessness—it reminds me of those holy men who, lost in a mystical concentration, become similarly immobile for long periods of time, oblivious to weather, the stares of the curious, and whatnot. But of course there is a positiveness about them; they've swapped one world for another, whereas I was simply paralyzed.

But suddenly another voice came from the dining room—Jane Mack's voice, very much upset.

"Todd! Is that Todd?"

There was an ancient urgency in that voice. I was on my feet and headed out of the galley in an instant. Jane was there, a terrified look on her face, and Harrison with her. The crewman who'd interrupted me seemed to have disappeared. Harrison and Marvin Rose were bending over the dining table, where, when I came closer, still dizzy from the gas, I saw Jeannine lying unconscious, her teeth clenched, her eyes rolled up, and her breath coming hard. Harrison was loosening her clothing while Marvin quickly examined her. Jane clutched my coat sleeve for an instant.

"What is it?" I asked Marvin sickly. My head was reeling, but no longer from the gas. I began to catch Jane's fright.

Marvin glanced up at me; he was not excited. "She had a convulsion."

Harrison was too busy with Jeannine to notice me.

"We shouldn't have let her come!" Jane cried to him.

"No use to say that, honey," Harrison said gently.

"Don't worry," Marvin smiled. "These things look worse than they are. They're not so unusual when a big fever hits a kid."

"Let's get her to the hospital!" I said. It was a terrifying thing to see her like that on the table. Harrison looked quickly around at me and then at Marvin.

"No, there's no reason to. Just get her home right fast. I'll get my bag and come over. It's probably just grippe or something."

"Are you sure, Marvin?" I demanded, perhaps a little angrily.

"Of course I'm sure," he said curtly, and turned to Harrison. "Give her an alcohol rubdown if she's still like this when you get home," he said. "Chances are she'll be asleep by the time I get there. These things pass off fast. I'll run get my stuff now."

He left. Harrison lifted Jeannine up in his arms at once—I had a terrible flash of envy!—and strode out, Jane following immediately behind. After a moment's uncertainty I blushed and ran after them, out to the top of the gangplank. How to tell them not to trust Marvin?

"I hope she'll be all right!" I called—a little too loudly, I suppose. Harrison was already halfway down the gangplank, but Jane turned back for a moment, distractedly.

"Oh," she said. "I thought you were coming." She looked at me more closely. "Don't you want to?"

This last had in it a small accusation, along with whatever else, and it stung, because I wanted to go with them very badly indeed. A number of things urgently needed saying, but there was no time. Quick decisions! Harrison was off the gangplank, unaware that Jane wasn't right behind him at the moment.

"I don't know how to act in these situations," I said firmly. "You'd better run. I'll call later on, I guess."

She ran, but I had seen a little wonder touch her eyes and the muscles around her mouth. Would it turn later into resentment or understanding?

"Jane?" I wanted to tell her to call me at once if anything serious developed—but either she was already out of earshot or else she ignored me in her haste. No matter.

So. I stood at the top of the gangplank for a minute, uncertain what to do. To return to the galley was out of the question now—the crewman was probably looking for me at that moment—and I had disinvolved myself from the Macks' emergency. I felt as helpless as after Dad's suicide.

Well, there was the Choptank River, into which a man might jump. But I did not trust Marvin. No, the moment was lost. And there was another thing that stayed me: something was different. Some qualitative change had occurred, instantly, down in the dining room. The fact is I had no reason to be concerned over little Jeannine, and yet my concern for that child was so intense, and had been so immediately forthcoming, that (I understood now) the first desperate sound of Jane's voice had snapped me out of a paralysis *which there was no reason to terminate*. No reason at all. Moreover, had I not, in abjuring my responsibility for Jeannine, for the first time in my life assumed it—for her, for her parents, and for myself? I was confused, and I refused to die that way. Things needed explaining; abstractions needed to be straightened out. To die now was simply out of the question, though I hated to spoil such a perfect day.

I saw a crewman come around the corner of the showboat down at the other end from me, and before he could notice me I showed my ticket stub to the man in the box office, re-entered the theater, and took my seat beside Capt. Osborn. I would tell him, if he asked me, that I'd gone to find the Men's Room, and that after some uncertainty I had found it.

But he didn't ask. On stage, Burley Joe Wells was winding up his act. The audience was shouting encouragement, and Prof. Eisen's accompaniment approached a crescendo.

"LADIES AND GENTLEMEN!" Capt. Adam hollered. "PLEASE MAKE READY FOR THE GREAT STEAMBOAT EXPLOSION! DO NOT LEAVE YOUR SEATS!"

Some women screamed, for apparently no transition had been made from whatever had been in progress to this new excitement. From the orchestra pit, under the rather frenzied music of the $7,500 Challenge Maritime Band, came a low, deep rumbling, as of tympani, its volume gradually increasing. From Burley Joe—now rising slowly from his knees, arms outstretched, eyeballs bulging—came a loud, hackle-raising hiss like escaping steam. The drums thundered on; trumpets and cornets whinnied like horses; children cried hysterically; Tambo and Bones hid behind their neighbors. Standing high up on the interlocutor's chair, Capt. Adam regarded his brood with an Olympian smile.

Like a monstrous black serpent, Burley Joe now stood poised on tiptoe, his massive arms over his head. The hissing and the music reached their greatest intensity; there was a double flash from the wings, a choked scream, a stunning explosion; the stage filled at once with thick white smoke.

An instant of complete silence. Evelyn Morton, on the front row, quietly fainted, and the Colonel caught her just before she slid off her chair. Then immediately Prof. Eisen tore into "Lucy Long," the smoke began drifting away, and the minstrels appeared in a laughing, dancing row on the stage: Tambo, Bones, J. Strudge, Burley Joe Wells (bowing), the two guitarists, Capt. Adam himself (bowing)—and with them Sweet Sally Starbuck and Miss Clara Mulloy, dewy-eyed and blowing kisses. The audience laughed—shocked, relieved—and exclaimed sharply to one another. Husbands looked at wives, and wives at children, with an instant's new eyes —eyes with which I'd been made familiar some ten minutes before.

"Lucy Long! Lucy Long!" The *Wonderful Panithi-*

opliconica, it turned out, was not more nor less than a grand old-fashioned minstrel walk-around—bones, tambourines, banjos, guitars. The minstrels danced, sang, leaped, cartwheeled. "Lucy Long" metamorphosed into "The Essence of Old Virginny"; faster and faster the minstrels cavorted, to a final, almost savage breakdown. The cymbals crashed, the performers bowed low, Tambo and Bones tumbled into the orchestra pit, and our wild applause saluted the curtains of the *Original & Unparalleled Floating Opera.*

XXIX. A parenthesis, a happy ending, a *Floating Opera*

If you do not understand by now that the end of my *Floating Opera* story must necessarily be calm and undramatic, then you have understood nothing at all, and once again I'm cursed with imperfect communication. Say what you will about the formal requirements of storytelling; this is my opera, and I shall lead you out of it as gently as I led you in. I've little use, as a principle, for slam-bang finishes such as Burley Joe's, whether genuine or contrived.

I helped Capt. Osborn to his feet (he was still shaken with the excitement of the Great Steamboat Explosion) and ushered him out with the crowd and back to the hotel, where Hurley Binder told us that Mr. Haecker was reported to be in satisfactory condition at the hospital. I lost no time in bidding Capt. Osborn good night and going to my room, for I had a great deal of rationalizing to get done before I could begin to think of sleeping that night.

I sat on the window sill and smoked a cigar for several minutes, regarding the cooling night, the traffic light below, the dark graveyard of Christ Episcopal Church across the corner, and the black expanse of the sky, the blacker because the stars were blotted out by the storm clouds overhead. Sheet lightning flickered frequently in the west and northwest, over the Post Office and behind the church steeple, and an occasional rumbling signaled the approach of the squall out over the Chesapeake. How like ponderous nature, so dramatically to change the weather when I had so delicately changed my mind! For that, it appeared, was what I'd done—unexcitedly, almost unwittingly. I remembered my evening's formulations, and going to them presently, added a parenthesis to my fifth proposition:

> V. There is, then, no "reason" for living (or for suicide).

That much, at least, I saw clearly now as I remembered my strange, short-lived paralysis. I hadn't reasoned completely from my premises before. To realize that nothing has absolute value is, surely, overwhelming, but if one goes no further from that proposition than to become a saint, a cynic, or a suicide on principle, one hasn't gone far enough. If nothing makes any final difference, that fact makes no final difference either, and there is no more reason to commit suicide, say, than not to, in the last analysis. Hamlet's question is, absolutely, meaningless. A narrow escape!

Where did that leave me? Well, for one thing it left me alive, for better or for worse. But that's about all, for it also left me rudderless, like a showboat without tugs, with nothing in the way of direction but inertia. Faced with the infinity of possible directions which the rejection of absolutes opens to one, and having no ultimate reason to choose any one over the other, one would, it seemed to me, *in all probability*, though not at all necessarily, go on behaving much as one did before, from habit and momentum, just as a rabbit shot on the run keeps running in the same direction until death overtakes him.

There was at least that. But the negativity of the programme I found profoundly distasteful. It was reasonable, but it was also sterile and uninteresting. To speak simply and honestly, it didn't sound like *fun*. Not only that: it didn't account for my refusal to die at least until I knew Jeannine was all right. There was nothing negative about my concern for her, though I had to assent that her life had no more absolute, objective value than did anything else. The value of that girl's life was only relative, as the value of everything else is only relative, either to ends or to individuals or to both. There was no escaping that; wherever I went, I had perforce to start from there. . . .

Quite suddenly I grew very excited; my spine tingled with excitement. For like that night in Baltimore when a dark alleyway turned me dazzled onto the bright flood of Monument Street, I now all at once found myself confronted with a new and unsuspected world. This (I can tell you now more clearly than I could have told you then) was the essence of it: if there are no absolutes, then a value is no less authentic, no less genuine, no less compelling, no less "real," for its being relative! It is one thing to say "Values are *only* relative"; quite another, and more thrilling, to remove the pejorative adverb and assert "There *are* relative values!" These, at least, we have, and if they are all we have, then *in no way whatsoever* are they inferior. A corner for you, there!

But God, this needed thinking about! Needed *time*, needed years to consider and explore! I laughed uneasily; everything was wide open again; I was back in the game! The *Inquiry*, the *Letter to My Father*, and especially that third peach basket, the investigation of myself had to be reopened at once—for certainly if I was ever going to explain to myself why Dad committed suicide, I must explain to him why I did not and (it seemed to me then) probably never would. Thinking of *time*, I remembered Marvin Rose's report on my heart, which I'd receive next day, and I laughed again. Never before had the uncertainty of that organ seemed of less moment to me! It was completely beside the point now whether my endocarditis was still among my infirmities or not; the problem (for which, bless nature, my heart made a handy symbol!)—was the same either way—and this for everybody—and the solution, if this new notion of mine should turn out to be one, was the same as well. At least for the time being; at least for *me*.

And that was enough—it sounded like a good way to operate.

I had to take a good long careful time, then, to tell Dad the story of *The Floating Opera*. Perhaps I would die in the middle of it, and perhaps I would die still confused, without ever getting things finally straightened out —perhaps, indeed, there could be no such thing as a final straightening-out. This was all right, too. But I would never, I resolved at that moment, kill myself in confusion!

This decided, I made a note to intercept my note to Jimmy Andrews, stubbed out my cigar, and without hesitation went downstairs to telephone the Macks, ignoring with a smile the absurd thunderstorm that just then broke over Cambridge.